Johann Friedrich Heinrich Wohlers, John Houghton

Memories of the Life of J.F.H. Wohlers

Missionary at Ruapuke, New Zealand

Johann Friedrich Heinrich Wohlers, John Houghton

Memories of the Life of J.F.H. Wohlers
Missionary at Ruapuke, New Zealand

ISBN/EAN: 9783337030780

Printed in Europe, USA, Canada, Australia, Japan

Cover: Foto ©Raphael Reischuk / pixelio.de

More available books at **www.hansebooks.com**

MEMORIES OF THE LIFE

OF J. F. H. WOHLERS,

MISSIONARY AT RUAPUKE, NEW ZEALAND.

An Autobiography.

TRANSLATED FROM THE GERMAN BY

JOHN HOUGHTON.

— —

" *Such men are the strong nails that keep the world together.* "

THE LITTLE MINISTER.

— —

DUNEDIN:

OTAGO DAILY TIMES & WITNESS NEWSPAPERS COMPANY, LTD.

MDCCCXCV.

INTRODUCTION.

J. F. H. WOHLERS was born a peasant in the village of Hoyerhagen, near Bremen, but a desire for the life of a missionary being developed in him, he went to New Zealand in 1843, under the auspices of the North German Missionary Society.

He settled in the first instance at Nelson, but finding no sphere there for missionary operations removed to the island of Ruapuke, in Foveaux Straits, then the residence of the principal native chiefs of the South Island, coming down the coast with Mr. Tuckett, the agent of the New Zealand Company, on his journey to select the site for the present settlement of Otago.

He converted communities, to use his own words, of loathsome savages sunk in degradation and poverty, both at Ruapuke and on the adjacent coasts of Stewart Island and the mainland, into prosperous communities of civilized human beings, receiving for many years no remuneration, but producing his own food out of the soil, and teaching the Maoris to do the same after a civilized manner. He preserved and fully records the old Maori mythology (a sublime one) which, even in his day, was only known to a few, as it was the religion of previous generations, the custodians of which all died before his own demise. He published the book of which this is a translation in Bremen, in 1883, and died at Stewart Island on the 7th of May, 1885, at the age of seventy-three.

Says Mr. James Anthony Froude in his Essay on Representative Men: "*The age of the saints has passed; they are no longer of any service to us: we must work* in their spirit, *but not along their road.* And in this sense we say that we have *no pattern great men, no biographies, no history,* which are of any service to us. It is the remarkable characteristic of the present time—as far as we can know, a new phenomenon since history began to be written—one more proof, if we wanted proof, that we are entering upon *another era.*"

The translator of THE MEMORIES OF THE LIFE OF J. F. H. WOHLERS submits that the present era is only a continuation of the old one—the Christian era—and that the rule still is, that when we have a pattern great man amongst us that we do not know it until he is dead, and " that he was in the world and the world knew him not " is as true to-day as it was eighteen centuries ago.

The author of this book lived and died amongst us, and as a great man we certainly did not know him. He wrote the " Memories of My Life " in his old age in his native tongue, and it has lain amongst us twelve years untranslated. His work was this : To make savages into Christian men and women, not in name only, but in very deed and truth, and to show in practice that " godliness is *profitable unto all things,* having *promise of the life that now is,* and of that which is to come." He saved people's souls, and their bodies too. He put into practice the maxim of the old monks, *Laborare est orare,* and did manual labour as well as his spiritual task as under the Great Taskmaster's eye.

In his somewhat narrow sphere he solved the social problem—that problem that is the despair of modern states-men, that labour unions, extensions of franchise, labour bills, and other Acts of Parliament are so vainly trying to solve. His materials were—and poorer ones could hardly be conceived—*First,* Men and women, loathsome savages, sunk in degradation and poverty, but still, like himself, made in the image of God ; *Second,* God Almighty's earth, a small, sterile, rocky island in the midst of a stormy strait, but still that earth that is the Lord's, and full of riches; *Third,* a little axe, a fowling piece, a bag of flour, a little salt, and no money at all ; but the Christian religion—that faith that moves mountains. His method was this : He combined religion and industry, and served God for no money at all, as much with the spade and plough as before the altar. He has gone to his longed-for home, but his work still goes on. His memory is still an active force in the field of his late labours.

The translator's acquaintance with the old world is but small. In the new continents he has passed a lifetime, and has seen such work as this man did in but one other place. On the coast of California are many adobe cathedrals, centuries old, some in ruins, some still in use and in good repair. They were founded by an order of Franciscan friars some three hundred years ago. The wild tribes of Indians which then inhabited California could not be reduced to order by the Spanish military authorities, and the coast of California for a length of five hundred miles was abandoned to a few of these friars, amongst whom were men of great learning and profound piety. With nothing but a rosary, a little holy water, and the Christian religion, they converted these wild men whom the soldiery could not tame. They taught them the arts of peace, that of irrigation, of the cultivation of wheat, of barley, of the vine, the olive and the fig, and they formed them into communities—not one, but twenty communities—of thousands of civilised men and women. They built these beautiful cathedrals of adobe, with cool transept and nave, with buttressed walls many feet in thickness, with shady corridors, and fountains gurgling in the plaza. They taught the Indians to breed sheep and cattle, horses and mules; and, exporting wool and hides to the parent country, received back goods in exchange, and amassed such wealth that they could afford to have their heavy altar services of solid gold. The missions Dolores, of Monterey, of Santa Barbara, San Luis Rey, San Luis Obispo, Santa Clara, Santa Inez, San Diego, San Buenaventura, and many others still tell of the work of these saints. With them, too, the practice was, *Laborare est orare.* And the translator submits that Mr. Froude's new era will dawn when all the saints learn that they are not here merely to pray, but to work as well—for to work is to pray; and that the solution of the social problem lies (as Mr. Carlyle suggests in his tale of Abbot Samson) in the combination of religion and agriculture first, and all other industry afterwards; for work is as holy as prayer, and "Six days shalt thou work" as much a divine command as "Remember the Sabbath day to keep it holy." Acts of Parliament cannot effect this. It must necessarily be a matter of slow growth, for the "Kingdom of Heaven," which is Peace on earth and good will towards men, "cometh not with observation."

The story told is that of a faithful husbandman—a true worker in the vineyard, and after a lifetime of toil, when earth had no more in store for him and his sole desire but for eternal rest, he calls himself an unprofitable servant! "Blessed are the poor in spirit, for theirs is the Kingdom of Heaven"

As Mr. J. M. Barrie says of one of the clergymen in the "Little Minister"—"Such men are the strong nails that keep the world together." They are the cement that joins the new era to the old one.

J. H.

INVERCARGILL, *1st July, 1895.*

CONTENTS.

MEMORIES OF THE LIFE OF
J. F. H. WÖHLERS.

CHAPTER I.

MY YOUTH.

THE years of childhood and of youth are in themselves of no great importance, still there is something in them that has a bearing on the later life. I was born on the 1st October, 1811 (a younger son amongst seven children), in Mahlenstorf, in the parish of Brücken, district of Hoya, where my father was a respected farmer. The neighbourhood and the district of Hoya lies far from cities. Civilisation in respect of the inhabitants was in a backward state. The reason was that the whole surrounding country was oppressed under the rule of the French conquest. Parents and children had to eat their sorrowful bread in the bitter sweat of their brow. The French had, as it was expressed, sucked the marrow out of the peasants' bones. My father had allowed my name to be registered by the mayor in the French registry as Heinrich Friedrich, but from hatred of the French had me baptized as Johann Friedrich Heinrich. I can only remember one Frenchman now. It was probably after the battle of Leipzig, when the Frenchmen were driven out of Germany heels over head. There was a cry in the house—a Frenchman! I ran out and saw a jaded cavalry soldier talking to my father at the door of the house. I still have a lively remembrance of his trembling voice, as well as his rusty scabbard.

It may be here remarked, by the way, that my father was a considerable man among the peasantry of the place, and for that reason, after the conclusion of the French occupation, was elected the so-called Alte Bremer Münze, by Peter Koster. I stuck to my arithmetic after school years were over, especially in the winter evenings, and in course of time worked the whole book through, with the exception of the appendices, which embraced algebraic examples, of which at that time I knew nothing. As I had no supervision, I had to make many unnecessary experiments, and work my way through a host of unnecessary figures (I did not then know the short method) before I could bring out the right answers to the difficult and involved problems.

I only turned my attention to arithmetic in my few leisure hours because all other avenues to learning were closed to me. I was not so well acquainted with any cultivated man as to be able to obtain books from him, as the upper classes had nothing in common with the peasantry.

Many a time I have broken my head over the High German language. In spite of all my endeavours I could not make it out why words which appeared to me quite the same were printed one time with a capital letter, and another time without; why sometimes there should be a "dem" and another time "den," and of similar puzzles many more. I could well believe that these things were not the result of chance. Sometimes I seemed to scent out a difference, and then the scent vanished again. Enough of this!

The labour of the peasant is as necessary to make a whole man as learning is, and one cannot support oneself with speculations about incomprehensible mysteries.

The condition of the peasant is always one of contentedness. Come along with me into the field! No; not now, now that I am an old man, and, after a life of labour, just yearn for eternal rest; but then, when I was yet a fresh and hearty peasant boy. It is early morning in the autumn seed time. As we rise the stars are yet in the sky; but when we have the horses harnessed to the ploughs, the dawn is broken, and we can see the furrows. The share cuts through the sod with a lively rustle, and turns the spit over with an easy fall, to cover up the sod all overgrown with weeds and thistles with the fresh clean earth from below. We dare not look back, or the plough might slide out of the furrow, and leave an ugly place in the field ; but still we can see the reddening dawn in front of us. What a sight ! It is as if the loved heavenly Father held his hand before the light, and amused the child on His lap by letting the light stream through His fingers.

> In the morning's purple glances,
>   Blazing on its wreath of rays,
> The youthful day in joyous dances ;
>   Me, too, he wakes with friendly hand,
> And uprise my grateful songs
>   In creation's joyous band.

God sweetens the long hours to the peasant, from early morn till late at night, with an inward joy which the quick movement in the bracing air, and the beauty of surrounding nature, produces as a gratuitous gift. Mowing grass is hard labour, but yet what greater joy than that of a young peasant, when at daybreak he is on the dewy meadow. How refreshed he feels after the short sleep, and how sweetly his sharp scythe hisses through the moisture-laden grass.

> I'm content the whole year round ;
>   In spring I plough the land ;
> Then springs the lark with upward bound,
>   A merry song he sings to God ;
> Then comes the lovely summer time ;
>   Then does my heart o'erflow ;
> Then when I wander in the prime,
>   So many thousand ears I see ;
> When comes the Jacob day along,
>   I swing my scythe,
>   I cut the corn,
> And take the grain to harvest home.
>
> In autumn look I upon my trees,
> See apples, pears, and plums thereon,
> And if they are ripe I shake them well ;
> So God rewards the peasant's toil.
> Then when sad winter comes,
> And my cottage is all white with snow,
> And all the fields as chalk are white ;
> The meadows then are thick with ice ;
> And when the lovely Sunday comes
> I dress myself with decent care,
> And go to church with quiet heart,
> And hark to what the preacher says.
>
> —*Spinning-room Song.*

Hoyerhagen (meaning probably Count's Park), the village and the common where I was born, lies in a woody region of great natural beauty, under a row of sandhills partly covered with needlewood (pines). Oak and beech woods spread themselves out on either side. These hills, evidently the sandhills of some earlier sea beach, are in places so high that one can see the spires and towers of Bremen from them, a distance of thirty miles or so. Hoyerhagen itself lies in the foreground of the low country. The many farmhouses lie mostly isolated, almost every one surrounded with its own groves of fruit and other trees in a great oak wood. On the edge of this wood, and partly between the farmhouses, there is a row of stream-like ponds, that are kept flowing by the annual overflowing of the Weser (I hear the wood has died out now, and the district has a more uniform appearance). The beauties of nature were daily before my eyes, and impressed my sensibilities more and more. They awakened, however, a keen desire for wider experiences, such as are available to townspeople, but closed to the peasantry. In a more uniform neighbourhood, such as that of my birthplace, with the heavy load of manual labour in early childhood, such a disposition had probably been less developed.

With all its natural beauties Hoyerhagen was a most dead-and-alive community, and, with regard to opportunities for mental acquisition, very poor in books. The few books that were to be found in houses for the most part lay unused, and could have been easily counted. There was the land catechism (a good book), exclusively for the school children; then the church hymn book; then there was the yearly land calendar; then an old prayer-book; a still older house postil, and last, an old Bible. In my estimation the Bible was the chief book, and then the calendar. I preserved the calendars from year to year, and consequently had quite an important collection. Sometimes I bought myself a little book from the bookbinder's, but these were of no great importance, and have vanished from my memory. On the other hand I have yet lively recollections of the lessons on the Bible and the calendar.

As a result of my want of books, and my great desire to read and learn, I soon made the discovery that the Bible contained a rich treasure of instruction. I learnt therefrom the biblical histories, learnt chapters and Psalms by heart, and thought over them afterwards, when I was driving and ploughing, whenever my thoughts were not required in attention to my work. This certainly had this good effect—although the natural man receives nothing of the spirit of God, it kept me in a sort of innocent naturalness. At all events I was free from many sins to which youth is liable.

Besides the Bible, my collection of calendars contained a valuable treasure of easily understandable information about astronomy, meteorology, and other pleasant bits of information, as well as patriotic and other songs. I learnt all this diligently. The patriotic songs stirred my whole heart with love for my German fatherland.

> I greet thee, dearest fatherland—
> I'm born for thee alone !
> To thee, with high uplifted hand,
> The child's true faith is sworn.
>
> My powers I do devote to thee—
> Thy welfare shall my honour be ;
> Be bann'd all mean and base desire
> From thy son's breast, oh fatherland !
>
> *—From the Calendar.*

But I was born a peasant, and a peasant I supposed I must remain. Not even as a soldier was I of any use—I was too small.

In accordance with good old custom, the peasantry always went regularly to church. I did not. Yet, if I could have heard explanations of the Bible, or, above all, something spiritual that would have helped my sinking belief, then had gladly gone. Instead of that, I was fed with lessons in housekeeping. When, for instance, the sermon was on the necessity of early rising, and a calculation was made as to how much time was saved in a year—or maybe in a lifetime—if one rose every morning an hour earlier ; that was a matter I could easily have reckoned up for myself. But what angered me beyond measur was that the whole affair was totally unnecessary.. By far the most of us hearers were obliged to be out of bed every morning at four; only a few could sleep till five; and some few had to get up at three. Surely that was early enough!

Such dissertations about common everyday affairs disgusted me with church going. In preference, therefore, I read at home, or went in summer time into a wood and dreamed the time away. I had not far to go. Close by the house the before-mentioned river-like pond flowed along, and here, between the still water and a blooming meadow, we had a little wood of high oaks, beeches, and other kinds of trees, as well as thick undergrowth of osiers, hazels, and such like. Here it was, as still and solemn as in some sublime temple of a Nature's God, the little insects enjoyed their short life—they wished no better. A gift of a few days was to them as good as all eternity. Why, then, should the heart of man be so drear? Why does it seem so strange and lonely in God's beautiful creation?

> The good God He lives for us all,
>   We all do stand in His right hand,
> Whether we roam in the Northern wild
>   Or in the Southern tropic land;
> The Father's eye it reaches far,
> It blesses all, it takes all in,
> And from the starry host of heaven
> Looks down on flower that lonely blows.
>
> *—Out of the Calendar.*

Is it true that a self-existent God lives that knows every green leaf and its web, and who thinks of the lonely man and his dark forebodings; or is there only a world soul, only half known to itself, that permeates all visible nature and unfolds itself through it, but which regards no single life? Ah! the solemn stillness in the temple of Nature may well instil a soft sadness, but it cannot satisfy the awakened yearning after something. What is it? What may Nathaniel have felt when he was alone under the fig tree, before Philip called him and led him to Christ? Or I went alone to the already-mentioned heights. Here lay spread out before me, right across to Verden, the thirty-mile-wide Weser valley, with hamlets and villages, spires and windmills, woods, fields, and meadows, and the woody Hoyerhagen in the foreground.

For love of us they deck them all,
The meadow, hill, and grove ;
The birds they sing from near and far,
With song they fill the air ;
The lark sings to us when at work,
At our sweet rest the nightingale.
And when the golden sun gets up,
And gold floods all the world ;
When everything in blossom stands,
And ears all fill the field,
This splendour all, then think I then,
For me, dear God, for me is made.

—From a School Song.

But how small one feels in the great creation. Here on the margin of a fragrant pine wood, where a solemn rustling wanders through the pine needles, the anxious foreboding rises once more that one is forsaken. One feels in the very home like a stranger in a strange land. Will it be different in a future life? Will even a peasant there have access to higher knowledge? Is there really a life after death, or is the belief a mere naked hope to be set against the certainty of the death that lies before us? Does life end with death? or do we not really know but that we have comforted ourselves with a vain belief? Is God a man that He should lie? Can He really hold out idle hopes to His children to make their short earthly life bearable? Not if He is really the God the Bible teaches.

A still summer evening. Twilight is gradually losing itself in night. A few faint streaks of the red fading evening glow gleam through the fruit trees and the far-away woods. A plum tree in full freshness stands before me. The leaves of the young shoots are in full sap, ready for their nightly rest, in such expressive manner, as if to say we correspond with our existence. I could not say this about myself. The world and nature when in their softest moods can give me no satisfaction. God appeared to me to be near in the visible creation, but immeasurably distant from the yearnings of my inner soul. A bat fluttering described an always returning circle. Poor creature! Helpless in flying—unskilled in running—and it dare not trust itself out in daylight. And yet it enjoys itself for its existence in its dark world. Even so the men of my condition are glad to be content in their ignorance, and men shun knowledge for fear it might bewilder them. But I could not be content. My whole soul yearned after higher light, and with this longing locked in my bosom I was obliged to move restlessly in a dark circle. I was acquainted with no cultivated man, knew no one to whom I could lay bare the longings and yearnings of my heart, or any one who would be able to understand me. If I spoke about the longings and yearnings of my heart I received the short answer—Bist narr! (you're a fool). I had also sufficient penetration to see that really there was a good deal of folly in me. This drove me to solitude.

It was the hereditary opinion that a peasant must trouble himself only about such matters as had been usual in previous generations—all other knowledge and speculation could only end in his ruin. And I, too, thought there was somewhat of truth in this. All younger sons in my rank of life placed their hopes and exerted their energies in the direction of some day being farmers themselves, whether by purchase, lease, or marriage. I never had such a wish, therefore, thought I, I was ruined already. But this thought in no way hindered me doing my duty in the service of my uncle at Hoyerhagen, and becoming a thorough farmer. I could load a cart with hay or corn, could turn as good a furrow, sow the seed as well and regularly as any other peasant who never thought at all. But I had no desire at all to be an independent farmer myself.

And so I arrived at my twenty-fifth year, and the road to higher knowledge was closed to me on all sides, and that by so high a wall that I could not even look over it. It is well that God preserved me from people with revolutionary ideas, *who want to improve the world without God and without Christianity.* If I had fallen into such hands, and they had represented to me that the entire parochial and civil organisation was a wrong one, and as a consequence I was wrongfully deprived of the opportunities of improvement, and it must be overturned, they might easily have led me astray and ruined me. But God's merciful hand was over me, and I knew it not.

CHAPTER II.

A WINDFALL AND ITS CONSEQUENCES.

I ALWAYS drove with pleasure to the mill, because, while the corn was being ground, I sometimes found something to read. The mill was in the parish of Vilsen—not in our parish of Hoyerhagen. Now, it happened once, when I went into the miller's room, that I saw printed papers lying on the table. I at once looked at them. There was a picture on the top representing the rays of the rising sun, and over it was written " The glory of the Lord is risen upon thee." Both the picture and the title touched my receptive mind. The rays of the rising sun in the early hours of the morning were always enchanting natural objects to me; and I had often read the words from the sixtieth chapter of Isaiah with awe, because they sounded so lovely, and because the chapter contained such sublime poetry. I knew by heart.

> Arise, shine, for thy light is come,
> And the glory of the Lord is risen upon thee.

It was no wonder that I was attracted by so good an impression of the meaning of the print. I read further : Merciful Missionary Leaf. These were strange words to me, but that did not trouble me ; the narratives of foreign lands and heathen were attractive. I asked the miller's wife to allow me to take the pamphlet away till my next trip to the mill, which I was willingly permitted to do. Yes, she seemed pleased, the good old wife (she was old-fashioned in her belief, and abhorred novelties), to distribute the pamphlets with a good conscience.

The finding of the missionary tract on the miller's table was, unknown to me at the time, the turning point of my life, and the hand of God can be clearly seen therein. The tracts were not regularly received by the people at the mill. I never saw them there before or after. As I heard later, Pastor Köhler, at Vilsen, had only sent them there that one time in order that the peasants, when they came to the mill, might read them there, and I—long anticipating something unknown to me, sought for it painfully—came and found them. I must say about this dear family of millers that some years later I found awakened Christianity in them.

The wide surrounding district suffered at that time from a spiritual drought. Real infidelity had, so far, made but little advance, but a dreadful indifference reigned supreme that was no better than unbelief. Some held on to the old-fashioned forms of piety; but there was no inner life, and where the voice of one calling for repentance was raised in the wilderness, as that of Pastor Köhler, at Vilsen, who demanded conversion of heart and an awakened Christian life, it was considered novelty, and those who held by old-fashioned ways feared it might bewilder them.

I have already remarked that I had a considerable stock of the yearly land calendar, because there were some good things to read in it; only I was sorry that I always had to wait a whole year before a new one was published. Here, now, was a publication that came out every fourteen days, and was just as good to read as a calendar. As I had heard in the mill that the Missionary Leaves could be got from Pastor Köhler, at Vilsen, I resolved on the occasion of my next journey to the mill to run over and order the publication. I had previously heard of Pastor Köhler. Some praised him up to heaven; others damned him down to hell. I was indifferent to both opinions, for I did not know him, and did not belong to his parish. As the upper classes had nothing in common with the peasantry I did not trouble myself about them. The ordering of the missionary publication was a matter of business; there was no necessity to see him in person. The pastor received me in a friendly manner, and appeared to be much astonished that a young peasant servant, for which he took me, and from the parish of Hoyerhagen, of his own accord should desire to have the missionary tract. As he still hesitated, and seemed to be in doubt whether or not I was in earnest, I asked how much the yearly subscription cost. He told me, and I laid the money on the table. Thereupon he laid the numbers together which had appeared since the beginning of the year, and as he reached me the packet I snatched it with eagerness and said, "Here I have secured a treasure of learning." I wondered why a man in such a high position could talk with an uncultivated peasant boy in so friendly and unrestrained a manner.

The reading and re-reading of the tracts awakened in me an inclination towards, and then a heartfelt sympathy for, the heathen, and a desire for their conversion to Christianity, and I waited with eager curiosity to know what the next number would bring. I soon remarked that in these leaves there was a different tone of piety from what I was accustomed to hear. This reminded me of the pious speeches which I had heard in my childhood from my mother and grandmother (now dead); but it made no further impression on me than that the wavering of my belief, which I had for a long time remarked, again received stability.

Although I always faithfully fulfilled my agricultural labours, which, however, gave me not the least inclination to become a farmer—as I always had a great thirst for knowledge, as if I suspected there was something unknown in its possession— it was natural that a longing should arise in me to be sent to the heathen myself—especially as nothing prevented my leaving my fatherland and my friends.

Although I had now read the missionary publication for a considerable time, I was still unacquainted with the institutions of the mission. I expected that the missionaries must be all men of university education, and had therefore no idea of becoming a missionary; but I read also of assistants, and for that office I considered myself eligible, and I never expected to be sent out in the uncultivated state of mind in which I then was. I was not quite without means (our district was beginning to recover itself from the French occupation), and intended to take a short course in a school of not too high a grade, at my own expense, if the superintendent of the mission thereupon would give me an occupation. There was only one man who could advise me in the matter—namely, Pastor Köhler at Vilsen, and in order to do this he ought to know all my intentions, my age, and circumstances. This was best done in writing. The art of writing which I had so far acquired was neither grammatical, nor did I always use the right words; but that made no difference, the pastor knew the language of the peasantry. I wrote him with the request that when I next had an opportunity of speaking to him he would let me hear what he thought about it.

The next time I went to him he took my hand and said, " You have quite surprised me with your writing." Then, after a few questions, which I answered, he said that nothing stood in my way—neither my age, my want of knowledge, or of means, would hinder my being taken into a missionary seminary ; but that in order that we might see whether the wish was of the Lord, or a mere flash in the pan (strohfeuer), I had better wait a year and say nothing about it. Both suggestions appeared to me to be right. The first, that I should wait a year, was so welcome to me that it appeared like a reprieve, for a thought came into my mind that had not hitherto occurred to me, to examine myself closely, and I wished in the very first place to be quite clear in my own mind as to what my real intentions and desires were. The other condition, to say nothing about it, I would have imposed myself if he had not done so. He was afraid that, perhaps, I had represented my purpose to myself in too attractive colours. I replied that no one would be likely to laugh at me. He thought that if they did it would not trouble me. But he did not know the depth of ignorance in our dead community. It was not a matter of bringing reproach on the name of Christ—the people did not even know what a mission was ; the word was never heard ; and the word heathen was supposed to mean wild men who ate live hens, feathers and all. If, therefore, I allowed my intention to be become known, people would have said that if I was not born a fool I was become one, and I was not yet ready to bear the public scorn for no purpose whatever. The conversation with the pastor made a deep impression on me. It gave rise to the thought I have mentioned. It would present itself to me that I was not yet converted myself, and consequently was not fit to undertake the conversion of the heathen.

The year of waiting is the most important of my life—it is the year of my second birth—and I always look back to it gratefully, although forty years have since passed by. I have already said that as I had nothing better I sought to bind up my faith in

the works of creation, that such attempts ended in a sort of soft
sorrowful sadness that at first was not unpleasant, but lost themselves in an anxious doubt whether there was a living God and a
life after death. Such doubts, with all sorts of disagreeable ideas
about my existence, sat upon my breast cold as a corpse. In the
previous time when I had read the missionary tract and taken
interest in the conversion of the heathen, it is true my doubts
had fled; but it appeared to me now as if the corpse was decaying,
and my inner consciousness filled with the putrid stink of my
sins. I understood now what this meant. "O wretched man
that I am, who shall deliver me from the body of this death."
I recognized that I had served and honoured the creature more
than the Creator, who is to be praised to all eternity. Amen.
So far I had only known Jesus Christ as the founder of our
religion, who had delivered us from the sins of ignorance and of
life, and brought the light of eternal life to the enlightenment of
the Christian nations. But these are poor considerations which
cannot content an anxious state of mind that yearns for life and
blessedness. My soul thirsted for God—the living God.

  I knew well from my catechism, which I had learnt by heart
in school and have not yet forgotten, what the conditions of
penitence —that is, the change of heart—were, namely, a lively
conviction and earnest repentance of our sins ; a confident reliance
on the mercy of God in Christ; an earnest striving to better oneself. If these portions of the catechism had enforced themselves on
my mind from their own power of conviction, I had been a converted
Christian years before. But that is as impossible as, in our
natural strength, to rise to heaven and bring Christ down, or to
go down to hell and fetch Christ from the grave. The Kingdom
of God does not come with any outward expression: it is within
us ; and when one gives oneself wholly to Christ, it becomes a
living power. No forcing of penitence is necessary. The renew-
ing of the heart within us comes as something quite new, worked
by God from inward outward.

  " For by grace are ye saved, through faith, and not of your-
selves. It is the gift of God, not of works, lest any man should
boast." I learnt to pray. Previously I knew no other method of

praying but that of repeating or thinking over a prayer I had learnt by heart, out of which I was able to extract but little devotion, now prayer flowed freely from my heart. Oh! sweet and heavenly devotion that flows from it freely into one's heart! Is there anyone who feels his heart drear and joyless?—let him go into his closet and close the door. Now he will discover that he is alone with God, with the invisible, ever-present God, who, in spite of our wickedness, loves us as the children of His heart. Let him kneel down—it is so joyfully solemn to bow the knee to God in the stillness of the little chamber—and pray to his Father in secret, as the words come straight from the heart. Our dear Heavenly Father understands the stammering of his weak children, and is pleased to hear it. He presses us to His heart. We feel it in the sublime devotion with which our heart is filled. And then the blessing with which we rise up and take away with us, that strengthens us to confident and joyful faith and all good, and in temptations mightily supports us! He who once knows this blessing will often seek the stillness of his chamber.

The change of heart is something so wonderful, so divine, that it does not permit itself to be compared with anything but a new birth. Other circumstances arise in life which move the heart mightily, but none of them change one's very heart. It is different with the new birth; by its means one is permanently inclined towards heavenly things. One attends to one's earthly affairs just as well as before, only with more conscientiousness and thoroughness, and therefore they succeed so much the better. One guards oneself against sin, and for that reason escapes many vexatious pursuits. But the inward consciousness, the new birth, is a secret of the soul with God, that only those can learn and know who not by men, but by God, are initiated into its mystery. It is like the new name and the new song in the Revelation of John.

A new song to sing,
That no other can,
To raise it to the Lamb,
The conqueror's path along.

Yes, to the Lamb who bears the sin of the world! On the cross Christ for us, Christ in us, where He wins an abiding place.

Virgins pure and holy,
Pictures all of Christ,
With His Spirit all are filled,
Him in all they see.

—Herder.

I had promised to say nothing of it that I wished to become
a missionary, and as my own inclination so entirely agreed with
this suggestion, I held my peace on the subject. From the
pleasures which young people generally love I silently withdrew
myself. This silence, doubtless, had its advantages. Not without
reason does Jesus say, "See thou tell no man." By talking of it,
whilst still new to me, I would only have done harm to myself
and no good to others; yet my quiet walking in the fear of God
could not remain unobserved, and I noticed that I was regarded
with a sort of holy awe. When occasion arose to lay blame or to
witness for the Lord I did it with a few words, and these were
always taken in good part. If, on the other hand, I had talked
much, it would have only aroused contempt and argument. This
silence, however, did not arise from my Christian knowledge—I
had no great acquisitions in this respect,—but from the promise
which I have previously mentioned.

Nor was I quite alone. Pastor Köhler could have easily
made me acquainted with converted Christians in his parish, but
he did not do it. Doubtless he had his reasons. I can see now
that he knew me most thoroughly, better than I knew myself.
Our conversations, when I fetched the Missionary Leaves, were
usually short, but I had on one occasion let fall that sometimes,
especially when my feelings were laid hold of by the contemplation of the works of God all around me, I had placed my thoughts
on paper, and in this way had filled many sheets. He told
me to bring him these papers. No one had seen them so far. I
hesitated, as I remarked my views had altered themselves very
considerably; but he wanted all the papers, and I must go through
them with him on my next visit. Naturally there was a lot of
nonsense in them, but they were written in such a manner that
one could learn from them what my disposition was.

In our work out of doors among the peasantry there is no
distinction of rank between the servant and the sons of the

household, but there is a distinction in the inside life of the house. Accordingly, I alone had a roomy, light bed chamber all to myself, with a chair, a little table, and an oil-lamp. On the table always lay my Bible, and in the chest of drawers lay writing materials and a few books which Pastor Köhler had lent me, among these the first volumes of Blumhardt's "History of Missions," embracing the first centuries of Christian chronology.

During the short Summer nights I had, with the exception of the Sunday afternoons, little time for reading; but as the nights became longer in the Autumn, of an evening, when all were in bed, I could sit still by my lamp and study Blumhardt's "History of Missions." I had often wondered whether other occurrences besides those related in the Bible were known in these ancient times, and here I found them. It was as if a whole new world of knowledge was laid open before me. It is no little matter, when one has been occupied all day with plough and harrow in the fresh air in the field, or has walked up and down with a heavy sack of seed on one's shoulders on newly ploughed land and sown the seed broadcast, to keep one's eyes open of an evening for the purpose of reading. But the spread of Christianity and its consequences under the Roman Emperors were to me so deeply interesting that I could have sat up with pleasure more than half the night if I had not promised Pastor Köhler on no account to deprive myself of the necessary sleep for the sake of study, and I would not break this promise secretly.

About half a year of the term of my probation had passed by. The time had not seemed long. It never occurred to me to count the months as young folks, who expect great things to happen at a certain date, are accustomed to do.

I was now acquainted with a man in an elevated position who could understand me. I could now have books and quench my thirst for knowledge as long as time was granted to me, and therewith I was content. And more than that— I had my Saviour Jesus Christ, and in Him a wealth of contentment that fills a deeper yearning in the soul than a thirst for knowledge.

CHAPTER III.

AN OCCUPATION IN BREMEN.

OWARDS Christmas I drove once more towards the mill, and after I had put the horses in the stall, while the corn was being ground, I went to Vilsen to Pastor Köhler. He was engaged in conversation with somebody, and had to keep me waiting a little while, with the remark that he had some good news for me. I could not guess what news this might be, and was still more astonished when, while the other visitor was about to go away and was taking his leave, the Pastor reached out his hand to me and said (pointing to me), " We must pray for this young man; he is going to the heathen." Then, when we were alone, he said he had written about me to Pastor Mallet, in Bremen, and had received an answer. He then read me a letter from Pastor Mallet, and the contents related that the committee had taken his letter into consideration, and had unanimously agreed that the young man was suitable for the service of Christ among the heathen, and he could come to Bremen at the New Year to be presented to the committee on the 2nd of January. This was a surprise.

On New Year's morning I rose at four, and started on the road to Bremen. It was a still, long, dark night, and the snow lay deep; but I knew all the roads for a mile, and then I came to the great thoroughfare. I can yet remember how happy I was with my Saviour, to whom I felt I could leave the result of my journey. I felt none of the earlier impatience for light of the days of my boorish ignorance. I had now the light of my Saviour, and if it should be His will that I should remain a peasant I was therewith content. In the afternoon I arrived at Bremen, and inquired my way to the church of St. Stephen. I had been in Bremen before with waggon and horses, and, in company with other peasants, had done business, and wondered at the high houses and many streets in the old city (altstadt); but now I was here alone, and about to speak with a city clergyman without introduction.

I walked round the church before I ventured to inquire where Pastor Mallet lived. At last I asked a child, who showed me the house at once. With a silent prayer I went into the house. On the threshold I asked a woman if the pastor was at home. The answer was—Yes. Could I speak to him? She thought not. A door opened at this moment, and a stately man, who had the appearance of a clergyman, stepped out. He came straight up to me, and before I could stammer out who I was and what I wanted, he said : " Ah, you are the young man of whom "—here he hesitated. " Yes," I said, " about whom Pastor Köhler has written to you." He took me by the hand and led me into a room, and as he saw my bashfulness he made me sit close beside him on the sofa, and calmed me in as friendly a manner as one would a nervous child, and this soon gave me confidence. As I observed that he was in a difficulty how to dispose of me, I said I could easily find lodging in a hostelry for a few days. " No," he said, " not in a hostelry ; wait, I will have my church servant called." He soon made his appearance, and I was handed over to him, with instructions to lodge me for a few days in a Christian family. And therewith the pastor gave him as many directions as to what he was to do with me, as if I were a child and might come to harm in Bremen. I was then in my 26th year, but on account of my small stature and fresh colour I appeared to be much younger. Amongst other things, the pastor said to the church servant that I knew no people, and that my pastor had been long dead. I was astonished to hear him say so, but did not dare to make any remark.

The church servant (his name was Bude) went with me to the street called " Way's End," to a master tailor of the name of Schierstein, and the family were willing to lodge me. I was un-accustomed to meeting townspeople, and therefore they and I spoke but little, but when I heard their pious conversation I thought, These people have in common what I so far have hidden in my heart. Here I was made acquainted with more Christian people, and it was always said before me that I knew no people, and that my pastor was dead long ago. At last I had to break in and say that our pastor was alive, only I had no further acquaintance with him than that I saw and heard him in the church; thereupon one of the friends said to me, "That is what we mean; it is true he has a bodily life, but spiritually he is dead." That I had to acknowledge. Soon I learnt further, that the expression that I knew no people at all did not mean that I had no acquaintances in Bremen, as I had understood it, but that I was not yet acquainted with new-born Christian people. Here I would now become acquainted with such. It was so good. It was a communion of the saints almost overpowering me.

On the evening of the 2nd of January I was to be presented to the committee. There was a mention, too, of a mission hour, and I could not quite make out which was the one, which the other. They told me, however, I need not disturb myself, as the church servant was instructed to keep me in the right way. He took me to a large hall and showed me my place at the upper end, not far from a table, and told me to stay there. The benches in the hall were gradually filled by people. There was no seat where I was placed, and I dared not leave the place. Standing was easy enough to me, but it occurred to me that I found myself in a conspicuous situation. Perhaps, thought I, this assembly is the committee, and I shall be examined here. At last Pastor Mallet came and held a mission hour, the first at which I had attended. At the conclusion, and as the people went away, he came to me, and now I saw that I had been thus placed that he might easily find me.

Pastor Mallet went with me out of the hall, and when we were in the street he drew my arm through his. This appeared to me almost too much condescension, but I submitted in silence. At last we went into a house (I think it was Burgomaster Nonnen's). Here in a room we found more gentlemen assembled. They seated themselves around a table, and I now saw what a committee was. I remained standing, because I thought I would have to undergo examination; but I was motioned to take my seat at the table. At first I was embarrassed, and did not know what was happening. A servant came in and brought a plate with confectionery. When he came to me I hesitated to take any, till a gentleman said to me I should take some, which I then did.

Thereupon I was drawn into conversation by the gentleman. The conversation became in time warm and still warmer, and I became at last so warm that I lost all my embarrassment, and was astonished at myself that I could express myself with clear voice and without hesitation so fluently in the unaccustomed High German language. Naturally my language could not be grammatical, and I noticed sometimes a good-humoured smile at my broad pronunciation. At last I was asked if I could find my lodgings alone. I gave the assurance that I had no trouble in finding my way in neighbourhoods with which I was unacquainted. I was then told I could go, and, early next morning, come to Pastor Mallet and he would inform me what the decision of the committee respecting me was. I was about to withdraw myself with a bow and a simple Good-night, but I was called back and compelled to shake every gentleman's hand.

The uncertainty about the decision I was to hear the next morning prevented my sleeping very well that night. There are times when we leave the result of great occasions quietly in God's hand, and with full acquiescence of the heart can say, "Thy will be done." At other times when perhaps the result is of far lesser importance, we can hardly arrive at such calm submission after much prayer. This shows us the wise education of our dear Heavenly Father. When He gives us such calm submission, then we know that His good Spirit rules our hearts, and that strengthens our faith and does us good. But that we should not be rebellious children at other times he allows us to struggle hard. Lord, if I only have Thee I ask no more from earth or heaven!

The next morning, as soon as I was presentable, I went to Pastor Mallet, for I had a walk of five miles before me, and the days were short and the weather cold. I found him in his work-room. He looked earnest and moved, as if he had been praying, and he said to me the committee had resolved in the name of God to take me up. He did not yet know to which institute they would send me, nor did he know the time. I should go back home, and when the time came he would write to Pastor Köhler. Then he laid his hand on my head and blessed me. The remembrance of this blessing has sometimes been an encouragement to me in my lonely missionary work.

On my journey homeward I took my way through Vilsen, where I arrived in the evening. I found Pastor Köhler in his study, and as he looked at me inquiringly, I said the committee in Bremen has resolved to take me up in the name of God. He was visibly moved. I narrated shortly what had happened to me in Bremen, and then said: " So far I have concealed my intention, but now I must tell it in the house, for I have taken care of the farm work for my uncle, and he must be on the look out for a man who can take my place." " Yes," he said, " now you can tell it." Then he took me into the dwelling room, and made me acquainted with his family, especially his mother and two sisters (he was not married)—we were country people of the same district. He was the son of the Obervogt at Bücken, the parish where Mahlenstorf, my birthplace, was situated. One of the sisters remembered having seen my father, Bauermeister Gerd Wöhlers, in their house doing business with her father. Pastor Köhler was the second pastor. The first (the superintendent) preached in such a manner that the glory of the Bible was lost, and as if Jesus Christ was merely a wise teacher. Köhler, however, resolutely preached Jesus Christ the Son of God and the Saviour of sinners. He was, moreover, a broad-minded man, and a friend of art and science. I still had a good hour to walk before I arrived at home ; but that was a small matter to me in a region where I knew all roads and by-ways on the darkest night. Arrived at the house, I saw my uncle and both aunts were curious to learn some news from me, and I narrated my affairs. I found that the matter was not unexpected by them. They had long seen that there was something going on.

I have just mentioned two aunts. One was my uncle's wife, and the other her and my mother's unmarried sister. This one loved me like a mother, but was willing to allow me to go to the heathen in the service of Jesus Christ. All were of one mind, that this would suit my inclination better than farming. They were old-fashioned, and had not experienced the new birth as I had lived it through in stillness. Still piety was more and more observed in the house; also, among my brothers and sister (we had six brothers and only one sister), who all lived at my birthplace and its neighbourhood (three hours distant from Hoyerhagen), a spiritual life began to be apparent, and has continued to thrive. To some of the neighbours it was ridiculous. Others, however, and they were the most numerous, thought there might well be somewhat of good in it, and they wished me the blessing of God.

CHAPTER IV.

IN THE MISSION HOUSE AT HAMBURG.

WHEN, after some time, I again visited Pastor Köhler, he said, "I have an invitation for you. Mrs. Olmann, of Bruckhöfen, would like you to call on her." "Oh," I said, "we are related." "Yes," he replied, "I have heard so. You will find there also spiritual relations. The old mother in the house just lives in the Word of God." Now, I had sometimes in my childhood visited this old mother with my grandmother. Later on, after my grandmother was dead, the visits were neglected, because the relationship was distant. When I related at home that I had received this invitation, my aunt (my mother's sister) was overjoyed that the old friendship would be renewed through me, and that by means of a spiritual relationship (I kept silence on the subject of my Christianity no longer). It was resolved that my uncle's daughter, a growing maiden, and myself should go next Sunday morning to the church at Vilsen, and hear Pastor Köhler preach (it was his Sunday), and then from there go with the Olmann family to Bruckhöfen. Our aunt could describe to us exactly how we should find Olmann's cherry orchard. All happened as arranged. We knew one another yet, although we had not seen one another for many years.

Madam Olmann (not to be confused with the old mother, the particular friend of my dead grandmother) had much to tell me. First, however, I will say that I found in her and in her house living Christianity. Some Christian neighbours used to visit it.

They had been awakened by Pastor Köhler, and were like the people I had learnt to know in Bremen—joyous, free Christians, like the pastor himself. Madam Olmann told me the pastor had told her of a young man from Hoyerhagen who intended to go to a mission school, and had the proposal made to her to collect the passage money for him. She was quite willing to give her assistance. Then she had met a lady from the district of the Vilser commonalty at Hoyerhagen, and asked if she could tell her from what house the young man came that intended to be a missionary. " Oh! don't you know ? " she replied, " that is one of the sons of Ahlers Gretchen." Then she remembered me, and went at once to Pastor Köhler and besought him to make no collection. The young man might not like it (she knew the self-respect of the Ahlers and Wöhlers); he came of a good family, and was not without means.

I will here confess for the first time an act of stupidity of which I was guilty a few weeks later, and upon which I always look back with disgust. One Sunday morning I went to the church at Vilsen. As it was still early I spoke to Pastor Köhler. He could not give me much attention, as he had to preach ; but I had the *entrée* to his dwelling-room. Here I met a candidate of theology, the son of the squire (amtsmann) of Brückhausen, a village near Vilsen. He was so friendly towards me that I loved him at once. As we went to church he compelled me to go with him to his seat. Owing to a feeling of friendship, and before my head had time to reflect, I gave way to him. But as we were in the squire's place (amtsmann) and amongst the upper classes I saw at once that I was in the wrong place, and that my presence there must give offence. I would have liked to crawl under the seat. I wished I was outside, but I could not get out without attracting attention, and was obliged therefore to sit it out. The candidate kept me at his side, and let me look over his book, but I could give it no attention. Since then I was always careful, as long as I was a peasant, not to give offence by intruding myself into the society of the upper classes.

In spite of this, the friendship thus commenced between myself and the candidate (his name was Merkel) continued to

ripen. Perhaps it was weakness on both sides that drew us together; but with this difference, that my head, although slower
than my heart, always in the end (if you gave it time enough)
obtained the supremacy, but with him the heart always ran away
with the head.

Later on, when I went into the district in the holidays, we
met at the mill, and he visited me at Hoyerhagen. And when I
was not there, he visited at the house, where, as my friend and a
favourite of my old aunt, he was always welcome. He became
pastor (in the common of Lüneberg) before I was sent out, and
I have visited him in his parish; but I heard to my sorrow that
his heart always overran his head, which brought him into
trouble.

The winter passed, and I heard nothing from Pastor Mallet;
but in the week after Easter a letter arrived, wherein I was
requested to go to Bremen as soon as possible, that I might be
sent to Hamburg from there. When I bid the pastor good-bye,
he said : " Beware of both pride and self-abasement." This warning
was of importance to me, for I was soon to come into a position
where I had need of it.

I little dreamed that at this last farewell to the dear Pastor
Köhler in this life I should see him no more. He died after a
few months of a fever, in the midst of his most blessed labours.
Soon afterwards died the superintendent—a Rationalist. When, a
few years later, I went to Vilsen in the holidays, we went to the
churchyard to see Pastor Köhler's grave. It was tidy, and planted
with flowers; that of the superintendent was neglected and overgrown with weeds. The Köhler family was no longer there, but
the faithful old servant was still there—the same who a few years
before had brought the missionary tracts which gave the direction
to my life to the mill, and had laid them on the table in the
miller's room, where I found them. We were both overjoyed and
overcome by our feelings to see one another in this life. He
belonged in a certain manner to the vicarage, for whenever a
pastor died or was removed he always remained in the house, and
was servant to the successor. He was now old, and had not long
to live.

When I took leave in Bremen of Pastor Mallet, he said: "You will find out a great many things such as I cannot tell you, but do not allow yourself to be bewildered. Hold fast to Christ; with Him we can go through, but without him we were lost in Paradise." His farewell warning was an anchor in my later difficulties.

I must here beg attention to another important warning, even if it was given in a spirit as if it had been that of Caiaphas. He, however, did not speak of himself, but he prophesied because that year he was high priest.

The day before my departure from Bremen to Hamburg I was commended to Aldermann Haase. He asked me if I wanted money for my journey. I said No, I was amply provided. Then, said he, his servant should go with me to the post-town and furnish the money for my passage. I replied, " I shall be very glad if your servant will go with me to the post-town, because I am unacquainted with it ; but you must allow me to pay for my fare myself, for if God calls me to the mission both what I have and am belong to the mission." Then he looked at me earnestly and said : " That God has called you to the mission service you must doubt no more." In later years this Alderman Haase became notorious on account of a sad defalcation. I am convinced, however, that what he said to me was uprightly spoken at the very least. He spoke to me as a member of the mission committee, and the admonition was in my later difficulties a source of strength to me.

Arrived in Hamburg, I found two pupils, with whom I was associated. As there was no domicile connected with the mission, we boarded and lodged with a Christian family. My installation with my fellow pupils, and the Christian people with whom we were on terms of intimacy, or those with whom we had any society, was different to what it had been in Bremen. There (in Bremen) Pastor Mallet had always laid it down with marked emphasis: He knows no one. I was received here, however, as still young in Christ, and my want of experience supplied in a friendly manner, and we got along very well together. In Hamburg, however, a refined Christianity was expected from me, and they were disappointed. I arrived in peasant's clothes, was unaccustomed to associate with townspeople, and inexperienced in Christian companionship. I do not know what the respective opinions on either side were, but I know that when I was presented in the evening to Candidate Brauer, who had most prominently undertaken the direction of our conduct, I felt I should have to call a halt here, and I was not mistaken.

One of my fellow pupils, Ochs, from the Würtemberg country, belonged by birth to the cultivated classes, and I could well understand that he could not associate with me. The other, Trost, was of the peasantry, but had for a long time past acquired the manners of the townspeople, and was much older than myself. In his company I seemed little more than a boy. As neither thought it worth the trouble to assist me heartily, I was always afraid of committing a breach of good manners, and managed matters so much the worse and showed myself still more clownish.

But there were certain of the people of our circle who always gave the tone, and these must be considered for a time as connected with my fellow pupils. They were mostly, judged by the standard of city tone and city manners, as uncultivated as the peasantry. A young Jesus may have been the same. But I missed in them the free, joyful, Christlike life that I had found amongst the people in the Vilsen community. These people had to bear with me, but they let me understand that they neither thought me to be called to the service of a missionary nor especially adapted for it.

Candidate Brauer had especially undertaken our training, but he could only give us a small modicum of instruction, because a meeting of the General Assembly was shortly to be held in Bremen, and he had to make preparation for it; other candidates had therefore to render assistance.

I have yet a lively recollection of the impression that the first hour of instruction in the German language made upon me. For the first time I held a German grammar in my hand, and I was asked what an article was. I bethought myself that so far I had heard of no other articles than the "Three chief articles of the Christian religion." I could hardly believe these were meant, and I made answer, "No." The candidate (Moraht, later on

Pastor at Mölln) shook his head doubtfully, and as a consequence I could never forget that hour. My position became still more doubtful. At the coming General Assembly a decision had to be arrived at relative to the establishment of a missionary institute and the election of an inspector, in case the North German Missionary Society did not dissolve, which was what the people in our circle desired, and for which they prayed, on account of a separation from the Reformed Church, so that an exclusively Lutheran society might take its place. If the Candidate Brauer should be elected inspector I thought my position secure; but if a man after the hearts of the earnest Lutherans should be chosen, l thought I might take my leave; and that very nearly happened to me. I had on that account very considerable attacks of diffidence. I fought and prayed over it; but Pastor Köhler had said to me: " Beware of both pride and self-abasement." I remembered also the admonition of Alderman Haase: " We must not doubt that God has called you to missionary service." I often strengthened myself with the thought that Pastor Mallet had told me all this beforehand, although I did not understand it at the time.

Before I came to Hamburg I had never heard of religious discord. I was induced by the reading of the merciful missionary tract to take part in the conversion of the heathen, and by the same means became intimately acquainted with the dear, widehearted Pastor Köhler. Then, without my knowing exactly how it happened, the Spirit of God had enlightened me and converted me to Jesus Christ. Thereon I was made acquainted with the dear Pastor Mallet and other liberal Christian people in Bremen, and with just as liberal people in the community at Vilsen.

But Lutheran and Reformed differences of opinion were not taken into consideration. All were hearty loving disciples of Jesus Christ. I had lived through it myself, and it was as certain to me as the certainty that there is a Weser river, and that its waters, which I had so often gazed on with awestruck feelings, lose themselves in still greater waters, amongst which they pour themselves. Now, to convince me that the believers in the Reformed Church were less righteous disciples of Jesus Christ, or had a lesser part in the Kingdom of Heaven, than the believers in the Lutheran Church, was as impossible as to try to convince me that there was no water in the Weser river.

When the General Assembly, which was held in the week after Whitsuntide, at Bremen, was closed, it was resolved at once to establish a missionary institute at Bremen, and candidate Brauer was elected inspector. This choice was a great comfort and joy to me, but a great disappointment to others who had great influence on my fellow pupils. Before a mission house could be built Brauer was to make a journey to Bremen and Basel personally to inspect the local mission houses. Dear Inspector Brauer was much misunderstood and abused. He had many enemies. He embittered the unbelievers by his blameless bearing towards infidelity (perhaps with more mildness than harshness), and the timid believers as well, because he joined himself, and with himself the Hamburg Mission Union to the Reformed North German Mission Union.

The Summer soon slipped by, while Brauer was away on his journey, and the pupils during this time were somewhat neglected. Candidates Moraht, Huber, and Reils gave us some lessons. Ochs those in the ancient languages, Trost and myself in the groundings of instruction, such as children of the upper classes have in a school for children. I learnt with eagerness, and as soon as the outer rind of my ignorance was pierced I learnt easily. I understood now what an article meant in grammar. I learnt to my satisfaction the difference between "dem" and "den," and other mistakes, over which I had formerly considerably puzzled myself. My teachers no longer shook their heads doubtfully over my unheard-of ignorance. I gained confidence again. My struggles, my wholesome disposition towards timidity, and anxiety being laid on one side, were overcome. I had enough to content me, both in Christ and in a satisfaction of my desire for learning.

At last Inspector Brauer came back from his journey, and then towards Autumn the mission house could be begun. At the same time Riemenschneider came from Berlin, and entered as a new pupil. We were soon intimate friends, for we both came from the committee in Bremen, were both of the Weser district, and spoke in leisure hours both the same Bremen Weser low German language. We had both great desire to learn, and both loved our inspector Brauer in our most inmost souls. Riemenschneider had had a better education than I had, and had later and better opportunities for self cultivation. But yet, by means of the instruction imparted to me in the summer in Hamburg, we both were on a level and made equal progress. In learning our lessons, so far as a matter of understanding them was concerned, I made more progress than he did, perhaps because I had greater health, and could bring greater exertion to bear on them; but in fineness of feeling, and in admiration of all that was noble and beautiful, he was my superior.

I had never been able to establish an intimate friendship with the other two pupils. The hindrance lay principally in the influences brought to bear upon them by timid Lutheran friends. One of them, Ochs, was thereby so much influenced against the inspector that it necessarily came to an open breach and division. Trost, the other, was a good-natured Christian, and less taken up with human institutions; but he was too old to be able to learn. It was impossible to him to learn a foreign language, which was unmistakeably needful for a missionary. He went, therefore, out of the mission house into the Rough house, where as overseer of the boys in their agricultural labours he was unmistakeably in his place, and it was a mistake to withdraw him later on from this occupation.

The years that I spent in the mission house—from October, 1837, till the end of 1842—were very pleasant years to me. Here I obtained in full measure, and always with a grateful heart, what in days of my peasant life, from childhood upwards, consciously and unconsciously, I had sought after with pain. Consciously I had sought an opening to obtain cultivation and knowledge; unconsciously, in my secret yearnings after something higher than knowledge, living faith in Jesus Christ and blessed communion with Him. Without this living faith opportunity for cultivation would not have given me full satisfaction. I learnt with eagerness, but I had enough sound sense to know

that I could never become a learned man.   He who begins in his
six-and-twentieth year cannot possibly make up for what ought
to be begun in his sixth year.   And then in the schools for higher
cultivation and the gymnasium, the thoughts are under control
from childhood upwards, and brought into working order ; but
with me, my thinking faculties in the years of their quickest
development had grown up wild and distorted amongst carts,
ploughs and harrows, and corn waggons; at the threshing floor ;
at towns and villages, with dreamy thoughts in lonely woods and
deserts.   That could no more be altered.   Wild flights of thought
and contradictions to the right ones will unmarked make their
appearance, even though afterwards seen through.

Pursuing the same line of thought, I must throw light in a
different direction.   It is not unknown to me that my present
condition is a different one to what it was in earlier years.   For
he who has grown up to years of manhood in a natural state can
only in his maturity work his way into the deeper contemplation
of matters which another who has been under culture from childhood attains as a pupil in the High School.   The former will
therefore write differently when close on to seventy years of age
than he would have done when between thirty and forty.
Earlier, deeper impressions, which have been outlived, which one
did not then know how to represent, obtain only in time of old
age clear form and substance.

But yet I grieve in no wise that my earlier years were lived
as a peasant ; indeed, on no account would I have had it otherwise ; for if I had been in a condition from childhood upwards to
go through the proper courses, through better schools right up to
the university, I should have looked upon it as a matter of course,
and I should not have had the enduring consciousness of looking
back with pleasure on the years of earnest seeking, ending in the
joyful finding.   Besides, I should have had less skill and inclination to educate these wild New Zealanders after they had first
been converted and a desire for·Christian manners and customs
had been awakened in them, and make them into respectable
members of human society, to effect which a cultivated teacher
was less effective than an experienced helper.   In addition, my

youthful labours in the fresh air had given me sound health and a hardy constitution, which stood me in good stead in carrying this out. The principle instruction in the mission house was the daily Bible Lesson. The extracts from the Bible were first gone through daily in questions and answers. Our Bibles were interleaved with white paper, and the right translations and more correct readings, as well as a few annotations, were at once written down, and then learnt by heart. Then we had to work out the whole in writing and lay it before the inspector. He showed us then where we had not got the right meaning, at all events not to his satisfaction. Such a method of ground work leads to confidence in the knowledge of the Scriptures. Besides that, we had lessons in the German and English languages, geography, natural history (embracing a considerable range), algebra, drawing, trignometry, music. I could make nothing of the last subject. Later on we had special lessons, which were at once reduced to writing, of which the most important were those about world and Church history, the development of Christian life, and dogmatic religion.

In the German language our inspector began quite a new method with us, in accordance with Woerst's method of learning language; but as I had already become acquainted with the customary grammatical methods, and had found the key in them to what was to me before a sealed book, I could not adapt myself to the new method, and I always had to go back to the old one in order to understand the new one, which is what ought not to have been. The new philosophical way may have its advantages under certain circumstances, but I believe I should have been more firmly grounded in the German language if the instruction had been continued in the old-fashioned method.

As Riemenschneider and I showed a desire for it, our inspector began to give us instruction in Latin and Greek, which was a matter of great joy to us. Later on, however, it was decided at a General Assembly that instruction in the old languages must cease, because it was too much, and other necessary studies might be neglected. The General Assembly was so far right, for we had in our last years very much to make up, and it is not everybody who is strong enough to bear the necessary strain, and besides, we could never expect to become so accomplished in the ancient languages as to be able to do justice to the treasures of knowledge and of what is noble and beautiful preserved therein. But yet learning these languages gives one an advantage in learning other languages, so that one can fearlessly attack a quite foreign language, and that is of considerable value.

Besides, the ancient languages had become so dear to me that I could not give them up. I continued therefore the study of them in the quiet of my hours of reflection. My health was so good that I could endure prolonged exertions. This was not all. I bought an old Hebrew grammar and book from an old Jew bookseller, and began to learn Hebrew. I did not do it in secret, for that would not have been right; but I drew as little attention to it as possible, for fear that it might be forbidden. I never asked the inspector for assistance when I came to a dead stop, but wended my way to the candidates, amongst others to Candidate Valett. He had mentioned what I was doing in the city, where I had friends—for I sometimes made an excursion into the city—namely, Dr. Wyneken (lawyer), Pastor Von Hanffstengel, Rector Sattler, and others. One day at dinner the inspector said to me, " We have found out to-day what you are." Astonished, I asked what that could be. " That you are a Jew," was the answer. I noticed now that he referred to my Hebrew. After dinner he handed me a Hebrew Old Testament, grammar, and dictionary—all new books, gifts from my friends in the city. Before we were sent out I had got so far that, with some help from a dictionary, I could read easy Latin books. I could read the Greek New Testament because the translation was known to me. I nearly knew the first three chapters of the first book of Moses in Hebrew by heart, and began to read myself into the Old Testament in it. I flattered myself with the hope of becoming proficient in these languages, and to be able to make progress in them in my leisure hours in New Zealand, but that was a mistake. There were no leisure hours there, but work, always work. Later on my house and all my books were burnt. It was all over then with striving after learning; but I did not relinquish the idea without inward grief. I recognised, however, that I would do wrong if I desired new books in the old languages.

Outside the mission house I had no intimate friends in Hamburg. The zealots for Church doctrine were too repellant, and the evangelically inclined believer had enough sense to see that it would be ill-advised to withdraw us from our studies for the sake of friendly intercourse. It was different with more remotely dwelling missionary friends, who lived at some distance from Hamburg. We could only visit these in the holidays, or in short excursions, for the sake of recreation as at Easter time, and here real true friendship, as with family relations, could be cultivated with a few rich friends in the city I have already named. Other dear friends we had in the family of the merchant Schlüter, Dr. Schatze, and Mr. Kober. Also in the castle, in the family of the squire (amtsmann) of Lindstow, we were always welcome. But what I enjoyed most of all such pleasant recreations was that with the dear pastor Lüders and his dear wife, and their very dear little children, at Groden, near Ritzebüttel. The little children since then have long become big. When I was in New Zealand I learnt that Pastor Lüders had received a call to the Vierlanden, near Hamburg.

It was a good regulation in our missionary institute that we were allowed to travel four weeks every Summer. Our views were widened, and we obtained confidence to move about unconstrainedly in strange places. The travelling was especially good for Riemenschneider and myself, for we had previously not been even outside our own home neighbourhood. We had seen no mountains or sea. Both mountains and sea from childhood I had earnestly wished to be allowed to see. It is true I had once or twice been in the neighbourhood of Nienburg and seen a part of the mountains near the Westphalian State as a blue streak in the far distant sky, and I had then wondered what it looked like both on and close to the mountains.

It was with high spirits that Riemenschneider and myself with a knapsack on our backs started out to see the world for the first time. We first went past Stade and Ritzebüttel, where we had a glimpse of the North Sea. But we did not find the impression of a flat surface, the gradually widening distant Elbe, so sublime as we had expected. Certainly we did not see the sea, but only the mouth of the Elbe. Thence we went past Bremen to my home in Hoyerhagen, where, however, we did not remain, for we wished to travel over a part of the Weser mountains. When we then came into the neighbourhood of Nienburg I could show Riemenschneider the blue streak of the mountains, the goal of our journey, in the far-away distance. At Gernsheim, on the road to Münden, we had the opportunity of seeing a glassworks and glassmaking.

The Weser mountains are small compared with other German mountains, but on us who had never seen mountains before they made a powerful impression. The wood-crowned heights with the beautiful lofty aisles of trees presented a magnificent sight. The Westphalian gate itself looks like an enormous breach in a dyke—only you must imagine a dyke five to eight hundred feet high. The Weser has here broken through a long mountain ridge in order to force its way out of the mountains into the plain, and be able to flow past the place where Bremen and Hoya stand. From the gate we mounted the mountain on the right hand (looking up the stream) 800ft. above the Weser. A metalled road led upwards through a dark avenue of trees. The soil of the wood was covered with blackberries on which the black fruit hung in quantity. Riemenschneider knew the blackberries well in baskets, as they are sold in the markets in Bremen, but he had never seen them growing naturally before. I could not get him away—he was for picking all the time. He had more pleasure in picking them than in buying them in Bremen.

A watchtower stood on the top, which we had seen already from a distance. In olden times it had been used for watching offensive operations. Arrived at the top, we found an old lady all alone sitting by the tower and spinning. She became quite lively when she saw us, and related she was a poor woman, and the authorities had given her the key of the tower to unlock it for visitors. She sat here many a day, and not a soul came up. We recompensed her at first with small silver, and then gave her a sustaining tract, with which she was overjoyed. From the top of the tower there was an enchanting view over the mountains into the valley of the Weser, and a wide view over the plain country, with the town and fortress, Preuss, in the neighbourhood of Münden. As the tower stands on a steep hill and overhangs the top, the feeling of standing up there all alone gave a little scope to one's imagination. It was entrancing—one seemed to sway in a starry air castle in the upper air.

We visited the old Schaumburg, the village of Bückeburg, and then went to Rinteln. We then visited the pastor of Langenholzhausen, to whom we had an introduction. I think his name was Rückert, but I am not sure. He obliged us to take a walk with him into the mountains, for (said he) he was a child of the mountains, and it gave him great pleasure to show us dwellers in the plain the beauty of the mountains and valleys. With pleasant conversation, during which he showed us the shells embedded in the chalk cliffs, we wandered into a lively little valley—and there we were surprised. We saw living waters gushing up out of the earth—many springs only a little distance from one another. Each had a little well, out of which the clearest of water welled up, and then bubbled forth in a little channel, making a little natural river, which joined with another, and all united together made a brook, which in a short distance drove a mill. The ground between the springs was not at all swampy, but hard and dry. The water was so clear and inviting that we could not help lifting it up with our hands and drinking it.

After the description of this still lively recollection of our first holiday tour, it will not be necessary to describe the impressions experienced in other journeys. We made a journey through Holstein, where there are pleasant lakes, and went once to the Lüneburg Common. It is now a wild waste common, with here and there solitary birds; and has, for one who has a feeling for the impressions of nature, something inspiring in it. Sometimes when we wished to make long journeys and had not much money, we found it advisable to part and journey alone, for then we could always reckon on hospitality. Friends of the mission, to whom it was easy to obtain introductions from place to place, were always overjoyed hospitably to entertain one, whereas there was not always room for two.

Accordingly I once made a journey through Mecklenburg and Pommerania to the island of Rugel, on which occasion 1 learnt to know and love many dear Christian friends. From the high chalk cliffs and rocks I obtained more magnificent sights of the ocean than the view the level banks of the Elbe had afforded. Once I made a long journey, mostly alone, too, through the Hartz mountains, and from there past Göttingen to Cassel, then to Thüringen and through the Thüringen forest, then back past Jena, Leipzig, Halle, and Magdeburg, and had the opportunity of seeing many cities and people. On this journey I used the privileges of hospitality, but to a small extent, for I was supplied with money from home, and 1 wished to exercise an independence in which I was somewhat wanting.

Good practice for practical missionary work was to be found in teaching in the Sunday School. In this way we could easily exercise ourselves, especially in teaching, and in preparation of comprehensible examples and narrations in biblical history acquired fluency of speech. Then we visited the scholars in their dwellings, and had an opportunity to become acquainted with their parents, and thus exercise ourselves in house visits in the spiritual interests of the occupants.

CHAPTER V.

AT SEA.

FROM the beginning I was convinced that the Missionary Society had to decide for us where our labours among the heathen lay, and I had therefore refrained from allowing myself any preference for any country or people; but when at last New Zealand was chosen, I could not rejoice over it. It was well known to me from the missionary papers that the English missionaries there, after long and apparently unsuccessful efforts, had won over the hearts of the natives to Christianity. The conversion was of such a nature that the early converison of the whole land to Christianity was to be expected. It is true there were still heathen districts where we could find work, but I could not get rid of the idea that, as New Zealand had become a British colony, and British settlers were going there, that we should appear to be sectarian intruders. I made no opposition, however, for the leaders of our society had their own good reasons for choosing New Zealand. Our mission was the first one, and great circumspection was necessary. A land difficult of access, a deadly climate, or other great hindrances which might easily wreck the mission; or, on the other hand, too long waiting for the first converts, might prove disadvantageous to a young missionary society that had not the standing of the North German Missionary Society. There was no need to fear such difficulties in New Zealand : the access was easy, the climate healthy, and the fields white for harvest.

I consented willingly from a sense of duty. The favourable conditions in New Zealand influenced me not in the slightest. A missionary who has given himself to the service of the Lord is indifferent to the dangers and difficulties before him. This is no heroic virtue; it is in this as in other respects of the nature of the matter. When, later on, the missionary amongst the heathen gets into danger or stumbles upon insurmountable difficulties, he may well be afraid—that is only human nature ; but at the time of his despatch the matter is no more considered by him than a student of theology would be afraid to study because, some time or other, he must mount the pulpit and preach, although when the time really comes, and for the first time he enters the pulpit, he must—he may well—tremble with dismay.

So far I had willingly accepted the choice made—viz., that of New Zealand—but when land was bought and we were directed to build a house on it ; when Trost was sent for from erecting the farm buildings at the rough house at Hofmeier ; when a waggon and farm implements were bought, which we were to take with us, then I became disheartened. I knew from my own experience that farming demanded hard, dull work from early morn till evening if it is not to be prosecuted at a loss, and the mere raising of food for one's own wants may be more costly than when it is bought. I knew that the fatigue of much manual labour would exhaust energies required for learning and teaching, as well as the zeal for missionary work proper. Sirach said that 2,000 years ago. "He who wants to learn the Scriptures can attend to no other labour, and if one wishes to learn one must do nothing else. How can he attend to learning who must plough, drive oxen with a whip, and do suchlike matters, and can talk of nothing but oxen. He must think how he can farm, and, late and early, must give the cows their fodder." (Sirach xxxviii., 25-7.) When I had an opportunity to lay it before the leader of the mission, I gave expression to my thoughts on the subject. To quell my fears I was told that, the first labours being over, things would be easier. Further, Trost would be sent as superintendent of the agricultural matters, and we would find the farm buildings a useful addition to the residence, and so on.

But I knew well what enormous labour it would entail to erect farm buildings in a wilderness. If even ever so plain a residence and lodging-house were erected, fences and ditches would have to be made, the wild land prepared for the plough, the necessary beasts attended to late and early, and other unexpected labours executed as occasion might require. I knew Trost, and knew that he would prove a good overseer ; but for manual labour his best years were already behind him, and the Missionary Society had not the means to supply many experienced workmen. What, therefore, had to be done had to be principally done with our own hands, or the farm would have to be worked at a loss. But as it was once decided that so it should be, I gave way, and was resolved to do my best, in accordance with my German nature. The English say the German does his duty without grumbling; the Englishman does his duty best whilst heartily grumbling.

I am inclined to think few theological students fresh from the High School, with any quantity of learning still buzzing about in their heads, would be inclined to undergo the high solemnity and sacredness of the ordination, and I felt this holy awe; but there was nothing else for it. I was ordained in

August, 1842, in the great church of St. Michael in Hamburg, by
the head pastor, Dr. Strauch. His text was: "Thou therefore
endure hardness as a good soldier of Jesus Christ." (Timothy ii.,
2, 3.) Feelings which are sacred to oneself and concern oneself alone, one keeps locked in one's own heart, and does not care
to speak about them.

In October of the same year another solemn service was
held in St. George's Church in Hamburg on behalf of us four
New Zealand missionaries and the missionary Valett, who was
destined for the East Indies, at which I gave a short address on
the words " Lift up your eyes and look on the fields, for they are
white already for harvest." Pastor Mallet delivered a powerful
address on the text, "All power in heaven and earth is given unto
me. Go ye, therefore, and teach all nations, baptizing them in
the name of the Father, of the Son, and of the Holy Ghost."

Just before our departure a solemn farewell to us was held
one evening in the mission house — Trost, Heine, Riemenschneider and myself — at which the particular duty of each
was allotted to him. The monetary affairs and account keeping
were allotted to me. All expenses were to be provided for out
of the mission chest, and exact accounts kept and forwarded. On
the whole this appeared right to me, but in one particular it went
against my German freedom-loving individuality, because all
private dealings in one's private property were cut off. No one
could incur the expense of a penny according to his own liking,
—whether it were the giving of an alms or the purchase of a
quarter of a pound of tobacco—without giving an account of it.
I asked, therefore, that each of us should be allowed five shillings
a month as pocket money, which he could spend as he liked, and
the request was at once willingly granted.

At last, at the end of the year 1842, on the day after
Christmas, came the day of our departure. The ship St. Paul,
Captain Schacht, which was to take us in addition to a considerable number of German emigrants to New Zealand, had already,
before it could take in the whole of its cargo, left the harbour of
Hamburg, and lay at anchor not far from the city. A steamer
crammed full · took us and the emigrants, as well as a few

gentlemen of the governing body of the New Zealand Land and
Emigration Society in Hamburg, to the ship. It was a moist
day—not exactly rainy, but so moist all over that you could
hardly tell land from water. Arrived at the St. Paul, and having
climbed on board, Riemenschneider and I had at once important
affairs to attend to. We were requested by the above-named
New Zealand society to undertake the spiritual welfare of the
emigrants in the ship, and we were at once asked to unite five
pairs of engaged couples, who by this means escaped the marriage
fees payable at home. The ceremony was performed in the
'tweendecks, underneath the large hatchway. The brides and
bridegrooms stood before us in a half-circle, close behind them, as
officials of the emigrants, stood the before-named gentlemen,
and around in the dark hold of the vessel, thickly packed, stood
the emigrants; above, over the combings, heads close to heads,
looked down, like the heads of angels, the fresh wind and weather-
reddened faces of the hardy sailors. Overhead in the watery sky
floated seagulls. It was a really joyous scene. The confusion of
starting did not disturb me, for I felt I was in my right place, and
that gave me confidence. Being the oldest of us two ordained
missionaries I gave a short discourse about Christmas and emigration. Joseph and Mary were obliged shortly after the first
Christmas to emigrate from Egypt with their child, the Saviour
of the world. We, too, began our emigration on Christmas. Let
us also take the child Jesus, born for our salvation, in our hearts
along with us, and cherish him there, and so on. Then I read a
short marriage service, and then Riemenschneider and I both went
to work and joined each pair separately together. Riemenschneider joined three, I two pairs. The newly made brides and
bridegrooms were then congratulated by the officials, and the
solemnity was at an end. The wind was unfavourable for our
journey over the North Sea; we had, therefore, to remain a week
at anchor in the Elbe. We had now opportunity to become acquainted with our travelling companions, but our feelings were
not much disposed towards companionship, because everybody
was too cold. One only saw blue faces looking out of heavy over-
coats. It was the middle of winter, and we missed the accustomed

stoves. At last, after the New Year, 1843, the weather appeared favourable for our journey to begin. It was a beautiful Winter's evening as we, in company with other vessels that were also waiting for a fair wind, put to sea. How beautiful the works of Creation are, and the dear God has given man the power not only to feel the beauty but to make himself like it. The sight of beautiful buildings and architecture uplifts the heart ; not less inspiring is the sight of large ships, when, with full sails and a graceful inclination, they plough their way through the waves.

For the last time I cast my glances once more towards the beloved Fatherland, now vanishing in the gloaming. There was only a little corner of it in sight, but it was German soil which my feet should press no more.

The fine weather did not last long. Even the first night it began to blow, and that dead ahead. Readers on land who have never been at sea may well wish to know how one feels in such a position. Now, when one goes to sea for the first time, and that in rough weather, sea sickness is certainly an important matter, and the reader must try it himself to discover what it is like, or he misses the principal experience of a sea voyage. In order to know how one feels we must go back to the days of our childhood, when, as children, we turned ourselves quickly round and round till everything around us appeared to turn round. Then we fell down quite giddy, and now the world seemed to drop down on one side and turn itself around sideways. Now let one imagine while we were so lying and thinking the giddiness had gone by, a power takes hold of us and swings us up and down in slow measures from side to side, sometimes head up and sometimes head down. We cry out, Let me go, I cannot stand it, I shall be sick. But the power is relentless. The long swayings go on without ceasing ; everything internal turns itself around, and that not for, may be, an hour, but all the time, day and night, till at last one gets used to it. But before this can happen all spirit is gone. With some the feeling of depression is so bad that complete indifference to anything, even life and death, sets in. If, for instance, you were told, the ship was sinking and you would all be drowned, you would listen with complete indifference, and if you thought it worth while to answer, the answer would be the sooner the better. In others, however, especially if of a hardy constitution, courage does not sink quite so far, but still they get pitifully low. Their imagination exercises itself in vain wishes, but of different kinds, never far removed from the sea; and, really, one feels inclined on no account to undertake the journey homeward again. If one could only, even in storm and rain, once more stand on firm ground again; if it were only a spot of wet sand on a seashore. But the long swayings go on, and one has no opportunity of refreshing oneself even a little. Then a cold trembling shudders through one, for we are in winter on the rough North Sea, and there is no stove in the ship. If one could only warm oneself a little—once more sit in a warm room, or even in a damp fisherman's hut, with a little window from above, and of glass made dark with the dirt of flies. But vain wishes. Unceasing are the swayings that cause everything inside to turn around.

But we must see once how a storm-tossed sea looks from a ship's deck. To do that, let us wrap ourselves up and work our way up the companion on to the deck. From our cabin, as the ship is leaning over to one side, one can see through the porthole the foaming crest of a high wave—a magnificent, horror-awakening sight. Arrived on deck, we see moving mountains of a grey-green colour, as if they had arisen from the broken gall of the seasick people. The captain stands quietly, in a waterproof coat, a sou'-wester on his head. We try to speak to him, but cannot get further than "Herr captain," when we lurch over to leeward and lean over the rail to sacrifice to the sea gods. At the same moment the captain takes a firm grip of us, so as to prevent our spewing ourselves overboard. At last, when the eruptions are somewhat subdued, we ask, gasping, "Is this a storm, captain?" "No," is the answer. "As long as we can fly a yard of canvas it is no storm." Now a little sail is set to make the ship ride a little easier, and then it is slowly hoisted to a place where we would not like to go.

But how does a storm-tossed sea really look from the deck of a ship? Dreary and void. The horizon is contracted, and while the whole appears large, any particular part does not appear so large. You see only a few large waves in the immediate neighbourhood, and overhead nothing at all, neither land nor water.

After a few days you get used to the unheard of swaying of the ship, and then the seasickness ceases. Cheerfulness and good spirits, which had vanished, come back again. At first you want your sea legs—you tumble about hither and thither; but we bring to mind that we are good skaters and accustomed to maintain our equilibrium amidst swaying movements without falling, and we soon learn to balance ourselves on the swaying ship without falling.

When we were at sea the smallpox broke out amongst some emigrants, who had caught the infection at some low lodging-house in Hamburg. The ship's doctor at once had the sick people removed to the hospital, to which he allowed no one to have access except himself and the necessary attendants. He would not even let us in, because, said he, as we had never even seen smallpox, we should undoubtedly catch it from the mere sight of it. If there were danger of death it would be otherwise, and he would let us in; but he was satisfied that, with the help of God and his professional skill, all would pull through. No one died of the complaint.

The ship's doctor—Dr. Goders, from Holstein—was a stately man of true German appearance. We were great friends. We were also fortunate enough to have a good captain. Captain Schacht was a large man. His large, handsome person at once commanded respect; and, furthermore, he was a thorough and experienced seaman. One could well see that he could be severe, but he was so loved and respected by the entire crew that he could always manage and govern by kindness. As the course at sea goes right on day and night in unbroken continuity, the captain cannot, of course, always be in charge, so he has two officers under him called first and second mates. These have passed their examinations in seamanship, and understand, therefore, how to navigate a ship over the wide sea and how to command the crew. In good weather the two mates change places in taking command every four hours, day and night, but if a storm should arise the captain takes the command himself. It would appear from this that the captain must have many idle days; but this is not the case. He is always conscious that he is responsible for the lives entrusted to his charge, as well as for the ship and her valuable cargo. His eyes are always on the alert, and observant to see if the officer in charge attends to his business, whether the man at the wheel steers properly, and, above all, if everything is in order and goes along all right, and that not only by day, but even by night. He often remains on deck till late hours, walking to and fro. Woe to him whom he finds asleep. Four men are on the watch every night to see that we do not come into collision with another ship.

The captain's wife and little child were also on board. She was a good, quiet woman, respected and loved by all. Every one of the crew would, if need have been, have laid down his life for her and her little Peter.

Landsmen are often of opinion that sailors, especially when on shore, are a reckless class of people. I have never had an opportunity of seeing such. At sea they are quite civil young people who behave themselves courteously and with civility, and one may, therefore, well like them. On a large ship like ours there are very young sailors, because old sailors would become giddy on the high masts. Landsmen who have never seen a large ship cannot imagine the height of the masts. A pine tree is not so high; it takes three or four. Of course only the thickest parts of the stems are used, joined together, to enable many sails to be set.

The life of the sailor is a noble calling in the great household of God. At the beginning of the world God blessed mankind with the words, "Be fruitful and multiply, and replenish the earth, and make it subject unto you." It is, therefore, His will that mankind should inhabit all lands and islands of the earth, that they may exchange their surplus products with one another, and that they may spread the religion of Jesus Christ amongst all peoples, until they all become disciples of Christ. In order to effect this, God has given man the gift of building large ships, and in order that the seaman should be able to find his way over the great wide sea, God has made a wonderful power of Nature— magnetism. This magnetism serves, doubtless, other still larger purposes, such as we poor dwellers in the earth cannot understand, but God has so made it that man could discover and use it as a reliable servant, and by means of an iron needle ascertain his position at sea. This needle rests on a free point, and can readily move in any direction, but always so that the one point is towards the north and the other towards the south. The seaman therefore knows the quarters of the heavens on the wide sea, when neither sun nor stars are to be seen. Of a truth the dear God, although unseen, has not left Himself without a witness. He has always given us directions that we should seek Him that we might feel and find Him; and, indeed, He is not far from everyone of us, for in Him we live and move and have our being as well on the dry land as on the flowing sea. It is good and comforting to truly believe that our dear Heavenly Father is always and everywhere close to us.

We are still in the North Sea. In the cold and stormy days and nights we were driven about in all directions, so that at last we were of opinion that we should be glad to be quit of it. Sometimes we got close to the entrance of the Channel, but were always driven back by a heavy gale—once close to the coast of Norway. We kept as far away as possible from the coast of Holland and Germany, because of its low shores and sandbanks. At last, early one morning I was awakened by the mate with the announcement, " We are entering the Channel."

It was not yet daybreak, and the coast of England only to be seen through rifts in the clouds. Two large beacons flared not very far from us—one up aloft on the castle, one down below at the town of Dover. We could see nothing of France on the other side of the Channel but a blazing beacon at the town of Calais. When the day broke we were already a considerable distance in the Channel; the far-away English coast glimmered through a light cloud belt. The land was covered with snow, and with the help of a telescope I discovered at last a single building. That is all that I have seen of that important country—England. In creeping through the channel we saw no more land.

After a slow passage through the Channel—for we had here only light winds, and those not always favourable—we arrived in the open ocean, the great Atlantic. The whole aspect is here more magnificent. The waves in the North Sea were short and choppy; in the Atlantic they rolled with a long and magnificent heave, and moved with a majestic roll. Porpoises—fishes—as large as pigs, played around.

> Ye dark blue waves,
> Whence roll you from ?
>   Come you from foreign strand ?
> Roll on your way, ye waves,
>   Back to the Fatherland !   —*Sailors' song.*

The North Sea is green in colour, but the Atlantic is of a beautiful blue colour, more beautiful than that of the sky that arches over the North German country. But the green colour in the North Sea is not a component part of the water itself, but because the sea is only 800 feet deep the bottom gleams through, and blends with the light in the water, making it green. But the blue in the Atlantic is in the water itself, just as one puts a little blue in the washtub; but it is in so small a quantity that it has to be many thousand feet deep before it can be observed; but then it is a beautiful blue. It is the same way with the air in which we live and move, for a little blue is mixed with it, and that is why the sky and distant mountains look blue. In substance, water and air are not so very different; one is a light, the other a heavy fluid. Sea water is so clear that if you tie a plate to a long line and lower it down with a lead, in a calm you can see it at a depth of a hundred feet. At last it looks as small as a little white shirt button.

So far we had sailed only between European countries; now we left behind not only Germany but all Europe, and sailed right out into the wide, wide world, whilst we made a little world of our own. Seasickness was a thing of long ago; the last smallpox patient was in the way of recovery; the air was warmer, the feelings more disposed to good fellowship. Our ship was full of emigrants to New Zealand—I have forgotten the number. They were from different districts of Germany. There were Catholics from Bavaria, Unionists from Prussia, Lutherans, Reformists, and a few Baptists from the North. We assembled the children daily for school, and on Sundays a service was held on deck, at which all gathered together. The captain had a few sails furled and the course so laid that the ship made the least possible motion, to give opportunity for quiet and meditation.

I must here remark that the population of our ship world consisted of three classes : (1) The sailors—I name them first. Honour to whom honour belongs, for without them our ship could not have got along at all. These consisted of the captain (his wife and child), the two mates, and the sailors—in all about thirty persons. The captain and mates for this journey had given up their own main cabins to passengers, and slept in side cabins. The common sailors and petty officers had their quarters in the forward part of the ship. (2) The cabin passengers, consisting of the agent of the Emigration Society with his numerous family, the ship's doctor, Riemenschneider, and myself. Heine and Trost, our associates, were lodged with the emigrants. (3) The emigrants. These had the great open space under the main deck, so called because it is placed between the saloon aft and the sailors' quarters at the forward end of the ship. The saloon, surrounded by a number of small and large berths, dressing rooms, and such like, was formed by a raised part of the ship, the upper deck of which formed a promenade for the cabin passengers. The steering wheel stood at the far end of this deck.

Admission to the raised quarter-deck was forbidden to the emigrants and the intermediate passengers, but we could go down to them. Riemenschneider and myself often went amongst the people, and conversed with them about ordinary and sacred matters, but we endeavoured to make no proselytes. We had nothing to do with the opinions of the different churches and sects. Amongst them we desired to know nothing but Jesus Christ, and Him crucified. In that way we won the confidence of all, including that of the Catholics. If souls are saved and become holy through Jesus Christ, it is all the same what church they belong to.

It was astonishing how these emigrants, who had come from different districts and were now packed together in so small a world, conducted themselves peaceably and courteously to one another. On land, in small distant villages, where only a few people are near, you often find envy, hatred, and backbiting—which may well arise, for the reason that the minds of people, when they have tired themselves in work and with worldly cares, cannot raise themselves to take part in wider and higher matters of general interest, and know of no other variety and recreation than to trouble themselves about the affairs of their neighbours and speak of them with censure. But the emigrants, on the other hand, in our little ship world, had no exhausting labour and no care for the morrow ; they did not need, therefore, the refreshing change of troubling themselves about their neighbours' affairs. The feeling of being cut off from the outside world by the wide sea drew them together in a friendly manner. Their courtesy towards one another went a little too far, for although they almost all belonged to the uncultivated classes, they called one another Mr., Madam, and Miss. We gave them these titles with pleasure, and this awakened a self respect in them and paved the way to a good understanding.

Our ship's company might have been a very loving one, if it had not been disturbed by a peculiar person. This was the agent of the New Zealand Emigration Society. He was a German, but had lived a long time in England, had married there, and was now going with his family to New Zealand. Riemenschneider and myself were his passengers, not the captain's. The Emigration Society had chartered the ship for the voyage and given it over to the agent. He was therefore a man of importance, and took upon himself the position of superintendent of the whole ship. In order to make his position felt, although he had no knowledge of seafaring matters, he began from time to time to give orders to the captain. When we were at last in the open sea, the captain spoke out roundly to him and said : " I have the sole command here, and brook no interference." But the agent wished to maintain his authority, if only in appearance, and sent, therefore, his orders to the captain in writing, on official paper, and folded in an official manner. The captain received the orders, wrote on them " Bs. Schw. " (*sic*), and laid them on one side.

The agent could exercise authority over the emigrants with more success. The Emigration Society had had bills of fare printed, on which was plainly shown how much was to be given out for each person every day in the week. If they had fared accordingly, the people would have fared well. But during their seasickness the people had but little appetite, and that a capricious one. The agent fell in with their wishes, and the people were fed as he thought proper, without reference to the bill of fare. But when the seasickness was over a good appetite set in, and the rations daily given out were not enough to satisfy their hunger. In the meantime, the agent had intimidated the people. On the least opposition to his authority, or anything that could be construed as such, a punishment of bread and water for a few days followed. If anyone wished to excuse himself, or maintain that he was in the right, the punishment was increased. Their hunger grew sharper day by day, and at last drove the people to ask, quite modestly, that the printed bill of fare should be followed. The agent declared this to be nothing less than mutiny, and threatened irons and chains. Once he so far forgot himself in his rage that he wished to put a man in irons who had said with reference to his order, "That is impossible." "Not for such a matter," said the captain. "I command it," said the agent. "I have charge of the ship. English law is the rule here." "Mate," said the captain. "Hoist our flag." The Hamburg flag soon waved from the peak, and the agent was powerless.

We and the ship's doctor naturally took sides with our German countrymen, the emigrants, in opposition to the agent, who wished to pass for an Englishman. But the doctor was not so bold as we were. In his professional duties he brooked, of course, no interference; but in other matters he was under the agent's orders, and had to hold his peace. It was quite different with Riemenschneider and myself: we were free people, and could speak out our minds. But moderate counsels had no effect. I am by nature very yielding, but when it goes too far I can be as stiffnecked as an obstinate man. The agent and I, therefore, came sometimes into direct antagonism. Once he declared before all the people he could no longer sit at table with me, and in future he would send me my dinner into my bedroom. I replied that I should not allow it. I was a cabin passenger, my passage money was paid, and if he ordered me from the cabin table I should find my sustenance somewhere else, and when we arrived at New Zealand he should find out who had to pay for it. Thereafter I took my meals with the mates in their own cabin. The captain dined with his wife in his own cabin. The sailors had nothing to do with the catering of the Emigration Society.

After three days we passed the line, as the degree is called, which is drawn right across the middle of the world between north and south. The agent came to me when I was walking the quarter-deck, in a friendly manner reached out his hand, and said: " Let us drop our quarrels on the other side of the line." I was moved at once, took his hand heartily, and the reconciliation was complete.

Soon afterwards the agent again expressed himself in scorn against the emigrants, and spoke spitefully about our associates, Heine and Trost. It was only with a great effort I could compel myself to be silent, for I did not wish at once to make a breach in our recent reconciliation.

When my feelings had subsided, I seated myself in a lonely corner, for I felt very hurt. The ship's doctor came to me, reached out his hand, and said: " I feel for you, but I am glad that you have controlled yourself." The old agent appeared to be in a better frame of mind, for we were invited by one of his children, in a friendly manner, to come into the cabin. The agent himself was not in sight, but it was evidently his doing, for grapes and a bottle of good wine were placed before us. The doctor thought it was suitable, under the circumstances and on such an important circle of the earth, that we should elevate our hearts with wine. Riemenschneider could drink no more wine on the ship, as it made him seasick. During the whole of the voyage he was seldom free from seasickness.

It was partly to be attributed to our influence that the people did not break out into rebellion, and that in time they were treated a little better by the agent.

Let us quit the subject of contentions of men, for the sights on the sea, the blending of colours in sky and water, are so beautiful—

> Over all the earth is fair
> But where man comes and makes a jar,

says Schiller.   That is true of sinful men without Christ.   Turks, and men like Turks, make a fruitful land into a dreary wilderness, and those who only wish to walk on ready-made roads must bend and tread uneven ones.   But those who are freed from sin by Jesus Christ and ennobled and enlightened by His spirit "shall make the wilderness and solitary place glad for them and the desert shall rejoice and blossom as the rose."   Be still! we are still on the great wide sea, and for a long time have seen no land. The sea has its natural beauty as well as the land.   Thereo later.

One day the captain said to us—Dr. Goders, Riemenschneider, and myself—"This evening I will tell you some news."   Anything fresh in our lonely world on the world sea was of importance. We would have liked to have heard it at once, but he would not satisfy our awakened curiosity before the appointed time. The evening came at last, and we should hear the news.   The narrative was not long, but we heard it with great attention. The captain merely said: "Early to-morrow morning at daybreak you shall see land."   Thereon we asked the mate, whose watch it was at the time mentioned, to wake us at the right time.   At daybreak we were on the poop, and sure enough we saw the tops of several mountains rise up out of the sea.   They looked in the dawn, through a fine light mist, like haycocks in a dewy meadow. This reminded me in a lively way of the time when I used to go into the meadow of an early morning.   We sailed between the African islands of a green coast range.   Soon, as we proceeded further, the mountains rose up higher, till the whole island of Santiago lay exposed to view on our left.   At the same time another island appeared on our right, named Fogo.   It appeared flat, and a large morning cloud lay over it, but this began to dissolve.   High in the air, through a rift in the clouds, right into which the morning sun shone, appeared a fiery glance.   " What is it?" we asked, astonished. "It is a mountain," said the sailor at the wheel. We could hardly believe it, for it was as high as heaven. We awaited with anxiety the disappearance of the cloud, for we wished very much to see the whole of the glory that it concealed. At last the cloud disappeared, and a very high, sharp, naked mountain peak, glancing in the rays of the morning sun, stood before us. It was an extinct volcano. Probably the island had received its name from it, for Fogo means fire.

Is it not wonderful that the captain knew so exactly the evening before that we should see land in the morning? He must have known exactly where we were, although it was long since we had seen any land. In order to know this, a remarkable clock is kept in the ship called a chronometer—that means a time measurer. This chronometer is made by the most skilful clock-makers, with such care that on a long voyage which may last a year or more it neither gains nor loses a second. At sea you must change your watches, as one sails east or west every day, so that they may show 12 at noon. The chronometer, however, always shows the astronomical time at Greenwich in England, and in accordance with this time the "Nautical Almanac" (a thick book full of figures) is calculated. The chronometer is locked up as a priceless treasure in a box, where it can easily swing, so as to take as little harm from the motion of the ship as possible, and the captain keeps the key. Every forenoon when the sun shines he opens the box, sits down in front of it with a slate, and looks narrowly at the chronometer. At the same time the mate stands with an instrument on the deck and measures exactly the height of the sun. When he has got it, he calls out "Stop!" and the captain quickly notes the hour, minute, and second that the chronometer at that moment shows, and writes underneath it the height of the sun as measured by the mate. Then at noon the mate is busy with the instrument again, and takes the height of the sun at its greatest altitude. Through this instrument you can see the sun climb up till at once, with a halt, she seems to stand still, but only for a second, and then begins to sink again. Now the two mates take calculated tables, sit down, and calculate in accordance with the two observations exactly where the ship is. The place is then marked on the chart and entered in the ship's log. The seaman's duty of yesterday is now at an end, and the new day begins. You see, then, that the sailor begins his day at mid-day—not at midnight, as the landsman does.

The chronometer ought to go so exactly that on a long sea voyage it neither loses nor gains a second ; but our captain used to say "The chronometer is made by the hand of man, and is therefore not as reliable as the heavenly chronometer which God has made—namely, the course of the stars." It is necessary, therefore, to compare the two from time to time to make sure that the chronometer is going right. This is done most easily on days when sun and moon can both be seen together. The position of each of these luminaries is then measured exactly with an instrument, and at the call " Stop !" the time on the chronometer noted to a second. It can then be calculated to a second whether the chronometer is right or not.

A second on the clock is a very small space of time, but to find a distant island or a distant harbour in the great ocean a second more or less makes an important difference in the calculation. The sailor, although his occupation is a magnificent one, must pay attention to very small matters, as in a well-ordered household trivial matters are taken into consideration. In the same way in our journey through life we can only have peace and joy in our minds and be comforted on our way in following Christ when we are true and conscientious in small matters.

For some time we have been in the tropics—that is a broad girdle round the earth, where it is always summer and always warm. But as in the Northern Hemisphere the sun at mid-day always appears in the south and in the southern one it appears in the north, so naturally in the middle—between north and south — there must be a belt where the sun at noonday is right overhead. But, as is well known, the sun moves one half-year northwards and the other half-year southwards, whence arise Summer and Winter. Along with the sun, the circle, where at noon it stands right overhead, must also move northwards and southwards. When (on June 21) the sun has got to the highest point north, it turns back, and the circle round the earth, where at its turning it shines at noon right overhead, is the northern tropic. Now it turns backwards till (on December 21) it has got far enough, and once more turns back, and the circle where it shines overhead at its returning is the southern tropic. In the middle—between the tropics—is the so-called line which divides the earth into two halves. The sun must cross the line twice a year—namely, on March 21 and September 21—at which time over the whole earth day and night are equal. Between the tropics day and night are almost always of equal length. The turning of the sun is caused by the inclination of the earth towards the sun, but with that we have here nothing to do.

One feels quite a peculiar feeling and a consciousness that one is very far from home when one can hardly bear the hot sun at noon, the rays of which right overhead are unbearable without coloured glasses, and one has no shadow when standing upright.

Countries which lie between the tropics on which the sun shines so hotly, as may be easily imagined, have a different vegetation and produce quite different fruits from the countries which lie in temperate zones in which Summer and Winter alternate. On the sea, too, there are quite different appearances. Here there are generally quite regular winds, but on the line there are often calms. The course of our ship was such that we generally had the wind on the side in which way a ship generally sails at her best. Our ship sailed about six miles (stunden) an hour. Now a ship is so built that it cuts sharply through the waves, and presents the least possible resistance to the water, and the quick sailing makes a beautiful hissing noise, and leaves a track of whirling water behind. Whizz! There flies up a flock of sparrows. Have they roosted there and picked up corn? No; there is no land for them to sit on—all is moving water. These are no sparrows. They are fish that fly up whirring and then dive into the waves again. Whirr! Another flock frightened by the ship fly up. I have observed two kinds of such fishes that swim with their fins in water and fly with them in the air. One sort appears to be about six inches long, flies always straight, and always in flocks. The others are somewhat longer, fly alone, and direct their flight at pleasure. Many of the latter sort fell on the deck of the ship at night.

Nature at sea is so beautiful that one cannot get enough of it. Here and there the pure spray of the waves dances in the sunshine in most beautiful rainbow tints. The sky is a beautiful blue, such as one cannot imagine in Germany. At sunrise and sunset so many glancing colours sparkle high in the heavens that the splendour of it cannot be described. One can wonder at the works of God quite close at hand. There are little sailors with ships no bigger than a child's hand. Each of them spreads a little glancing sail. Ship and sail both shimmer in the gayest colours. If our ship gets too close to them, they take in sail at once and dive beneath the waves. The little creatures are like a little galley, and they always sail on a wind.

A remarkable appearance in these latitudes are the sealights. If you come on deck on a dark night you will see far and near ghostly forms rise up out of the sea and disappear again. If you look down over the side of the ship and have a homely landsman's imagination you will receive the impression that there is a row of bright light rooms underneath the ship, from the open windows of which the light streams in snowy white on the surrounding land. The cause of the ghostly forms is that here and there the water in the combs of the waves is broken into spray, which lights up in the darkness. That of the appearance over the side of the ship is the disturbance of the water by the movement of the ship making it phosphorescent. For the same reason you see that the ship draws a long streak of fire behind her. Sometimes in gentle breezes the whole sea looks on a dark night as if it were thickly strewn with stars, every star appearing and immediately disappearing for a second. Sometimes when it rains the sea seems to sparkle with innumerable sparks of fire struck out by the falling rain drops. When a fish shoots through the water he makes a fiery streak. If you stir sea water in a pail the whole pailful is lit up. The light is caused by millions of little animals that shine in the darkness when they are stirred. They are so small, however, that they cannot be seen with the naked eye.

God displays his power and glory everywhere in his great creation—as well in the world of the smallest creatures, invisible to the naked eye, that light up the warm sea by night, as in the starry heavens, where at His command the worlds run their never-ending course. It is uplifting to pray to this God, who guards the great as well as small, and to be able to call Him Father through Jesus Christ.

"Oh Lord, how manifold are Thy works! in wisdom hast Thou made them all; the earth is full of Thy riches! So is this great and wide sea, wherein are things creeping innumerable, both small and great beasts. There go the ships; there is that leviathan, whom Thou hast made to play therein. These wait all upon Thee that Thou mayest give them their meat in due season. That Thou givest them they gather. Thou openest Thine hand, they are filled with good. Thou hidest Thy face, they are troubled. Thou takest away their breath, they die and return to their dust. Thou sendest forth Thy Spirit, they are created; and Thou renewest the face of the earth." (Psalms civ., 24-30.)

One evening I went on deck, and as I allowed my glance to sweep over the starry heavens I saw that quite new constellations were coming into sight in the south, while the old well-known northern ones were sinking so low down that I could hardly recognise them again. "Mr. Mate," said I, in an anxious tone, "can we see the North Pole Star any more?" "Yes," he said, "we can just see it." "Where is it?" "There!" Yes, there it was still, quite low down on the horizon. The star that in Germany stands at a considerable altitude, and can be found every night and every hour at the same place, and round which the whole vault of heaven appears to turn, was now sunk close to the rim of the earth. I gazed at it long, the star well known from my youth up, for now I saw it for the last time. Here, in the south, we have no Pole Star: the starry vault turns round a starless point. On the other hand, we have beautiful shining constellations and a glowing "milky way," compared to which the northern one is a feeble shimmer.

We had once a double marriage. Four no longer young persons—they made two pairs—became enamoured of one another under the warm tropic sky. The first we heard of this love story was a cry of strife among the emigrants. It was discovered that an elderly but very dressy widow was the aggressive party. She was ordered on to the poop and scolded by the agent for her breach of the peace. "Yes," she replied, quite unabashed, "I have boxed my daughter's ears (already married) because she wishes to prevent my marrying." Being questioned by the agent, she then said that she had become engaged. The fortunate bridegroom was a quiet old bachelor, to whom a well-dressed widow was a great attraction The agent said that she should have her wish, and the daughter had no power to prevent her mother marrying. Soon another pair appeared. The agent prepared the papers in an official manner, on the strength of which we called them up and married them.

Ordinarily, the voyage from Europe to New Zealand is made without stoppage ; but our ship was so full of people and merchandise that there was no room to spare to carry all the fresh water necessary. It was therefore decided in Hamburg that we should call at Bahia, a port in the empire of Brazil, South America, and fill up such water casks as had been emptied. (Sea water, as is well known, cannot be drunk because it is so salt, and contains other bitter minerals.) We were very glad, because it gave us an opportunity to see a country in the tropics " where pepper grows."

Bahia is a large city, but the streets look quite different to those of a German seaport. Instead of waggons and coaches you see here troops of pitch-black men, nearly naked, who carry goods or palanquins hanging on long poles, in which ladies and gentlemen sit, and run with them to the tune of a monotonous song. The language here is Portuguese, and most of the white inhabitants are of Portuguese extraction. There are also whites of other nations, as well as a number of Germans, who had no opportunities of religious services. Riemenschneider held an open-air service with them in the city, whilst I performed divine service on the ship, and an armchair was presented to him as a mark of esteem. The blacks, who are by far the greatest number of the inhabitants, are of African extraction. They were then still slaves, who were bought and sold by their white owners.

A never-ending hot Summer reigns here. White people from northern countries must go about under the shade of an umbrella, otherwise they cannot bear the heat of the rays of the sun. All vegetable growths are quite different to what they are in Germany. The town is so large that we could not get out into the country; but in the gardens in the suburbs we saw high cocoanut trees, bamboos, sugar canes, coffee plants, orange and lemon trees loaded with ripe and green fruit, and many other plants and fruits. The oranges here, ripe from the trees, are so large and of so delicate a flavour that those we get in Germany are not to be compared with them. Besides, there are a number of the most beautiful fruits, " good to eat and lovely to look on," amongst which the best flavoured is the banana. I hope our missionaries in West Africa may have such cooling, pleasant, and beautiful fruits on their stations.

Our captain was acquainted with German merchants living here, and took us to call on them. On the whole, I have no very lively recollection of our intercourse in Bahia, and cannot describe it very accurately. One recollection, however, still remains.

Only a student of theology (and I had just risen from the study) can tell how attractive is the study of Church history and monastic life in the Middle Ages. Here I found myself translated into the Middle Ages, for Bahia is of the Catholic religion of the Middle Ages, and has a number of monasteries. The chapels of the monasteries were open, at all events I found them always open at a certain time towards evening, "in the cool of the day," when they were sought by those desiring meditation. Little black female slaves kneeled by the side of their white mistresses on the floor— (there were no seats)—while the solemn songs of unseen singers echoed from above. In the chapels of the monasteries there were men's voices; in the convents those of women.

One evening later on I saw, while passing, the chapel of a cloister lit up and open. I entered. In the middle stood an open coffin, a corpse lay in it on a bier, and around it stood a circle of monks in rough clothes singing songs. At the head of the corpse stood a man in holy orders, in the robes of a bishop, who swayed a censer with fragrant incense. Perhaps he was the abbot of the cloister. I stood alone by the circle of the monks, naturally with head uncovered, attentive and in a devout posture. I forgot the present and imagined myself far back in the Middle Ages. At last the coffin was screwed down, and carried away on the bier by the monks. l followed. The way lead through a cloister, then through a hall, in which stood writing desks.

With my thoughts steeped in the Middle Ages, when twilight covered the Church and darkness all the sciences, and only in a few monasteries did light shine through, thought I, here is a place where a gleam of light may well break through. The way led through other chambers, down a flight of steps into an underground vault. Here was an open grave. The corpse was placed down close by, and then a paternoster said in the Latin tongue. That was all I understood. They then left the corpse there, and retraced their steps. On the way back I was in the middle of the company of monks. No word was spoken, and no one looked angrily at me. Perhaps they thought I had followed out of respect for the deceased. I took him for a dead monk, but learnt afterwards that he was probably a recently deceased high official.

I liked the great heat here. On recollecting the cold days in the rough North Sea in midwinter, I felt as if I were in Paradise.

After we had again started on our voyage and had sailed for some time in a south-easterly direction on the wide ocean, we came to the southern tropic circle, and into a zone once more where Summer and Winter change places with one another as they do in the north, but with this difference: that in the Southern Hemisphere it is Summer when it is Winter in the northern one. At noon the sun was in the northern sky.

Wherever one is on the wide sea, and however far from land, one always has the society of the sea-birds, which swim on the waves and fly in the air. The smallest of them are not larger than swallows, the largest, called albatrosses, measure eleven feet across the wings. It is remarkable for how long a time these birds can sail about in the air without perceptibly moving their wings. We caught some on stray fishhooks, which we lowered down with a piece of meat on a cork and allowed it to drag after the ship. The ship's cook—a coal-black negro—knew what to make out of them. He first skinned them—the fat under the skin is full of oil; he then boiled them in water and fried them. These birds build on uninhabited islands, where their dung lies heaped up for thousands of years, which, under the name of guano, is sold for manure.

No one in the ship doubted that the captain and the mates would find the far-away island of New Zealand in the wide ocean, although only a few could understand how it was possible. Their undoubted confidence was therefore faith without sight; but they could understand with their reason that their faith was truth. They had seen the great commercial city of Hamburg and its harbour full of great ships, where goods which were to be sent over the seas were loaded, and those which had come from over the seas were discharged. It was, therefore, clear to reason that the ships could find their way across the seas.

The conditions are the same with respect to the Christian religion which the Bible teaches us. We cannot explain it all clearly, but we can understand with our reason that our faith is truth. The great city with its harbour full of shipping is the world with its countries and peoples, and the belief in the Bible shows itself in its operation. Those peoples who have a free Bible and use it are the wisest, most cultivated, and noble of all the nations upon the earth. The ennobling effect of the Bible has manifested itself for thousands of years, Other teachings, even if they have produced a certain civilization and philosophy, are in their effects far behind the effects of a belief in the Bible in the free development of the human spirit, in the ennobling of the human heart, in the merciful consideration of one's fellow creatures and contemplation of the visible world. New theories—or still more, old ones warmed up, and spiced with a few new discoveries —which disturb the belief in the Bible, and profess to bring mankind to still greater happiness, have all come to nought; and theories without the Bible and God, which are intended to produce such happiness, but do not do it, and which for a time easily find credulous adherents, always result as the deeds of the celebrated

Spanish knight, Don Quixote did, who always wanted to conquer kingdoms, but never did it, and who wished to make his credulous shield-bearer, Sancho Panza, into a governor of a state, but could not do it.

Now I have got into this channel I must row along in it a little longer. I do not expect to convince all unbelievers, for it is human nature that a man does not easily change his belief, be it true, erroneous, or false. Often there is insight in it. The belief that there is no God, and, above all, no spiritual life, and therewith that there is no immortality of the soul, is also faith without sight, which does not weigh properly the reasons of, and the difference between, the good which the belief in the Bible really effects, and the good which the want of belief in God should effect but does not. Those, however, who are inclined to follow the atheists, as credulous shield-bearers, should bethink themselves and begin to seek the truth which historic experience teaches.

Scientific investigations are worthy of all honour, and the more we search into the dark secrets of Nature so much the better. Much that science has really discovered has given help to a better understanding of the Bible. Scientific men may content themselves with theories, for these may lead to truth, as astrology has led to astronomy ; alchemy to chemistry.

Theologians have only this against them—that they endeavour to induce the unlearned and the easily convinced ones to accept the theories without God, which always prove unfruitful, as materialism in Germany, or evolution in England, in which a God who does nothing is propounded. But the noble masters of science do not do this ; only those of a sorrowful countenance who are much followed by credulous Sancho Panzas on donkeys.

I will readily believe that a few great spirits (spoken figuratively, for they themselves believe in no spirit), in their enthusiasm for their belief that there is no God, may be noble, honourable men. But these have not to thank their atheism for these virtues, but their Christian training. They still breathe the spiritual air of Christendom, although they will not analyze this ennobling air, for it must be spiritually instituted, and that might lead them to be Christian believers themselves. But if they are still strong enough, by God's will, to choose the good and refuse the evil, it is not so with their weaker neighbours, who cannot be good without a belief in a Holy God. If these believe no more in a God who rewards them, and in a life after death, they will, according to their belief, no longer be such fools, merely for the sake of the beauty of virtue, as to avoid vice.

No belief, neither for nor against the divine education of men and in men, can be fully proven, but one has results to show —the other none ; and the great thought, " I believe in God the Father, the Almighty, maker of heaven and earth," is more sublime than the little one, There is no God, because he is not necessary.

No cultivated man doubts that there is, in accordance with our conceptions, an all-pervading power, by means of which we hold our existence on this earth; a power that flows forth from the sun — unfolds the flower with its odours—that makes birds to sing—that keep the globe in its course—and one that, starting from a still higher source, keeps the sun in its course. Reason stands still here, or one might rise still higher. Now, without being credulous, let one believe that above this lifeless power there is also a living, self-conscious, self-contained, all-knowing Being, that fills the whole creation, and, according to His goodwill and pleasure, rules everything and everyone, and devotes personal attention to the largest as well as the smallest matters in it.

> High o'er towers Thy inexhaustible being
> The reason weak of poor mankind,
> And how Thou work'st, and what Thy counsel be,
> Not known to angels e'en ;
> How dare I, dust, e'en undertake
> To sound thy depths, oh God.

The soul of man cannot content itself either with a dry atheism or with a weak, ineffective godhood. It must believe. It anticipates a God who takes an interest in his creation—who can rejoice over the gambols of the lamb—who rejoices when a hungry child eats a piece of bread and butter—who, not to spoil us, remains concealed, but takes part in our joy when we wander amongst lovely flowers—who holds us by the hand when we are in

danger of falling—who comforts us in sorrow and trouble—a God
to whom we can pray.

> Our Father, who art in heaven !
> Lord Thou hast made and knowest me ;
> My downsitting and uprising knowest Thou ;
> My thoughts Thou understand'st afar ;
> I walk or lie, so art Thou near,
> And seest all my ways.
> Whither shall I Thy Spirit flee ?
> Where from Thy countenance escape ?
> Fly I to heaven, lo, Thou art there ;
> Lie down in hell, there art Thou, too !
> Take I the wings of morning,
> And fly to furthest sea,
> There shall Thy hand lead—
> There Thy right hand shall guide me.

CHAPTER VI.

IN NEW ZEALAND.

AFTER a long voyage over the wide sea, whereon for a long
time we had seen no land, we saw at last, agreeing
exactly with the ship's calculations, the mountains of
New Zealand rising up out of the sea.   Neither the captain nor the
mates had been in New Zealand before ; and in a land at that
time still uncivilised our seamen could expect no lighthouses or
other landmarks.   But not far from the bight in which our destination—Nelson—lay, there was marked on the chart a remarkable
cleft rock.   Our captain had chosen this as the point where he
wished to make the land, and had hit it right off.   It was a great
naked upright rock on the side of a mountain, where at some time
a large piece had broken away and fallen off.   From this place
we could easily find the harbour of Nelson.

On nearing the land we found a remarkable difference in the
temperature.   It was the middle of June, and therefore winter
here ; and in the latter part of our voyage we had had raw and
cold winds.   We now sailed, as if changed by enchantment, with
soft winds in warm sunshine, and in an air as sweet and mild as
a warm Spring day among blooming fruit trees in the old home.

Thought I, is this a New Zealand Winter? If so, we need no stove. But there I was wrong. There are often warm Winter days here : but on shore they are generally accompanied by hard night frosts, and then there are more raw wet days than fine ones in Winter.

The climate is normally milder here than in North Germany, for the Nelson district lies in a latitude about 41 deg. south, but North Germany is about 53. New Zealand is, therefore, a great deal nearer the sun than North Germany. One must take into consideration, moreover, that the Southern Hemisphere is much more raw than the northern one, which may readily be caused by the greater area of water. If it were not for this difference, Nelson in New Zealand ought to have a climate like Naples in Italy, which it is very far from having.

New Zealand is divided in the middle by a strait called Cook Strait, and thus divided into two large islands. The southern island stretches northwards here in two large mountain ranges, which form a bay between them—the large bay now called Tasman, formerly Blind Bay. Towards the south, in the narrowing den of this bay, the town of Nelson is situated, on a good natural harbour, which is formed by a cleft in the rocks, against which the waves have formed a heavy boulder bank and made a dry bank with a good entrance at one end. On the landward side, between the harbour and the high mountains, is room enough for an important city, which will be here some day, but which consisted on our arrival of only a few scattered wooden houses.

The mountains here are higher and bolder than any I had seen in Germany—either those of the Hartz or the Thüringen Forest. In Germany they are clothed with a delicate green, and have graceful and elegant slopes ; here in Nelson they are stark, upright, nearly naked, as if they had only just come up out of the sea and had not yet learned good manners. They are mostly covered with a brown fern, which, when it has once taken hold, and is not interfered with by man, will not allow the intrusion of any other plant. And the woods here, the mountains as well as the valleys, have neither the smiling grace of our shady woods nor the friendly gloom of the pine forests in Germany. Shortly, the green of the New Zealand woods is weaker than that of Germany.

After we had landed and made the acquaintance of a few English settlers, we at once made inquiry about the natives, and then learned that in the neighbourhood of Nelson there were none. We thought they might live further inland, but soon learnt that was not the case, that in this great southern island there were but few natives, and that these few lived in widely scattered places on the sea coast. For our intended farm buildings no suitable mission station could, therefore, be found. When we applied to the two English missionaries already stationed here, one of whom belonged to the Episcopalian and the other to the Wesleyan Church, we learnt that all the natives of the whole of New Zealand were already under spiritual guidance. It is true many were still heathens, but almost all had already adopted Christian customs and had native Christian teachers amongst them. Our prospects were therefore gloomy; but I was not altogether unprepared to learn this.

We wished to retain our independence as missionaries of the North German Missionary Society, and were very unwilling, therefore, to interfere with the labours of others.

What was to be done? Cruise round New Zealand and look at the different places ourselves? That is easily said, and what was really replied to us from Hamburg; but our North German Missionary Society was not rich enough to spare us the passage money. Here you cannot travel as far with a pound as you can in Germany with a Prussian dollar. There are no roads, the mountains insurmountable, the woods impenetrable. One could only journey by ship, and none were going to the places we wished to examine. Under such circumstances, and as long as we had not made ourselves acquainted with the country, and had no proper survey of the country, travelling would not be of much use to us. There were four of us—and what was to be done with our agricultural implements?

It seemed to us the most advisable, and at the same time the least expensive, thing to do to carry out the original plan made at our departure and build a residence, until we could become better acquainted with the land and people, and trust in God, that in His own time He would show us our missionary work.

As a preliminary, we were obliged to remain in the city to land our goods and place them under cover. For the latter purpose a room in the New Zealand Company's warehouse was allotted to us. For our own use we hired a little hut behind the wood—there was then still a wood within the limits of the town, but this shortly after disappeared. The board hut was small, and there was no furniture in it. That did not trouble us much. We slept quite well on the floor. This had this advantage, that when we woke of a morning and looked for daylight, we need only look at the floor close by, for the hut stood on blocks, and there were cracks between the boards of the floor, between which the light shone. In a small room that had no floor there was a hearth, and no lack of firewood. There were no cooking utensils, but Riemenschneider had the sense to see what was absolutely necessary and what could be dispensed with. Without him, we other three would have been mere fools in making the arrangements. Enough! We soon made the place so habitable that we could accept a visit from the captain, his wife, and the ship's doctor.

It is necessary here shortly to give the history of the settlement of Nelson, in order to explain how our society came to buy land there. There was a New Zealand Land and Emigration Society established in England, from which great things were expected—even so far as to hope it might become like the then still existing rich East India Company. Through its agents—the brothers Wakefield, the one commander and the other captain in the fleet—the company had sold large tracts of land for very small prices. Whilst the then acquired lands were being surveyed in New Zealand, the company in England began to sell them by their numbers. The prospects of the company looked so profitable that buyers were soon found. Not all were willing to go to New Zealand themselves, but they intended to sell their lands after a few years with great profit, or else to lease them, and thus draw good interest on their money.

The first settlement was at the north side of Cook Strait and named Wellington, and as the land found so good a sale in London the company resolved to lay out another on a larger scale on the other side of Cook Strait, and called it Nelson. Notification of this was made public in 1841. It was notified that the settlement would consist of 201,000 acres of land in 1,000 allotments of 201 acres each—namely, 1 acre in the town, 50 in the neighbourhood, and 150 in the country. The purchase money for an allotment was fixed at £300. The buyer received a free cabin passage and a free carriage of his goods to boot. The proposal looked so profitable upon paper that a branch of the New Zealand Company of London was established at Hamburg. Our missionary society was thereby tempted to buy an allotment in the Nelson settlement. Three hundred pounds, a small sum in rich England, was truly a large sum for our missionary society, but they saved thereby the passage money of their missionaries, and obtained also a foothold in New Zealand. The favourable descriptions in the advertisements were made by people in London who had never seen New Zealand, and were sitting comfortably in their offices, and the real lands in the overgrown wilds, and the inaccessible solitude of New Zealand, never appeared in them.

Tasman Bay, with the adjoining bay—Massacre Bay, now called Golden Bay,—forms a hollow in a mountain range, from which a few fertile valleys spread out of the mountains. At the southern end of the bay, and a continuation of it, there is a fruitful plain called Waimea, but of small extent, because the land all round soon rises into hills and mountains. Between the hills and mountains there are a few fertile valleys. But altogether included they fall far short of an area of 201,000 acres of agricultural land. The founders of this settlement had omitted the high mountains on the map. Land for agriculture had, therefore, to be sought far removed from Nelson, and it was not accessible by land.

I must here relate an occurrence that took place about the time of our arrival at Nelson. In order to find agricultural land the surveyors had to coast round the jutting mountain range, and reach the banks of the Wairau River, which empties itself on the eastern side. Soon afterwards some chiefs of high rank, from whom the New Zealand Company had bought land, came from the North Island to the head agent at Nelson, Captain Wakefield, and pointed out to him that they had only sold land in Tasman Bay, but not land in the river bed of the Wairau; and if they were to sell this land, for which they had little inclination, they wanted a higher price. The agent, on the other hand, declared he had bought land on both sides of Cook Strait, and the Wairau Valley along with it. The chiefs warned him to withdraw the surveyors or it might lead to bloodshed; but the agent paid no attention to the warning, and the surveyors were sent to the Wairau. Soon after complaints came from the surveyors that the natives were hindering them in their work, and that they had burnt down the hut which they had built. It must here be mentioned that the natives had carried all the effects of the surveyors outside, and had misappropriated none of them, and then set fire to the hut, which was built of scrub. Captain Wakefield, the agent, then took police officers with him to the Wairau in order to prosecute the incendiaries, as he called them. But the natives did not yet understand such a process. Their passions were aroused by this treatment, and Captain Wakefield and others, in all twenty-two persons, were killed. This terrifying news reached Nelson a few days after our arrival.

After describing these matters I can return to us four missionaries. We wanted to go on to our land and begin our farm buildings. Our instructions ran that we were to build on our 150 acres in the country, but these were not yet surveyed, and in the state of affairs then existing there was little prospect that they would be; but the fifty neighbouring acres were surveyed. This was land enough for us to begin our homestead, and as it was ten hours distant from Nelson, it was far enough away. This district, on the road from the town of Nelson to our place, was not quite empty; always at a distance of two or three hours you met a hut with a small piece of cultivated land, where some one had settled down. The road to our land in the valley of Moutere lay through the already-mentioned Waimea Plain, mostly free from timber, but two rivers and a few creeks, which at their ordinary level were easily fordable, had to be crossed.

The valley of Moutere is about two hours' distant from the Waimea Plain in a north-easterly direction, and separated from the sea by a broad strip of hill land.   This strip consisted of cold steep hills and narrow valleys ; these joined and spread out, either into the plain, the sea, or the valley of Moutere.   On the south-east side of the valley the high land soon rises into mountains. On this side it is all covered with thick wood.   Clumps and patches of bush stretch out into the valley, here about half-a-mile wide, and extend partly over it.   The little river Moutere, which receives streamlets on either side, flows through it, and is a beautiful fruitful valley.   From the heights, towards the west, you see high wooded mountains with gorges like rifts.   It is true one cannot see the waterfalls, but one can see plainly the gaps in the woods where they fall over the cliffs.   Over their heads range the white tops of mountains, reaching above the snow line.   At times bitter winds blow from these mountains into an otherwise lovely valley.   The word Moutere means a group, like islands. Geologically, this district consists of the detritus from the western mountain ranges that in process of elevation slipped away from it, then filled up part of the sea, and was then washed by the rains into gorges and valleys.

Our fifty acre patch lay in a side valley, just where it emerges into the main valley.   The upper half of this place was the main valley, which was quite over-grown with high thick wood. A part of this wood covered the lower corner of our land, and a little higher a tongue of wood ran right across it, and divided it into two unequal parts.   The smaller part, just suitable for a fruit and vegetable garden and the necessary buildings, had a stream flowing through it.   It then ran into the main valley and up the road, already laid off, but not yet made.   The stream flowed the whole length through our land, and soon afterwards fell into the Moutere.   It was really a beautiful piece of land, and only an hour distant from our nearest neighbour, and there was a reasonable expectation that in time a road would be made to it.

But this is mere description, and to what end?   We are not yet out and at work.   No, indeed; but I wanted the reader just once to look over the lovely landscape, if not with his eyes, yet in thought, and discover there what I discovered.

> O Lord of power and might !
> O Lord, Thy goodness reaches far—
> Far as the clouds do stretch.

CHAPTER VII.

SETTLEMENT IN THE VALLEY OF MOUTERE.

AT last we were to go out. I had been out there before, knew the road, the neighbourhood, and the neighbours, and knew how to find our land. It must here be remembered that it was Winter, and that the beginning of a settlement in the wilderness is full of difficulties. Trost and Riemenschneider did not take kindly to it. The first was too old, and the latter not hardy enough at first. But Heine and I did not think it advisable to go alone : we took a young peasant, one of the German emigrants, with us. A few things, consisting of provisions and tools, we despatched to Upper Moutere on a bullock cart drawn by two oxen. The roads being very uneven, and the distance a ten hours' journey, the oxen could not take much. We stayed over night in the upper valley with a settler, and the next morning we packed as many of our things as we could carry on our backs and started for our land, that still lay an hour away down the valley. The road was not yet made, for we were the advance guard in the wilderness. There had been a sharp frost in the night, and the ice on some of the swamps would bear our weight. Some broke through with us, for we were heavily laden, and sometimes we fell knee deep into the water. It was pretty cold to the feet and legs, but it did not harm us, as we kept going. Swamps in New Zealand have, as a rule, a firm bottom, so there is no danger of sinking in them. In other places the road lay through narrow tracks which the surveyors had cut through the wood ; over tree trunks, thick and thin ; through dark woods, with high trees with thick undergrowth, so that the whole place from the ground to the tree tops was full of vines and creepers. The woods in New Zealand remain green all through the Winter.

Arrived at our land, the first thing to be done was to find a dry place and wash ourselves. The heavy, grasslike, sometimes six foot high, vegetable growth, which stood untouched in the wilderness before there were any cattle, had stood from year to year and made an impenetrable mass. We then cut poles—the wood was quite near,—which we stood up for roof trees, and covered them with grass. Then, as it was already evening, we made a fire and prepared our supper. That was so much done. When tired with the day's work, and our meals spiced with hunger, we could warm ourselves at the fire and rest in our own hut. All was still in the solitude of night. Only now and then an owl in the wood called out " More pork " in English—but it is not likely the owls here have already learnt English. The voice calls out exactly " Koo-koo" (the Maori name of this owl) : each vowel, although flowing together, is distinctly heard. It is not to be wondered at that the settlers, who had got hungry working in the wilderness, understood it as " More pork."

The next day the hut was properly covered and made water-tight. Timber was then felled—there was no want of it here— and preparations were made for building a roomy dwelling. After a few days we found that we were not quite alone here. The chief surveyor, in order to assist our settlement, had sent a few labourers to make the road to our place more approachable. That was fortunate for us, as we should soon find out.

One day it came on to rain heavily, and as we crept into our hut we congratulated ourselves that our roof was watertight and we could dry ourselves comfortably by the fire. We went to rest with these comfortable feelings, whilst the rushing of the brook and the roar of the cataracts from the mountains sang us to sleep.

Half asleep in the night, I bethought me that the clothes on my body were not quite dry, but before I could settle the point I heard our labourer cry out, " Get up! I am in water already!" That waked me up. The still glowing embers on the hearth began to hiss and go out. Soon we were in black darkness, and we could feel the water rising. We ought, therefore, to leave the hut at once and fly. Heine wanted to take to the mountains at once. "This is the way," said he, "the people must have fled at the deluge." I called him back, however, and told him to follow me, for I had seen the hut of the roadmakers the day before, and thought it stood on higher ground. We made our way in that direction. The night was too dark to seek out the best places, and we had sometimes to walk in water up to the armpits. We raised our voices in the meantime, called out, and were answered. Soon we saw the bright light of the hut. Here we found a friendly reception, and could dry ourselves at the fire. That was delightful. We recognised the mercy of God, who had protected us in our ignorance in settling in the wilderness, and had so lead matters that the roadmen were sent here, according to man's thoughts, to make a passable road, according to God's goodness; also to be able to take us into their hut, for otherwise we had passed a night of misery in wet clothes on the mountains, which, for a tender constitution, might have been too much.

The next day, as the rain during the night had already left off, the water went down, and we could go back to our hut again. Everything we had been obliged to leave behind was wet through, and our next work was to dry our things. After we had done this, and had erected the hut again, we could go on with the building of our house. The direction of the whole affair lay with me. I have a certain faculty of contrivance, but adhered too closely to homelike ways and methods, and lacked experience in rough architecture of the bush. If I had then had the experience which I now have, I could have made myself a much more comfortable dwelling with half the labour—it is true, of a rougher exterior aspect, but for that reason it would have been so much the more picturesque.

As soon as the new house was, in a measure, habitable (the walls were at first only thatched with grass), I went alone to Nelson to fetch our goods and our companions. On the way I went to a skipper (recommended to me by the chief land surveyor) who lived about two hours' distant from our land on the sea coast, and made arrangements with him to go to Nelson with his large boat and fetch us and our things across. From thence my road

lay for a considerable distance across the steep hill land. The
fern and such like growth, it is true, were burnt off, and the road
easy to find by the land marks of the land surveyors, but it was
a damp day, and the road was slippery, so that in climbing a
mountain one's feet slid a little backward every step. I am a
child of the plain, and always thought it must be more beautiful
in the mountain, but a deep narrow gorge up which I had to go,
and another high mountain which I saw before me just as steep,
convinced me that even if it is more beautiful in the mountains
it is much easier in the plains. I was like a certain milkmaid
who walked from the dry land into the swamp on a wet day, slid
on the slippery path, fell down, spilt the milk, and then broke out
with the complaint—

> O, the poor dry ground,
> I wish I were on it again ;
> If it is not very rich up there
> It's not as slippery as here.

Perhaps it was the exertions in the mountains that made me
feel quite exhausted when I arrived at Nelson in the evening. I
had only experienced this weakness once before—namely, on the
occasion of the great fire in Hamburg, which lasted three days,
when with some others I vainly tried to save the Church of St.
Peter, and the whole night long had carried water up high steps
to the top of the tower. Here at Nelson my muscles refused all
further service. However, I stepped into the house of an Englishman with whom I was acquainted, and must have looked very
miserable, for the people asked anxiously what they could do for
me. I assured them that I only suffered from exhaustion. They
gave me a little brandy, sugar, and hot water, which so refreshed
me that I could soon proceed on my journey to town, where Trost
and Riemenschneider still lived. Riemenschneider had already
made friends among the Englishmen, and had received hospitable
invitations of free quarters. We were glad, therefore, to allow
him to remain here and work amongst the Germans, because as
a city man, and for that reason not of a very strong constitution,
he was not at all used to such work as we had before us. Trost
went along with me.

The boat came and took our goods in. The heavy implements that have to be drawn by cattle we left behind, because we
could not yet make any use of them, and because we should have
had to carry them for an hour. After a good passage over a
bight of the bay we landed at our skipper's dwelling, and put
our things under cover in a shed. From here they could be carted
about an hour's distance towards the upper Moutere valley, but
for the distance of another hour we had to carry them ourselves.
Until we could get a conveyance, they lay at the landing-place
in an open shed, and I went every day to see that nothing was
missing, and then every day I carried a good load home. When
I was loading up I thought, I will get a little of it along anyhow,
and what is there is there, and every time I took a good load
home. Carriage is very high here, and it is not much that two
oxen can carry over the hills. For a time the carrying went on
very slowly, but two hours is a long road with a heavy load on one's
back, that gets heavier at the end with every step. The desire
to save time, which helped to load, did not help to carry. I did not
die of it, however. When we had got the remainder carted, we
all had to go to work and stick to the carrying. It is true it
was only an hour's distance, but it was quite far enough. If we had
brought our farm waggon with us we should have had to carry it on
our backs in pieces, but a waggon is not made for people to carry.

In my time people used to say in the old German Home
country—that is, people who did not care to have much to do with
missions—such things as this: "The young people only go to the
heathen that they can have an easy life there as missionaries."
But there was no easy life here. I have been a peasant a long
time, and I know what hard work is. I have never worked so
hard as a peasant in Germany as I have worked as a missionary
in New Zealand, and such labour as a peasant never pleased me.
One might here interject that such labours were exceptional, and
were not those proper to a mission. That may be, but a missionary who works among the savage heathen, far from civilized
society, and has not much money—and a German missionary
must always get along with very little, if he does not wish to
sink down into savage brutality, from which may God preserve

him—has always, and in many ways, to bear greater hardships than a farm labourer in Germany.

If anyone, who in the beginning of these Memoirs may have perhaps discovered a discontent with my position as peasant, should, therefore, think that on that account I had made no happy choice in my change of occupation, I should make the reply that it was not comfort that I then so ardently desired, but knowledge suitable to my inclinations ; that my previous yearnings arose not from presumption or perversity, but from the stress of longing which God had given to me, and which would be satisfied, and which actually was at last after long search (and the waiting has done me much good) to my full satisfaction discovered in the calling of a missionary. Exhausting labours and other hardships to which I had been used from youth up, and which give me, as a rule, but little trouble, I take along with it willingly and thankfully as a wholesome additional blessing.

As missionaries among the heathen readily undergo greater hardships than have been needful for them in the Home country, we may understand that they themselves have experienced the power of the Spirit of Jesus Christ. They have not only learnt the meaning of the words " If any man will come after me let him deny himself, and take up his cross and follow me," but inwardly appropriated the spirit of the meaning, and made it part of themselves. That is a different thing to the rationalistic proposition to copy Christ in one's own strength, from which only miserable caricatures arise. No, they live in Christ, and Christ in them. "Therefore, they are like-minded with Jesus Christ, who, being in the form of God, deemed it not robbery to be equal with God, but made Himself of no reputation, and took upon Him the form of a servant, and was made in the likeness of men, and being found in fashion as a man He humbled Himself, and became obedient to death, even the death of the cross ; wherefore God so hath highly exalted Him, and given Him a name which is above every name, that at the name of Jesus every knee shall bow, of things in heaven, and things in earth, and things under the earth ; and that every tongue should confess that Jesus Christ is Lord to the glory of God the Father.'

In the middle of the above magnificent passage stands " Even the death of the cross." This incomprehensible deed of God, which no human understanding can grasp, is the gravamen of salvation. Through it mankind and the heart of every disciple of Christ is born again. From it flows mercy to all mankind; through it we have forgiveness of sins, life and blessedness, and at the same time our whole being is crucified with Christ, buried in death, in order that as Christ is risen from the dead through the glory of the Father, so we also may walk in newness of life.

> I cannot fathom the wonders of the sun,
> Nor its course or construction,
> But the light of the sun
> And its heat I can enjoy ;
> Nor can my soul the lofty reasons
> Of Jesus' offer e'en discover,
> But the divinity of the deed
> My heart may well enjoy.

Not only are the missionaries inspired with the spirit of Jesus Christ in their labours, which makes them joyful, and willing to deny themselves to take up their cross daily and follow Him; but even the friends of the missionaries at Home, who cannot go to the heathen themselves, may help the missionaries in foreign countries with their prayers and their hearty sympathy. Millions of Christian souls have enjoyed this blessed communion of the spirit of Christ to their own blessing, and their labours testify that this spirit is the spirit of truth.

Our new residence had so far neither door nor window. Roof and walls were thatched in the first instance with a sort of grass. The whole inside was all one room, and therefore roomy. In the small hut we slept in our clothes on straw on the ground. Here we could make bedsteads. This is the way these are made. You get the wood and cut four stakes, two longer and two shorter poles, and a few sticks. You then drive the stakes into the earth inside the house where you want your bed; fasten the poles on as beams; put the sticks on like perches, and the bedstead is finished. Tying anything up is a very simple matter here. You need only go out of your house and cut off a long broad blade-like leaf of the wild New Zealand flax, which grows everywhere. Split it lengthwise, according to taste, and you have the strongest and most pliant of strings that you can wish. There is yet much to say about this remarkable plant which the dear God has doubtless made for more important uses of human industry than merely to be used as string ; but this can be more suitably done at some other time.

It is something so lovely and joyful to see with one's own eyes how the hitherto quite neglected solitude begins to become inhabited, not by huntsmen and combatants, but by men who build huts, and begin to turn the wilderness into a garden. One forgets the hardships that were necessarily associated with it. Hard work goes on with pleasure and joy, and when you sit in the evening in the still rough and unpolished house around a fire, which burns in a cheerful way inside the room, one forgets all the conveniences which are considered indispensably necessary in civilized life ; indeed, at present, they would be inconvenient.

Dwellers in Germany can hardly imagine the loneliness of a New Zealand landscape. There one is accustomed to see the mark of the hand of man everywhere. Towers and barns, waggon roads and footpaths ; and where there are no people, there are still animals, tame or wild. Here there is solitude everywhere. In our still valley there were then no animals, so that it was not even necessary to fence in our garden. As is well known, originally there were no quadrupeds in New Zealand. The two kinds of dogs and rats, which were found here by Europeans, probably came here with the natives. Neither are there any snakes here. There are a few lizards, but no frogs or toads. I should, therefore, never hear the croak of the frogs on the warm Spring evenings.

Soon we were to have German neighbours. The slaughter of the twenty-two citizens of Nelson considerably disheartened the settlement. No advance was made. Trade and commerce relied on the wages paid by the New Zealand Company, and the money that a few settlers had brought from Home. These latter were afraid to part with it, as they did not feel sure of ever getting it back. It was a bad time, therefore, for the working classes, who had to live on their earnings. This was hard on the German emigrants. Some of the most energetic had already found work and places to build huts; others were still helpless. Under these distressing circumstances, the chief surveyor, Mr. Tuckett, who undertook the management of the settlement since Mr. Wakefield's death, determined to send a number of impoverished German families into our neighbourhood, the Moutere Valley. With this in view he gave them the contract to make the road in our valley passable, at a fair and reasonable price. They were at once to be provided with provisions, and at the same time a piece of land for a dwelling could be laid off, which in time they could either buy or else give up again. Besides working on the road—with reference to which there was no great hurry—they were advised not to neglect to cultivate for themselves. They were then brought to the place, bag and baggage, at the cost of the company, by water, where our things had landed. The women and children were at first left here (there were a few empty huts here, made by previous road makers, inhabited now only by rats, which they could hunt out), while the leader went over with the men; and in our neighbourhood, a little further down the valley, where the company had retained a section for themselves, a piece of land was measured off for each family, and so that there might be no dispute about the choice he let the men raffle for which piece each one should have. Huts were now quickly built, wives and children and goods fetched across. It was a beautiful sight to see the band coming out of the dark wood into the open near our house.

Now it was lively in the valley hitherto as still as death. One cheered the other up. Unforeseen difficulties which would have placed a solitary man in a thousand plights were courageously overcome in a feeling of neighbourly friendliness, and then laughed at. The arrivals had built their huts on the edge of the wood. The position was beautiful, but it was not then known that it was liable to floods. A man who lived in his hut all alone (at that time he was not married) one rainy day had dried his clothes before the fire and then gone to bed in them. In the night he woke with a feeling that his clothes had become wet again of their own accord. He felt with his hand, and came to the conclusion that his hut stood in the water. Then he waded out.

Outside the unexpected water looked very terrible in the dark night. With an anxious voice he called out to his neighbour, " Have you got any water ? " " No," said the neighbour, who thought he was thirsty and wanted a drink, " we have none in the house." His wife, however, shocked at his anxious voice, thought his hut was on fire, jumped out of bed and went plump up to the knees in water.

There were some German tradesmen in the neighbourhood who could have finished building our hut, but that would have cost money, and we were obliged to be careful; we did the work, therefore, ourselves. We had only the window frames (the glass for which we had brought from Nelson) and the doors made. We caulked the walls of the house and plastered it with clay, which we worked with naked feet. We further sawed boards, for we had brought saws and other tools with us from Hamburg. I was the only one who had a little skill in sawing. Filing and setting the saws I did not yet trust myself to do, for I saw that a good or bad filing would make a great difference in the labour. The trees were already felled, because the road makers, who were hewing a way through the wood, had been obliged to fell heavy trees. We needed merely to saw the most suitable ones into lengths and then roll them on to the scaffold we had made over the ditch at the side of the road.

You would look in vain for German trees in these woods, and it requires considerable botanical knowledge to know their species, but they contain large supplies of most excellent, serviceable, and building timber amongst them—woods with beautiful veins, out of which beautiful joinery can be made. The pine trees, with their high straight stems, are the most valuable trees in these woods. You cannot properly call them fir trees, for they have very small leaves ; some are like cypress, some are like the fringe on an officer's epaulet, they have little likeness to fir spines. Their branches, too, are arranged in a different manner to those of the German fir tree, and the wood is harder and heavier.

There was but little game in our valley. Parrots, wild pigeons, and wild ducks, which are plentiful in many parts of New Zealand, seldom visited us. Sometimes you might shoot a woodcock. I think this bird is of the woodcock kind, but it is a solitary bird, and has no wings; instead of these it has short arm-like projections, with short feathers, and at the end a sharp curved nail. Of edible fishes there were only eels in the creeks and rivers. A sort of sprat from three to four inches long, and of the thickness of a quill, were present in number, but were of little use. Probably this is only the young of a sea fish about nine inches long, and of similar shape, that goes up the rivers at certain times of the year, and, perhaps, is of the salmon order. In some larger rivers there are lampreys, but very few other sorts of fish; but all appear to be more or less like sea fish. European fresh-water fish, as well as many useful plants and animals, must yet be introduced by the settlers.

Riemenschneider undertook the spiritual care of the Germans, and, at times, of those who had remained in the neighbourhood of Nelson. The hard labour during the week made me but little inclined to preach on Sundays, and when Riemenschneider was there I took a rest. As he travelled a good deal, and came into touch with a good many people, he had opportunity to make in-quiry about the natives. We learnt that in the neighbourhood of Tasman Bay there were three little native villages, a day's journey remote from each other and from us. The inhabitants had for a long time been under the care of the before-mentioned English missionaries at Nelson. These, as well as the Episco-palian and Wesleyan ones, had laboured before amongst the natives of the North Island, and were called here when the Englishmen settled at Nelson, where they worked as pastor amongst their own countrymen and the natives. Among the latter (as they could only visit them from time to time) they had native assistants. We had, therefore, to wait, and in the meantime work at our farm buildings. With the arrival of the Spring our garden, under Trost's care, began to flourish and to bloom, and we would soon have vegetables out of it. Our housekeeping was very economical, and the eels which I caught from time to time were a great assistance. When I look back at that time I feel bound to relate an occasion of great embarrassment, which, at the time, I bore in silence. I had charge of the cash, and it was my duty to keep accounts; and I certainly thought I had put down exactly every expenditure in the account book. In the first confusion I had no time for a long time to balance my accounts, and when I did this in the course of time I found a deficit. The cashbox held over a pound less than the account book showed. When, after dinner, the others had lain down for an hour to rest, I sat over my account book and vainly sought to find the error. I might have confessed the error to my companions, and then, with their consent, entered it in the book as an unexplainable loss, but I had not the courage. You well know that when in a house a certain duty is committed to you and neglected, every companion would feel it as unpleasant as if the reflection was on himself, and would rightly be blamed as well as he who made the loss. I could not, therefore, bear that the slightest feeling of reflection should arise amongst us, and resolved to make good the deficiency myself in silence. This was, however, not so easily done, for my private purse (money which I had brought from home with me) was nearly empty with helping our countrymen, as in the bad times they had come to the verge of poverty. The few shillings I had I gave up with pleasure, but they did not cover the deficiency. The remainder, therefore, I must seek to make good out of my monthly pocket-money of five shillings. I must, therefore, for several months give up my tobacco smoking. The pound of tobacco cost five shillings. It is true this little self-denial was easy to bear, but when I went down of an evening with my fishhook to catch eels, made a bright fire on the bank that lighted up the surface of the water on which the feathers of my hook were swimming in the darkness, to show by their movement when an eel was firmly fixed on, then, at the midnight fire on a lonely creek, I would very much have liked a pipe of tobacco. At other times I did not feel the want of it.

The intention with which we began the building of our residence—namely, to do with little money and work hard ourselves--was the safest, even if a slow one, for colonists. For my part, although I worked at it thoroughly, I had no heart in it. This building could not be our future mission station. There could be no thought of such a thing, and it became more and more clear to me that our labour in the hope of, in time, being able to sell or lease the building in an improved state, was a hopeless one, for where, amongst so few inhabitants, there is so much waste land, either tenant or buyer is not easily found. True, it might be the case after many years, but our labours could not extend that far. A sort of doubt as to the reason why we laboured so hard always hovered in the background. Here we could not stay. Our mission was to the heathen, not to the colonists. The cure of the Germans could not satisfy us.

In my time in Germany one often heard the saying, " There are plenty of heathen here ; they should be converted first before missionaries are sent to foreign lands." People who were always ready with such remarks did not feel themselves called on to help themselves in the conversion of the heathen at home, for they did mostly nothing, either for the heathen at home or afar. Now, it is true that the soul of a German sinner is just as valuable in the sight of God as the soul of a far-away heathen ; but the original instruction to missionaries was not to convert a soul here and there, but to make all peoples of the world disciples of Christ. This is the definite charge of the Saviour to the missionary (Matt. xxviii., 19). The sinful and heathenlike people at home are in no way forgotten. In fact, the mission to the heathen has called forth the home or internal mission. It is the consequence of it, and the more the mission to the heathen is developed the greater blessing it receives at home. He who pays attention to the signs of the times may see the hand of God at work.

To try curiously to know the future from the prophecies of the Bible is an unfruitful task. One cannot rightly understand for what purpose God has given us prophecy, except to recognise it in its fulfilment. This is of great importance in strengthening our faith. Now, for our present time, we have a prophecy in view, enclosed in a little light picture, which represents the state of missions in our time as truly, and in all respects as faithfully, as a well executed photograph. Read Rev. xiv., 6, 7—" And I saw another angel fly in the midst of heaven, having the everlasting

gospel to preach unto them that dwell on the earth, and to
every nation, and kindred, and tongue, and people, saying with a
loud voice: Fear God, and give glory to Him, for the hour of His
judgment is come: and worship Him that made heaven, and earth,
and the sea, and the fountains of waters."

CHAPTER VIII.

I SEEK AND FIND MAORIS.

THE New Zealand Society (called company here) had juris-
diction in Church matters. A branch of this company was
originally instituted in Scotland, which laid itself out to
found a settlement of the Free Church of Scotland in New Zealand,
to which only members of this Church should be forwarded as
emigrants. The chief surveyor, Frederick Tuckett, at Nelson,
received, therefore, instructions to search the then almost unknown
east coast of the Middle Island for a suitable place for this settlement. This Mr. Tuckett was a pious, intelligent man. He was
a member of the Society of Friends, commonly called Quakers.
In his all-round love of mankind he made no difference between
one religion and another. Jews, heathens, Turks, and Christians
were alike to him. In his love of his brethren he did not inquire
after their convictions, but looked for a belief that with upright
Christian piety is active in deeds of love. As my disposition was
naturally similar, soon after our first acquaintance we became
good friends; but I could never feel myself his equal in our
friendship. That was not because of his high position in the
Colony, but because of his knowledge of commerce and his general
experience, which was far in advance of mine; and because of
his high-minded, humane and Christian character. Perhaps this
unconsciousness of such a difference resulted in our friendship
being so firm and lasting. As it was now committed to him to
look for a suitable site for the Scotch settlement, he offered me a
free passage with him to the South, with a view to there finding

a suitable field for labour as a missionary. With the consent of my companions I readily accepted this offer.

As far as I recollect it must have been towards the end of February, 1844, that we were ready for the journey. Mr. Tuckett had chartered for our voyage of discovery a good two-masted schooner, called the Debora. Mr. Tuckett, a few surveyors and labourers, Dr. Munro, and myself, took our places in the hold. The captain, who also took his family with him, had his cabin full of passengers. There were, besides, some Nelson gentlemen, who took the opportunity to look at the yet unknown southern part of New Zealand, and a Wesleyan missionary of the name of Creed, with his wife and child, who came from the North Island, and was to relieve missionary Watkin on the lonely east coast towards the south. It seemed that everywhere all over New Zealand, wherever there were natives, there were missionaries too.

Since our arrival in New Zealand, and even in my previous anticipations, I carried about a depressing feeling with me that the whole mission field was already occupied for a long time past, whilst in other lands the people were dwelling in dark heathendom, without any missionaries at all. The consciousness that we were only the first outpost, sent out, as it were, as a feeler for a suitable sphere of operations for our company, and that I must accommodate myself to the attainment of this object, did not altogether remove this feeling of unrest. But when I was once on shipboard again, and the anchor weighed, I felt my spirits rise, and the feeling of the wind blowing on my face was a pleasant one. Towards evening we arrived at Massacre Bay—so called because some sailors of the Dutchman Tasman were there murdered by the natives—where a few natives still lived, but the bay was so wrapped in clouds that we could only see the coast indistinctly. In the west the setting sun was sinking, and the rays were reflected in the east in a wreath of rays, but the wreath was marked with streaks of darker colour. Later, the moon, nearly at the full, rose over the eastern mountains, and let the silver beams of its countenance shine on the gently swelling ocean. Moonshine in New Zealand is very beautiful, especially when it falls on a high mountainous coast.

The mountain range that runs eastward from Tasman Bay into Cook Strait is very jugged and torn, and has many branching sounds which run up far inland—deep valleys lower than the surface of the sea (*sic*). Eastward is the great bay called Cloudy Bay, into which the River Wairau flows.

The next day we landed at Wellington, also a settlement of the New Zealand Company on the north side of Cook Strait, situate on a large harbour, or rather many inlets. Here we took a magistrate on board, who was to superintend the transactions between the natives and the company, as the Government thought, after the slaughter at the Wairau, that this was necessary. I obtained here, from the Wesleyan missionary, whose name was well known southwards on the east coast, a letter of introduction to the natives in the south. The Wesleyans had two stations on the east coast, one in the neighbourhood of Cloudy Bay, the other further south. From Wellington we went south to Banks Peninsula. Southward from Cloudy Bay the mountains on the coast stand out boldly to somewhere about the forty-third degree of southern latitude; from there they bend back westward, and leave an important plain between them and the sea, up to about the forty-fifth degree of latitude. Towards the middle—about the forty-fourth degree—there is a commanding promontory called Banks Peninsula. Captain Cook, who took it for a peninsula, and marked it on his chart with a long neck, probably mistook for sea the larger lagoon to the south of it. This is separated from the sea by a long strip of land running west, with an opening at its western end. He probably thought this went all round the mountain range, which it does not do. This promontory has many inlets, which form good harbours. We sailed into one of the most northern ones, then called Port Cooper, now Lyttelton. In another inlet not far distant there were a few natives who had noticed our arrival, and soon came round to see us. A few of them came in a boat to see what we wanted. Among these there was a great chief, named Tuhawaiki in Maori, Bloody Jack by the Englishmen, because in his English, which he had learnt mostly from rough whalers and sealers, he often used the low word, "bloody." His own place of residence was on the island of Ruapuke, in the south; but he travelled a great deal, because his influence and authority extended from the furthest southern point up to here. He had long seen that the knowledge of the Europeans was better than the narrow views of his country-men, and had, therefore, made connections with them. This, with his own prominent position, had given him great authority. He had also adopted European customs, such as those he was in the midst of, but more on the bad than the good side. I did not then know that Ruapuke, his place of residence, would become mine as well. I showed him my introduction to the southern Maoris; he handed it to his companion and had it read to him, and then said I should be welcome. He could not read himself. When in his dealings with Europeans he had to sign important papers, he drew the beautiful spiral curves and lines with which his face was tattooed. Such documents are still in existence, and are admitted in evidence in legal proceedings having reference to the ownership of land. The prospect of soon having a European colony in his district was of great importance to him; but he was prudent, and kept such of his thoughts as might have any bearing on the proposed purchase of land to himself.

It may here be remarked that the natives of New Zealand call themselves Maori, and foreigners, Pakeha, words which have no other meaning in their language. The pronunciation, as well as the sound, of the vowels is the same as German. In dipthongs the sound begins with the first letter and then flows over to the next ending on one syllable; for instance, Maori, just like Mowry. Vowels which do not flow together, like "u," "a," are pronounced as separate syllables.

Mr. Tuckett resolved to examine the interior of the country from this place—at that time it was a mere wilderness without trace of man or beast. He wished to see whether the soil was fruitful or otherwise, and especially whether it was adapted for the proposed Scottish settlement. With this intention he prepared provisions and tools for roadmaking and examination of the soil, his companions assisting. It happened that he could not find his pocket compass, which was a thing abso-lutely necessary to him. As I did not intend to make any explorations I lent him mine, from which act certain consequences arose.

The next day was Sunday. Early in the morning the missionary Creed, whom I have already named, asked me if I was inclined to go with him to a Maori village which he was informed was only a few hours' distant, to hold divine service there. Of course I was so inclined, because I could thus learn some missionary work. He knew the Maori language, and the day before the natives had told him if he climbed a certain mountain he could see Port Levi from it, where their village lay. Accordingly, we started out and climbed the mountain. I left it to him to find the road, for it was he who had made inquiry, not I. The climbing was not difficult, for a European who intended to establish a sheep run here, had already burnt away the wild undergrowth, but we found the mountain very high. Was it the right one? When we had at last climbed to the top we found ourselves on a sharp, cold mountain ridge. Here we were surprised with a remarkable appearance which presented itself to our eyes on the other side of the mountain.

We are all well enough acquainted with the clouds above us, and I had often wondered how it would look if one could look down from above on the clouds hovering over the earth. Such an appearance was here presented to us. We had climbed up the side of the mountain, by which we had come into bright sunshine ; on the other side the sun shone on a sea of clouds as far as the eye could reach. From thence the clouds were being driven by a wind of considerable strength against the mountain ridge, and there piled up. Here they were leaping and rolling over one another, and thus gave the sun an opportunity of making ever-changing and glancing rainbows amongst them. In the whirling movements here and there mountain tops were for a short time visible, whose wet sides glittered in the sun. The whole gave one an impression of a sort of enchanted bed of giants' children, who wake in the morning, rub their eyes, shake the glistening coverlid, and then bury their heads with rosy, perspiring cheeks under the bed clothes again.

The conjuror's game did not last long. Soon the sea of clouds rolled over the brow of the mountain, so that we were wrapped in thick fog, in which we could hardly see three paces before us. We sat down in the hope that it would soon clear up. The ground consisted of small broken rock. The pieces were just suitable for building a little wall in play. My hands will not be still when I have nothing to do. My thoughts soon put themselves into action, and I soon built a little wall. Then I thought that it might be offensive to my companion that I should thus employ myself on Sunday, and left off; but could not make up my mind to destroy my wall.

As the clouds would not withdraw, we started on our way again as well as we could along the steep mountain ridge in hopes that we were going in the direction of the valley which ends in the inlet, Port Levi, where the Maori village is. Now I missed my pocket compass, for as we could only see a few steps it was impossible to avoid certain gaps in the mountain ridge, and to keep the right direction. We passed horrible masses of rock which had a fantastic appearance in the cloudy mist.

At last we heard birds singing, and thus knew that we neared a wood and had reached the lower regions, for on the high mountains all was bare. Soon we reached the edge of a wood which was invisible until we were close to it. In the thick wet fog it had a forlorn and forbidding look. We ventured confidently into it in the hope that once through it we should reach the desired valley. The trees were short and bent, with little undergrowth, because on the rocky ridge no high trees could get a foothold. At first we broke a few branches off here and there, in order that we might find our way back when we wanted. As we got further in and lower down the mountain the clouds got lighter, but the wood more dense, for the New Zealand woods are thickly clothed with leaves from the base to the top, and the lower foliage is a rusty parti-coloured green. At last we thought we saw an opening in the woods, but it was only an avalanche, where a part of the steep mountain side, trees and all, had fallen into the valley below. As this gap was on the side of the mountain, where we hoped to find the valley with the Maori village, we climbed up the side of it, holding on by trees and branches. When we at last arrived at the bottom of the valley we found ourselves in a narrow dark cleft, down which a stream rushed. The wood was impenetrable on account of the many supplejacks and the quantity of undergrowth, but the stream had cut a deep channel in the ground in which we could walk upright under the overhanging boughs. The water whirled around and among blocks of rock on which we had to walk, so that now and then we had to wade in the water. Our walk in the dark wood in the deep valley of the mountains had been a great deal more agreeable if we had been more certain of our way, and the fear of having lost it had not caused us considerable anxiety. We could not rid ourselves of a doubt that we had not climbed the right mountain, and, if so, that in the thick mist, with neither sun nor compass to guide us, we had not kept the right direction in the windings and turnings of the mountain ridge. As we went further down the valley our stream was joined by others, and became deeper and wider. Instead of walking on the rocks we could only pass from one to another, and often fell deep into the water. We were fully conscious that such jumping and scrambling was not without serious danger, because if one of us had broken a bone both had probably been hopelessly lost. Most mercifully God preserved us from dangerous falls.

After a long climb down the mountain, in the bed of the river, we arrived at last out of the wood into a spreading valley with a level surface. It looked black and uninviting, for you could see that the vegetable growth a short time before had been burnt off in a large fire, we could there walk in a clear space. In a few places where there had been scrub, we had to work our way through the yet standing blackened and jagged stumps and stems, and these tore our clothes and blackened them. Before us lay the opening of the valley, which, to all appearance, ran down to the sea, and we still entertained the hope there to find the Maori village. It was already evening, and the sky still covered with thick clouds, so that we could not ascertain the position of the sun. Once I thought I saw a gleam through the clouds, but a cold shudder ran through me. The gleam was on the right hand, it should have been on the left.

When we reached the end of the valley it was already dusk. We came to a lagoon across which we could not see, but its banks had not the firmness of a beach whereon waves break. It was moist and swampy. We tasted the water, it was brackish, but not seawater. Now we knew that we were at the great lagoon Waihora (later on called Ellesmere) that stands at the southern side of Banks Peninsula, our goal was on the northern side. Here we were now lost, hungry and tired, in a wild' waste. No sign of human beings to be seen. No roof and no food was to be had, and the day was done. We turned away from the swampy bank and climbed a spur of a mountain. Here we knelt down and prayed. Missionary Creed prayed aloud in the English language, which I understood, I then prayed in German, which he did not understand. I could not then express myself in English, and he wished that I should pray out loud from my heart in the language I was accustomed to at home. After the prayer we had fresh courage. We then went undismayed along the mountain spur to a wood in order there to find a lodging for the night. On the way we found a wild turnip which we plucked and took for our supper. It had a few large leaves but not much root. This turnip was originally introduced into New Zealand by Captain Cook, was then spread abroad by the natives, and now grows wild in many places; it bears leaves without a proper turnip root.

On the edge of the wood we found traces (in the shape of a scaffolding to place provisions on) that years ago a Maori garden had been here. But it was all overgrown, and no path was to be seen. We found an old fallen tree whose roots were hollow and roomy enough for us both to sleep in. Without fire, and in our light clothes, it would have been a poor lodging if, fortunately, I had not had materials for making fire with me. These consisted of flint, steel, and tinder. I do not know how I happened to have these in my pocket, for I carried no tobacco pipe. Such an old-fashioned way of striking a light was driven out of fashion by the use of matches, and I should have already laid it on one side if a memory had not clung to it. The steel, with a pouch ornamented by fair hands, with glass pearls, had been given to me as a memento in Hamburg. Without this steel and tinder we could have hardly lived in the following nights among the high cold

mountains. Such apparently unimportant matters as the gift of
a beautiful flint and steel case may by God's providence be so
guided as to lead to the salvation of a man's life. We lighted
our fire, roasted our turnip with its leaves, divided and ate it with
thankfulness, and laid down to sleep in the hollow tree, while we
kept up a warm fire before the opening. The next morning I
looked for wild carrots, as the place seemed to have been an old
Maori plantation, but found none but a little handful hardly larger
than peas. In the meantime my companion had killed a bird
about the size of a sparrow. The prey was roasted at the fire,
divided, and eaten with thankfulness. My fire materials were
then examined, for we might have to pass another night in the
wilderness. It happened that my tinder was nearly exhausted,
but missionary Creed knew how to help. He tore a piece off his
shirt, burnt it into tinder, and that filled my pouch again. After
prayer we broke up again.

We intended to go back the way we came. Climbing up the
rocks in the bed of the rushing stream was, however, much harder
work than coming down. From time to time we drank deep
draughts of the water. This gave us a feeling of hunger, and the
imagination would dwell on a table covered with cold meats ;
but that was not unpleasant. As we met many brooks, as they
united, it was impossible again to know the one by which we
had come down. We did not make much of this, for we concluded they all came from the same ridge, and that, when we
arrived at the top of it, we should have to journey to the left.
After wearisome climbing over stones and rocks, and wading
through much water, we reached the end of the creek at last,
but not the landslip. Now we had sometimes to break through
the undergrowth of the wood, sometimes to crawl under it on
all fours, and thus wearily climb the mountain. At last this
was overcome, and we got into the open, but a steep, high
mountain side, with thick undergrowth as high as a man, stood
before us. We had to climb it to reach the top, for there the
ground consists of stones, in which no plant can grow. On the
sides, on the other hand, where good soil had been washed down
from the top and found a resting place, the growth was thick

and dense, as the dead stalks and leaves remained there from year to year. We had to break through it. As the toughest (not the largest) I went in advance, tore with both hands, and bent with my arms the dense mass asunder, and when I had thus made an opening, gave my companion a shove from behind and then climbed up myself. With every effort as we got higher the growth became thinner, and in time we gained the top.

We found ourselves now in a wild unknown mountain range. The view was contracted. For a short distance above us floated thick clouds. It is a horrible sensation to be in a solitary mountain, without inhabitant, and to have the clouds so near that you see you have to go into the darkness. We had hoped the air would clear, so that we could tell the direction of the mountains, but there was no prospect of this. We climbed along the comb, and soon arrived at the thick, wet fog. Here we could again allay hunger by drinking clear water, as a great deal was collected from the clouds in little hollows in the rock. But the day came to an end; evening was near; and there was no wood to make a fire. "Be still," said my companion. "Yes, praised be God, there are birds singing. There must be wood where birds are singing." We climbed down the side of the mountain, and found ourselves at last on the edge of a wood. The precipice was so steep that when we had made a fire and camped for the night, only the trees and bush were between us and an unknown depth. I was so tired that I could not pray much, and fell at once into a deep sleep. After a couple of hours I awoke quite refreshed, and could now undertake the maintenance of the fire.

The following morning—Tuesday, the third day of our wanderings—we started again. There was nothing to eat here. We looked for the edible berries of a bush (belonging to the order of fuchsias), but found so few that we had to give it up. Now we had to climb the ridge again. Everything was still enveloped in thick cloud. We were often in doubt when the ridges parted, or seemed to part, which one we should choose. "Brother Wöhlers," said Missionary Creed to me more and more, "Shall we die here?" "No"—I would always answer him with confidence—"Our pilgrimage is not at an end yet." I do not know whence my confidence came; may be God gave it me, and because I had a stronger constitution I could more easily bear it. Moreover, my strong confidence had this good effect, that it encouraged my companion when he lost heart, and enabled him to make further exertions.

This dangerous loss of our road was much harder on him than on me, for he had a young wife and a little child on the ship, and it was a great trial to him that they would suffer great anxiety on his account. Still we could always allay our hunger by drinking of the clear water that had fallen into the clefts in the rock. The long wandering up and down high solitary mountains in cold and horrible mist at last reduces one's strength.

I began to look sharply at the ground when we were walking on smaller ridges, for I hoped to see some signs of a road. "Stop!" said I at last, "we were here on Sunday morning. I built this wall with my own hands"—and I knew that I had done it. Now we knew that we were not more than about three hours' distant from Port Cooper, where our ship lay at anchor. But now the difficulty was to find the direction in the thick fog. We tried one direction that appeared likely to us, but we soon came to so yawning an abyss that we shuddered before it. We went back, therefore, and tried another spur running in a similar direction, but again came to a yawning abyss, either really or apparently so. In the meantime the night had fallen, and we had to decide to prepare our bed. Fortunately we had got so far down that we could find a few clumps of creeping pines. We therefore began to break off a supply of twigs, and gather them together. Whilst I was doing it, without knowing it, I fell over fast asleep. When my companion thus found me he picked me up, shook me well, and at last had to beat me till I was so far awake that I could light a fire. As the tinder burnt I gave it into his hands, and at once fell fast asleep again. In the meantime he made a fire and drew me to a warm place. After a couple of hours I woke up quite refreshed, and could now undertake the maintenance of the fire.

The following morning—Wednesday, the fourth day of our wanderings—we again rose and went down the mountain. We soon got out of the clouds and saw already through the lower strata the gleaming surface of Port Cooper. Soon after we saw the masts of the schooner Debora. Now we were saved. As at last we neared the strand we saw a boat push off to fetch us. Our clothes hung in rags, and we had a very torn and blackened appearance. After a moderate meal of warm oatmeal, and a good long sleep, our exhausted energies were fully restored. We were not free from blame in thus having lost ourselves, for we trusted ourselves without guide and without compass on a wild mountain range.

The direction just to go up to the mountain, from whence Port Levi could be seen, meant, probably, not the top of the mountain, but a side spur.

Such was Banks Peninsula in those days. Now, after thirty-four years, this wild mountain range is turned into useful sheep runs. European settlers have burnt away the useless growth in the wild over-grown country and the mountain ranges, and sown the seed of useful grasses in the soil, so that now sheep run there by thousands. Surveyors have long ago delineated the different mountain ranges on their maps.

A few natives lived on Banks Peninsula and the neighbourhood, and Mr. Tuckett wished that I should remain amongst them. This did not appear advisable to me, for the Wesleyans already had a missionary station to the north of here in Cloudy Bay, and another to the southward in Waikouaiti, and I could not decide to push myself in between, besides there were native teachers here already. I would rather go quite to the south where, at all events, I should have one clear side. But who knows what might have happened if we had found the Maori village and the Maoris had asked me to become their missionary there. In the uncertainty of finding a suitable field for missionary work I might have looked upon it as a call and accepted it. It would not do now, however, as Mr. Tuckett had finished the examination of the land, and wished to sail southward to see if he could not find better land there. I saw the hand of God in it that I could not remain here, for I should not have liked to see the conditions that afterwards existed grow up around me.   For after a few years another branch of the New Zealand Company was formed in England, a union of the Episcopalian Church, which would only accept members of that Church as emigrants to New Zealand, and this neighbourhood was chosen for this settlement. If the Church authorities had found me at work amongst the natives they would, as is their custom, have greeted and treated me in a friendly manner—and that would have been very pleasant to me—but the friendship would have had the aim of incorporating us into their Church, and that personally I did not desire.   I love Christianity as the Bible teaches it, which includes all disciples of Jesus, but I cannot bear to be in an exclusive Church coerced by human rules.

According to the geological chart, Banks Peninsula, originally a mountain isolated from the flat coast, consists of igneous rocks. The large plain to the westward consists of newer stratified rocks (upper mesozoic and tertiary).   This formation extends sometimes narrow, sometimes broad, the whole length of the east coast.   The western mountains consist of older stratified rocks (lower mesozoic and palæozoic).   This formation extends to Cook Strait — to nearly the forty-fifth and a-half degree of latitude westward—therefrom along the whole length of the east coast the high mountains consist of metamorphic rocks (granites).   This formation extends between the forty-fourth and forty-sixth degree of latitude right across the land to the east coast.   Ruapuke and Stewart Island also belong to this formation.   The great plain near Banks Peninsula is watered by many swift flowing and therefore straight rivers that take their rise in the high Western Alps, and in their course through the mountains receive many tributaries.   The flat coasts of the plains are only broken by the rivers' mouths and have no inlets.   North-easterly, from Banks Peninsula, is the Forty Mile, and south-westerly the Ninety Mile Beach.

We sailed now southward to Waikouaiti, where we had to land missionary Creed and his family.   Halfway down some natives lived at a place called Moeraki.   As it was known—

through the Wesleyan mission post there—that there was a footpath to Waikouaiti, Mr. Tuckett was landed with some companions in the neighbourhood. He invited me to go with him, which I declined, and he thought I had lost my courage on Banks Peninsula. That was not the case. I should gladly have made the journey with him, but my clothes and shoes did not allow of it. They were not made like those of the surveyors—to climb over sharp stones and through thorny scrub. I had already destroyed a suit on Banks Peninsula and spoilt a pair of boots, and what I had left I carried in a not over-full portmanteau. There was no opening for me among the natives there, as they were already under Wesleyan care. Waikouaiti was at the time the seat of the John Jones, of Sydney, celebrated for the extent of his kingdom. He was without cultivation, and not without rudeness; but he understood how to make money and acquire lands after the manner of the worldly-wise, which covers a multitude of . . . He carried on an extensive whale-fishery here, and employed many Maoris and Europeans. The latter consisted, to a large extent, of a class of reckless people from the Australian Colonies, whither England at that time transported great criminals. They brought the Maoris no virtues, and John Jones came to see that he would be able to rely better upon his men if there was a little of the fear of God amongst them. He applied, therefore, to the Methodists (Wesleyans) in Sydney, and requested them to found a mission station at his whale fishery in New Zealand, where he would build a house for them. Missionary Watkin, who had worked for many years in the Fiji Islands and could not bear the climate there any longer, was at that time with his family in Sydney, and to him was the post allocated, Besides being pious he was a clever and experienced man, and knew how to take people the right way, and his labours were, with the blessing of God, successful as well among the Maoris as the Europeans. John Jones used to acknowledge this, but yet he complained that his best men would not work on the Sabbath day. It was not a very desirable place for an elderly missionary. When we had cast anchor in the bay, missionary Watkin came on board and shook hands with his successor. "Missionary

Creed," he said, half joking, "welcome to purgatory." He was now called to Wellington to take the superintendence of a few Wesleyan communities.

The whale fishing is carried on from the coasts as well as from ships. As is well known, the whales are warm-blooded animals. They must, therefore, at short intervals, come to the surface to breathe. They suckle their young, which are here called calves. At certain times of the year the so-called cows, or mother fish, come to the coasts to calve, in still waters in the bays. They are then killed from the land with boats, while the ships attack the bulls outside. Watches are set on the heights on land, and when a whale is seen, which is known by the spouting of the water that they send up through their breathing holes, the boats are manned and the hunt begins. The steersman occupies the first position in a boat, and good whalers compete with one another to obtain the position. One requires both to steer as well as command well, for it is necessary to bring the boat as close as possible to the huge creature with as little danger as possible, in order that the harpooner may cast his harpoon into him, which is furnished with a barb, and a long line attached to it. Care must be taken to keep the boat out of reach of his tail, for he could easily break it into smithereens. The creature must not be allowed to get under the boat, for with a light blow he could throw it and all the crew out of the water high into the air. When the harpoon is fast the whale drags the boat away with it, and every time when he comes up to breathe another lance is thrown into his body. It is really contrary to humanity that the great sea creatures should be so cruelly killed by men, especially when a mother fish, dying, still seeks to rescue her young; but both are killed without mercy.

Waikouaiti Bay is no harbour, but a good anchorage, which is sheltered from the prevailing south-west winds, but exposed to the easterly ones. Small schooners can run into the river which empties itself into the bay, where, when they are across the bar, which is thrown up where the stream and the breakers meet, they can find still and deep water. The landscape is beautiful. It consists of hills and mountains of moderate size, with valleys and little flats, intersected by small streams. The soil is fruitful, and the place adapted for a prosperous little town. Now, after thirty-four years, there is an important village there, built by European settlers. According to the geological chart, the coast range from here to Otago consists of igneous rocks. It appears, however, that the granite formation, which is not far from here, has already broken through in some few places, for single round mountains, like breasts, raise themselves aloft here, and on the top of these rocky points the granite breaks out.

Not long after our arrival in this bight Mr. Tuckett began his land journey. He ordered his surveyors to measure the bay, and ascertain the depth of the water, but this was forbidden by the magistrate whom the Government had sent with us, because the land still belonged to the natives. Mr. Tuckett pointed out that there was no intention of surveying any land, but merely to measure an anchorage, and for trade and commerce it was of great importance that the still unknown harbours and anchorages should be exactly marked on the chart. But the magistrate insisted that his instructions were that no surveying instruments were to be landed until the land had been formally and legally purchased from the natives. Mr. Tuckett, however, would not give way, and the measurements were completed in spite of the remonstrance of the magistrate.

It is said of the Quakers that they are for peace at any price, and that this is impracticable for this common world. The first is quite true as far as regards shedding blood; the rest is not true. Mr. Tuckett was a conscientious Quaker, and yet in all respects a practical man. He could take a stand and carry his intention through when he was satisfied it was the right one.

From Waikouaiti Bay we sailed southward across a large half-moon-shaped bay, three or four German miles wide, to the harbour of Otago. The coast here is fully fifty feet to one hundred feet high. At that time there was no lighthouse or other landmark for the sailor, and we could see nothing of the entrance to the harbour. We had, however, brought with us from Waikouaiti, as pilot, a man well acquainted with the place—a European who, as a sealer, knew all harbours and anchorages. It looked as if he would steer the vessel right on to the rocky headlands. Soon a level surface of water, between the steep cliffs, was to be seen, and as we went into it another opening made its appearance, and most charmingly surprised, we arrived in a beautiful harbour, like a broad stream enclosed in soft, wooded hills, from which the bright songs of birds could be heard on both sides. It was not a stream, but an arm of the sea, about six German miles long, and a quarter to half a mile broad. We sailed about half-way up the harbour and then cast anchor. A little higher up this harbour is divided into two by two jutting bluffs and a little island in the middle. Near the mouth of the harbour a native village might be seen, but I had no opportunity to see it.

The next day all went in a boat to the end of the harbour. Here we found a beautiful hilly country. Mr. Tuckett, with his strong long legs, climbed the hills and over-looked the landscape. He was delighted with the beautiful wide valleys which he saw both far and near. At that time this whole region was an uninhabited wilderness, and now, after thirty-four years, there is a rich town here called Dunedin, with over 20,000 inhabitants, which is making rapid strides.

Southward from Otago, the Taieri, an important river, empties itself into the sea, in the neighbourhood of which are many fruitful valleys. The next large river south is the Molyneux (Maori name, Matau), now called Clutha by the Scotch. In its upper course it is connected with the alpine lakes, and with its tributaries flows through fruitful valleys and plains. Still further south, at the easterly entrance of Foveaux Strait is the Mataura, a river also with fertile banks. All these three large rivers have bars at their mouths, where river and sea meet, large ships cannot, therefore, enter them. Northward of Otago the land is just as fertile. At that time the watershed of all these rivers was quite unknown, but now it is all accurately surveyed, marked on charts, and intersected by roads and railroads. On the hills and mountains flocks of sheep and cattle feed by thousands. In the valleys and plains there are well-to-do farm houses, and in the gorges of the mountains rich gold diggings. Iron and coal are also in abundance. No wonder that Dunedin has become so rich

a city in a few years. Mr. Tuckett, after he had examined the
whole of the East Coast, from north to south, rightly appreciated
the value of the district, and, therefore, chose Otago as the centre
of the settlement of the community consisting of members of the
Free Church of Scotland. None of the provinces of New Zealand
has become so populous and wealthy as the Province of Otago.
The settlement (the first settlers came here four years later) was,
it is true, founded by the Free Presbyterian Church of Scotland ;
but any exclusiveness was soon broken through from outside,
as, attracted by the fruitful land, and especially by the gold
discovery, immigrants from all lands and of all persuasions flowed
in. For all that, from there to Southland the Scottish element
has remained predominant.

From Otago we sailed to Molyneux Bay, where we took in
Mr. Tuckett with his companions, who had made the journey by
land in order to see the country from Otago to here. We then
went on to Foveaux Strait.

In pursuance of the inquiries that I had made from place to
place (especially I had obtained much information from our pilot),
I was convinced that the Island of Ruapuke, at the eastern end
of Foveaux Strait, would be the most suitable place for my
missionary work. On this little island, about eight miles long
and four miles wide, situate between Stewart Island and the
mainland, dwelt the largest number of natives of this southern
district. It was the residence of the distinguished people of the
race and of the most exalted chieftains, and the centre and
gathering place of the Maoris, who were scattered all over the
country.

The vessel was on the road to Bluff Harbour, and whilst we
were passing the Island of Ruapuke I got into a boat with
my belongings—consisting of a portmanteau, two woollen rugs,
a fowling-piece, a little axe, and handsaw, besides a sack of flour
and some salt which I had bought from the captain—and our pilot
steered toward the beach. (I was advised by the English
missionaries at Nelson not to take many things with me, because
there was fear that the savages in the south might take them
away from me ; besides, I have a dislike to travelling with a large

quantity of luggage.) The name of the pilot, Edward Palmer, deserves to be remembered, for he is yet proud of having landed me at Ruapuke. On the voyage he was lead to peace with God by missionary Watkin, and then learnt to conduct his affairs properly, and now lives at peace with a suitable income as an old but hearty man. " Godliness is profitable unto all things, having the promise of the life that now is and of that which is to come." A number of Maoris had already assembled on the beach to hear what news the approaching boat would bring. Our pilot, well known here, told them shortly—the language was half English and half Maori—that he brought a missionary who would remain with them. Thereupon I was landed with all my things on the backs of the Maoris, and the boat rowed back to the ship, not to keep it standing off and on too long. It was the middle of May, 1844, that I landed here.

CHAPTER IX.

THE BEGINNING AT RUAPUKE.

AT last I was amongst the savages in New Zealand, whose language I did not yet even understand. Some were clothed in large English blankets, in which their athletic forms and graceful bearing looked as stately as the ancient Greeks in their robes. Most of them, however, wore clothes, and in some cases only ragged pieces of them, which were made of the thread of the so-called New Zealand flax woven with their own fingers. A short distance from the beach stood a village consisting of very low dwellings with doors which were barely two feet high and broad so that one could only crawl in on all fours. A little higher up there was another opening of the same size to let light and air in and stinks out. I was now taken to a house that was built in European fashion, and belonged to the absent chief, named Tuhawaiki (commonly called Bloody Jack), whom I had already met on Banks Peninsula. This princely dwelling was, however, only a rough cottage built of boards,

with a thatched roof, and a door and two small square windows
in the front. The interior consisted of two small bedrooms, in
which the bedsteads were fashioned after those in a ship's cabin,
and a lean-to which served as kitchen and dwelling-room. Seats
there were none, but an old pail was turned upside down for me.
The cottage was filled with people who belonged to the family of
the chief and his household. A bed was allotted to me for my
separate use, but I had to share the room with another. A few
slept on the floor. Many slept on the flat ground in the kitchen.
Roasted potatoes were lying all around close to them. And this
was the chief's dwelling. In the huts of the common people it
was still more miserable. If the prophecy could then have come
to me that in twenty-five years all the people would be walking
about washed and in clean European clothes, and would live in
comfortable, cleanly-fashioned houses like respectable Europeans,
I should not have been able to believe it.

You could only call the Maoris here savages, still they were
no longer heathens. After long, apparently resultless, labours of
the missionaries in the north, their teaching was at last taken to
heart by the Maoris there, and they became, instead of dirty,
loutish and cruel men, kind and orderly disciples of Christ.
This created so great a revolution that the whole Maori people
were affected by it, and the shock was felt to the furthermost
end, and had results even in this far south.   Then the Wesleyan
missionary at Waikouaiti came on mission journeys to the south,
and appointed baptized natives as teachers. A year after my
arrival the Anglican Bishop of New Zealand (Dr. Selwyn) came
here and also appointed baptized natives as teachers. Furthermore,
travelling evangelists of both persuasions had already introduced
both forms of Christian services. Accordingly I found Christian
usages already in practice here. Besides Sunday and twice a
week services, every morning and evening meetings for prayer
were held, both by the Wesleyans and the Anglicans. As I
attended these meetings and saw how and in what a babbling and
thoughtless way the teachers read their lessons, and in what a
thoughtless way the people conducted themselves, I thought, I
perceive that in all things ye are too superstitious (really too

much afraid of God). Still what more could be expected at the time. These forms of Christianity, although still without its spirit, had already effected an astonishingly large amount of good in them. They had already given up murder and cannibalisms, and especially all cruel and gross sins which had formerly existed amongst them as something quite common.

An Irishman lived here with his Maori wife (he himself was absent) and their son: the boy knew some English. I had been able to use him as interpreter; but I saw I could not effect much that way, and that it would be much more advisable to devote my whole time to learning the Maori language. For this I had now every opportunity. On my journey through Wellington I had already possessed myself of a Maori grammar, a translated English Prayer Book, and New Testament, and studied them on board ship. Here I could learn the pronunciation. A few here could read already, and these were always ready to sit by me and read with me in the New Testament, in which each of us read his verse in turn. I noticed the pronunciation carefully, and gladly allowed myself to be taught how to pronounce the words. At the same time, my ears got accustomed to understand the sound, for one may be able to read a language which one has learnt and understand nothing of it, when hearing the people, whose language it is, speak it. The organs of speech, moreover, must be practised before one can give the sounds their proper expression. The Maori says of such foreigners who speak their language, but not after their fashion, that they " bite their words."

When the Irishman (he was a Catholic) came back from his journey, he invited me to take up my residence in his house. This, however, I declined, not because he was a Catholic—for in our circumstances no difference of belief must be taken into consideration—but because I wished to be for a time in a house where nothing was spoken but Maori. He pressed me to take my meals in his house, to which he would call me when required. I accepted this, for where I was staying the preparation of the food was entirely wanting in cleanliness. There were three meals a day in the house of the Irishman. These consisted of fat

seabirds (of which more hereafter), potatoes, and damper. The
latter is a damp bread made out of flour and water, kneaded,
without yeast, and baked in hot ashes. This method of life
agreed with me well enough, for I was yet in my full strength,
and had a healthy stomach, and I should gladly have shared the
expense with him if I had been better supplied with money or
had expectations of soon receiving remittances. I dare not
remain long in the dwelling where I was, unless I wished to
sink into the filthy ways of the Maori, and a missionary dare not
do this. Soon after my arrival, I made the acquaintance of the
then still young high chief Topi, who stood next in rank to
Tuhawaiki—a friendly man, but a little unstable, so that one
could not always rely upon him. He was kind enough to offer
me a house, but I must not enter it where it stood. It was
tapu—holy—because his first wife had died there, and, beside
me, he dare not speak to anyone who was not of high birth.
Those of high birth were superior to the tapu, because they were
either holy themselves or else separated from the common people
by the possession of a higher nature.

Superior Europeans, the class to which the missionaries
belonged, were considered by the chieftain race as equal in birth
to themselves, but they had to take care to preserve the respect
of the chieftain race for themselves, for if they were despised by
the upper classes still greater contempt was at once accorded to
them by the common people. The house, which was only built
in a lonely place for the sick woman to die in, in order that the
dwelling house might not become tapu, had, therefore, to be
removed and built again in another place, for which purpose Topi
had already chosen one. This lay under a hill, by a little lake of
fresh water, and was sheltered from the sea winds by a beautiful
green bush (belonging to the order of veronica). The place
pleased me much, as it was far enough removed from the Maori
huts to be clear of their stinks and mess, and at the same time
from thence one could reach all the villages of the island on the
best roads.

In my time one used to hear people in Germany speaking of
the dear heathen as if it would be a pleasure to live with such

amiable people. But this is a great mistake. Wild heathen, in spite of their occasional good temper, and of the occasional noble disposition of the high chieftains, are a class of men sunk so low that they disgust one who has been brought up in Christian customs. They are so dirty in their whole method of life that they stink of it. Still, the servant is not higher than the master, and as the son of God, Jesus Christ, abased Himself to the lowest of mankind to lift them to a Christian life by His life, sufferings and death, and gave us lost sinners eternal life, so His servants in following Him must not shrink from what is disgusting. And when the heathen disgust us it is our duty to make them into men, after the image of God, so that one may love them.

Mr. Tuckett had promised to stop here on his return journey, and I must, therefore, make preparation to send a short report by him to Nelson, and send word whether a field for us four missionaries was to be found here. When I had visited the different villages with the natives, and looked into their population, I came to the conclusion that somewhere about two hundred people lived here, old and young. It is true a few* of them were here only on a visit, but this made no difference, for it appeared that visitors often came here, which made this island so important. When I made inquiry about the inhabitants of the opposite coasts, on both sides of the strait, I was always told that there were only a very few, who lived in small, widely-scattered villages. It appeared to me, therefore, that only one missionary was necessary in this small population. It was further to be considered that if all four of us settled down here, we should be regarded with suspicion. I had not lived long amongst the people. As a single foreigner I was welcome; as a missionary I was indifferent to them. None of the already existing sects had any idea of placing themselves under my ministry, because I was neither an Anglican nor a Wesleyan. At no price would the natives part with any land on this island. Four of us would have required to cultivate a considerable piece to supply us with the necessary food, and the suspicion would at once have fallen upon us that we wished to obtain land surreptitiously. The slaughter of the English at the Wairau was long known of here, and was represented as if the

Maoris has won a splendid conquest over land robbers. Under these circumstances I could not advise my brethren at Nelson to follow me.

A few weeks after he had examined the neighbourhood of Bluff Harbour, and that of the New and Jacob Rivers, Mr. Tuckett came back and landed at Ruapuke. He said that he had found a large plain in the south, but that the soil, with the exception of the swampy land on the banks of the great rivers, was not as fruitful as that in the neighbourhood of Otago. He had, therefore, decided upon that place as the starting point of the Scottish settlement, from which it might spread in all directions. He therefore requested the Maoris, who could speak, to come to Otago soon, and arrange the price of an agreed portion in open meeting.

The great plain in the south of the Middle Island of New Zealand resembles the plains of North Germany. On the banks of the great rivers there are strips of rich swampy land; the remainder consists of agricultural land. It is good soil when manured, but the present agriculturists (at the time when I write) will not undertake this as long as land is to be had which will bear without manure. The agricultural land, because there is more rain here than in Germany, is intersected by many streams, so that when it is once worked it would make good meadows, and there is no want of scattered woods. I lately saw in a statistical publication that the average yield of wheat over the whole of New Zealand is thirty and a-half bushels per acre. If a reckoning were made of the Otago division alone, the yield would be considerably higher. If they reckon the bushel at sixty pounds (and good wheat weighs more), and the acre at one hundred and sixty rods, German farmers may calculate the yield of New Zealand soil. It is true that so far only the best land has been worked, but nothing like the care is expended on the preparation of the soil that is devoted to it in well-conducted properties at Home.

In time the promised dwelling was built for me. It was fifteen feet long and nine wide. The walls from the ground to the roof were four feet high, and the door of the house not quite so high. Walls and roof were thatched with freshly-plucked grass, and the whole looked liked a haystack. I was offered servants as well, but I knew well these would expect to be paid, and wages are much higher in New Zealand than in Germany. I therefore declined this courteously and served myself. Gifts of potatoes and fish I accepted gratefully. The most necessary cooking utensils I could get from the Irishman already named, who carried on something of a huckster's business.

My house was now a good settler's hut. When I was at home I was seldom alone. From daybreak till dusk my hut was always full of visitors. None came when it was dark, for they were all afraid in the dark, and I was sometimes asked if ghosts never troubled me at night. Many only came to lie 'lazily in my way. In time I had to courteously forbid this idle lying in my hut. Others who came to read the New Testament with me, or had something to say to me, I received in a friendly manner. The latter only came to tell me their dreams, or quite unimportant occurrences. Then I took a piece of paper and told them to speak slowly that I might understand it, and wrote their narratives down word for word. If there was a word or an expression which I did not understand I had it explained to me. At first they thought I was only scratching with a pen, but when I read it out to them at the end they were very much astonished that I could write as fast as a man could speak, whilst they have to draw for a long time before they can even make a letter. When the evening came I studied the language from these papers. If one goes to a people that has no literature (translations from foreign languages are not their own literature) to learn their language you must do so from narratives which are given by word of mouth. It may here be remarked that one can write the Maori language faster than a European one because no syllables have more than two letters. If a syllable does not consist of only one vowel it must end with a vowel with not more than one consonant before it. The " ng " and " wh " have only the effect of a single consonant. In dipthongs which run together when spoken slowly you hear the sound of two syllables. The language has five vowels as the German has, and ten consonants " h," " f," " m," " n," " ng," " p,"

" r," " t," " w," " wh," therefore ten times five and five are fifty-five sounds (formerly not so many as the syllables " wo," " wu," " who," " whu " were wanting). The words, however, can be quite long enough.

Learning a foreign language was never a great difficulty to me. I could consequently now make myself understood by the people. If anyone should here remark that I cannot even yet write the German language well, I might reply that for thirty-four years I have had no conversation with German people, and in that time something may well be forgotten (the translator may perhaps be permitted here to remark that it is thirty-five years since he left Germany, and can fully understand what the narrator feels), and, furthermore, that I only learnt to speak the high German a few years before I left Germany. My old head now gets so tired with daily teaching spelling, reading, writing and arithmetic in the school in English that even with better knowledge I cannot always avoid making mistakes.

Now I may remark that the Maoris for fifty years past were still in the stone age, and that, therefore, many advantages and occupations of civilised peoples were unknown to them, their language, therefore, could have no word to represent them. You cannot, as in German, manufacture a suitable word out of the German language, and one is therefore often weak and helpless in translating, although the Maori language is enriched with many conceptions and ideas. In translating the Bible this is less troublesome because the Bible suits all peoples. As far as earlier conceptions require, the language supplies any idea with great accuracy, in some things even greater so than the German. To mention one instance only, the German language leaves an uncertainty whether, in the case of the pronoun " we," the person addressed is in, or excluded—the Maori language never. I have wondered that even German authors, who certainly work with thoroughness, as well as others, copying foreigners, represent the Maori language as so helpless that it is obliged to form a plural by the prefix of a meaningless particle " nga." But " nga " is by no means a meaningless particle, but the quite plain and proper plural article, and as a plural article as grammatical as that of the

German language, and one which the English language does not possess.

I began now to hold meetings in the Maori villages, which I visited from time to time, one after another, These consisted of short extempore prayers, the reading of a chapter, and explanatory remarks. I naturally did not refer to sectarian differences. This was more easily avoided when the whole village community consisted of one sect. It was more difficult when they were mixed ; still, it generally happened that the gathering consisted mostly of a few of both persuasions. Sometimes I was asked which of the two Churches (the Anglican or the Wesleyan) was the best. When I replied that they were both churches of Jesus Christ, I received the answer that they knew that well ; it was the same as if a man had two wives ; but they wanted to know which was the head, which the subordinate wife. Those of the Anglican persuasion maintained their Church was to be compared with the head wife, the Wesleyans with that of the subordinate one, which these naturally contested, and even maintained that theirs was the better and most beloved, on which some rude Anglicans replied that theirs was a " he wahine Paremu " (a concubine). Further, I was asked, as the Anglicans had more prayers in their prayer-book than the Wesleyans, which was in the right ; or, if the Anglicans assembled one evening for school teaching, whilst on the same evening the Wesleyans had a sermon, which was right. Many questions about quite indifferent matters were asked. When I said these were matters of no importance, and they should trouble themselves more about their own sins and their own salvation, and through belief have Christ dwelling more in their hearts, this did not satisfy them at all. Instead of striving after holiness, they had much rather dispute about sectarian differences, in which they could let out their scorn for one another. They would thus become much more satisfied with themselves, and lust of the eye, lust of the flesh, and the pride of life have freer play than when living in the Word of God without sectarian disputes. These Church communities were, of course, not founded on convictions—the Maoris had, so far, no creeds, but entered on already-existing party lines.

What a blessing it would be for missions if all Evangelical Missionary Societies would act in accordance with the principles of the London and North German ones, and refrain from introducing the old-existing historical differences amougst the heathen communities!

The contention that one must present the Churches of the Home Country in all the details of their constitution to the heathen, and endow them with the entire creeds, because otherwise in their development they would have to go through all the battles which the Churches at Home have had to fight, is quite a mistaken one. With strange peoples in future centuries quite different disputes will arise to those through which the Church of the Home Country has had to fight its way. There is only one battle common to them all and at all times—that is, the battle against the worldliness of their members. This is not to be driven out with Church regulations, but by a loving heart that seeks the lost, and a true, hearty promulgation of the simple Gospel as Jesus and the Apostles did it.

If the missionaries of the different Missionary Societies could work in districts separated from one another, the differences of opinion of the Churches would do less harm to the conversion of the heathen. The meeting of the missionaries of different sects, in our disturbed time and in a time of so great enterprise, and with the ever-spreading expansion of missions, is not to be avoided. We read at the end of Daniel: "Seal up the writing till the last time, and many will come over and find great understanding." In the English Bible this sentence is thus translated: "Many shall run to and fro, and knowledge shall be increased." I am not so learned as to be able to tell which translation is the more correct. If the English is the more correct, it would admittedly suit our time, when one can travel so quickly all over the world, when knowledge has already been much increased and is always being still further increased, so that we even use the lightning of heaven as our messenger. Why, then, should the great missionary work of our Heavenly King be so hindered with small and hair-splitting ideas, and the conversion of the heathen be maintained by old Church institutions? If only the converted are saved, it is all the same whether they get to heaven out of close, exclusive churches or out of free communities.

If, after the manner of the old settlers, I had sought earthly inconveniences in my hut, I should have soon found them in smoke and draughts. But I sought for no unnecessary unpleasantness in my life as a settler. I had brought strips of glass, made of spare pieces, from a glazier in Nelson, with me. With my hand-saw, axe, and pocket knife, I made wooden frames in which I fastened the panes, not much larger than playing cards. Now I had windows, and was no longer troubled with draughts through the openings for light in the walls. Another opening which the builders had left for the smoke to issue was uncomfortable, as the prevailing wind blew into it, and blew back the smoke into the hut in a desperate manner. I had, therefore, to close this opening, and let the smoke find its way through the roof. This was more comfortable, but it had this disadvantage, that it made everything in the hut smoky. My woollen blankets, which were originally white, received a decidedly rusty-brown appearance. Now I cut a hole through the roof, and fastened upright poles into it after the form of a chimney, fastened sticks across them, and plastered my new chimney inside and out with clay. Then I lit a fire and went out to see the effect, and right enough the smoke went straight up from my chimney as it does in a civilised country. In time the grass on my walls dried up so much that the wind could blow through. I had then to take the grass away, fasten twigs on the walls, and then coat them with clay. There was another great trouble to overcome, my bed was always full of fleas which the dirtiness of the Maoris daily brought me. When I made my bed I could see them exercising in it, horse and foot ; whoever has seen fleas *en masse* will understand what I mean. I had, therefore, to make a division wall, so that neither Maoris nor their fleas could come into my bed chamber. The whole house was fifteen feet long and nine feet broad. At one end I made the bedroom, nine feet by four feet ; in the other, where the door was, I made the kitchen, nine feet by five feet ; in the middle, the reception room, nine feet by six feet. The walls were carefully plastered with clay to make them flea-tight.

Then I got a few boards (I got them from the Irishman who used to go round trading) and made steps and doors. The latter were not much more than four feet high, because the side walls were so low. I had previously made a table and chair. When the Maoris came, and they had finished their talk, I told them in a friendly way to go, to break them of their lazy habit of sitting in my house. Then I took my broom, swept the room, and strewed fresh sand. This was done three or four times in a day, and I achieved a certain amount of cleanliness. I could not manage the warming of my house for a long time. At last, in my wanderings through the island, I discovered some flat pieces of rock which had been loosened from granite blocks. I hewed these carefully into squares, made a sledge, and hauled them home. Then with clay I built them into the shape of a stove. Now my settlement in a comfortable little dwelling was effected.

When Spring came I had to think of making a garden, for the presents of potatoes ceased to be made. In my simplicity, as I gave the people credit for more kindness of heart than they had, I did not at first know that the Maoris expected for their gifts a return of still greater ones. It happened once that a man brought me, quite unexpectedly, a big pig for killing. It was very opportune, and as I thought he brought it out of kindness and love for me, I was very much pleased. Later, the man demanded a return of more than the pig was worth, and I was obliged to give it. Pigs at that time were only very small, and as they mostly fed on worms which the foul seaweed bred on the beach, they were of a very fishy flavour. This, however, did not trouble me much, for when one only has rough food, and not much of that, taste adapts itself to circumstances.

I enclosed, therefore, a place for my garden close to my hut. The Maoris were astonished at my labour—such a handsome woven fence they had not yet seen—and, therefore, willingly gave me potatoes to plant. When the Maoris who had a voice in the matter came back from the land sale in Otago, they brought me, from Mr. Tuckett, vegetable and flower seeds for my garden, as well as some coffee, tea, sugar, and wine. First I will tell about the seeds of vegetables only.   Peas, cabbages, turnips, and carrots would grow ; the others died, because of the cold, wet Spring air, caused by the cooling of the cold southern sea water.   Of the flower seeds only the hardier sorts would stand.   But these were flowers of the most conspicuous kind.   Looking out of my window in Summer you might have seen a variegated bed of flowers.   The Maoris were also astonished at this, and it was of assistance to elevate their minds, for the sense of beauty which, in a better bygone time they had possessed, had disappeared in later generations.

Concerning the wine, Mr. Tuckett wrote me that he sent it because I belonged to a persuasion that takes the sacrament in a spiritual manner externally, whilst it understands it in a spiritual manner internally.   We were, however, far from prepared to take the Holy Supper at Ruapuke, but I was overjoyed to find that he was so broadminded as to honour those of another persuasion in this manner.

We now come back to Ruapuke.   There were seven little villages, which all lay on the sea beach in the inlets all around the island.   I visited these villages one after another on week days for devotional meetings, and always towards evening, when the people had finished their labours in the field.

When with time I became more fluent in the language, I began to hold divine service regularly on Sundays, and to preach in turns at every place every Sunday.   The desire for Christian fellowship at that time was so weak that the people would not go from one village to another to hold a service in common.   I tried to speak in a very simple manner, and to make my meanings clear by illustrations taken from their own life.   In this manner, in time, I secured their attention ; so far they had thought that serving God consisted of merely patiently sitting through the time.   At first I wrote my sermons and then learnt them by heart, and as they came best from my heart if I wrote them very plainly, it had this good effect, that in time the Maoris became desirous of having my written sermons to read them and have them read to them.   As a reward for them I had presents of fish and such like.   Later on, when my labours increased, I had not always time to write, and I found then, that by means of reflection alone, I could learn a sermon by heart.

We shall soon come on to holy ground in this history, but before we tread on it this will be the proper place to give a short description of the island and the people.

CHAPTER X.

THE ISLAND AND ITS INHABITANTS.

THE island of Ruapuke is about eight miles long and four miles in diameter. The coast consists of inlets and rocky bluffs. If it were within easy distance of North Germany, where the country is so flat and uniform, it would be a favourite resort. It has great natural beauty, and has an impressive appearance. Gigantic waves break on the bluffs with a sound like thunder, especially after stormy weather, and drive a great mass of water broken into spray sometimes seventy feet high, from which height it sinks again slowly like a faint bluish veil. In the inlets the waves, when they strike the beach and roll on the sand, lift themselves like walls of water. The upper combs bend over forwards, and throw themselves over with a thundering crash, burying a quantity of air, that escapes from the foam of the broken water masses with a crackling, hissing, and blowing sound. Now the broken mass foams hissing up a wide stretch of beach, then rushes back, making the pebbles roll and clatter. "Hitherto shalt thou come, and no further; here shall thy proud waves be stayed" (Job); and "Though the waves thereof toss themselves, yet shall they not prevail" (Jeremiah).

Let us cast our eye over the landscape. Round hills not over 200 feet high, huge bare masses of rock, soft flats, wood, bush and meadow alternate with one another. Little lakes, too, with fresh water (but no fishes), and lagoons of salt water are not wanting. If from the height you let your sight fall on the wide sea you can notice the round curve of our earth quite plainly. In the direction of Stewart Island you look over a charmingly beautiful sea, graced with little rocks and islands toward the high mountains of this island, the highest of which is about 4,000 feet. Across at the Middle Island you see the long low coast line of the plains and the high mountains over it in the blue distance. The hill at the Bluff is close to Bluff Harbour, about thirteen miles from Ruapuke, and is about 800 feet high. From some heights you can see the high mountains of the Takitumu, so named after one of the canoes in which the ancestors of the present Maoris some 800 years ago came from Savai Island, one of the Samoan Group. The formation of this island is granite. The high jagged rocks and the round hills consist of hard fine-grained granite. the cliffs of the coast, however, they are coarse grained, and the constituent parts not so well mixed, and merge into an inferior kind of rock. At a few places blocks of basalt are to be found. A few of the granite heights are partly denuded of earth, and form magnificent cliffs. Of rivers there is, of course, nothing to be said, not even of proper streams, because no point of the island is far enough from the sea, the rain water, therefore, easily flows off. In former years I once wrote, and it was printed, too, that the drinking water had a brown colour, but that only refers to the lake out of which I then drank. Later on I found that at most places good clear water can be got. If you look around between the granite blocks, which in almost every place stick up out of the soil, and search for a damp place, you can dig for a spring, and need not dig deep. I will later on speak of the fruitfulness and usefulness of the soil when the appropriate time comes. At this time, in the first year of my residence, with the exception of a few potato plantations, it was yet in a wild state. The open places where the New Zealand flax had not got the upper hand were overgrown with hard cutting reeds. The great reed stalks which grow here on dry ground are larger and stronger than the brittle German reeds. The leaves are so sharp that if one does not take care they will cut the hand to the bone. You can see the little teeth, like little saw teeth, on the sides of the leaves with the naked eye. In the shade of the dark woods grow the fern trees, as if they were ashamed of not being palms. On the average they are about ten feet high and four inches in diameter; they have beautiful fronds, shaped like a branching palm. The stems are used as fences. Of the rosaceæ there are only a few kinds of brambles, but these bear but little, and that only a small fruit.

As I have already mentioned the songs of birds several times—and we have lovely singers here—it is suitable that I should say some more about them. The most excellent singer is the Koparapara. It is of the size of a lark, only a little more slender. It does not, however, belong to the tribe of larks, but, as I imagine, to the jays. Its grey colour is relieved by a blue shimmer. It is a wood bird, but gladly comes into the open to get honey out of the flowers. Since fruit trees were introduced here, he likes to come in companies—between ten and twelve—to visit the fruit gardens during the best of their bloom. Then, when they have satisfied their thirst for honey, they sometimes all sit in one tree and sing a merry song, as if they wished to express their gratitude in this way. They keep such good time that a musician can write their notes down. The sound is loud and metallic, like the clear sound of a bell. Verily, the birds of the air should teach men to praise God! " Ask now the beasts and they shall teach thee, and the fowls of the air shall tell thee, or speak to the earth and it shall answer thee, and the fishes in the sea shall tell thee, who knoweth not that the hand of the Lord hath wrought in this." (Job.)

Another somewhat larger bird of the same species is the Tui. He sings less, but he is remarkable for his black coat, and two snow-white feathers that hang under his throat make him look ridiculously like a parson. He is a honey-sucker, and very skilful at sucking the honey out of the flax.

This plant is remarkable for its rich store of honey. The New Zealand flax, growing here everywhere, belongs to the order of lilies. One kind of the same grows as a sort of reed in swampy places in North Germany. This has, however, no flax threads in its leaves, whilst the New Zealand flax is full of them. In other respects the leaves, the flowers, and seed vessels are very similar, the New Zealand plant, however, is much larger, and the flowers are reddish, whilst the German ones, as far as I can recollect, are yellow. The reed-like leaves are here four to six feet high, and the flower or seed stalks eight to ten feet long. These stalks are about an inch in diameter. They have a hard rind, and internally, when they are dry, they are filled with a cork-like substance. They are, therefore, light, and useful for making garden fences to keep the poultry out. At the bottom, the leaves contain a kind of gum, which could be used for polishing furniture, if it were not soluble in water and did not soon draw the water out of damp air. You can fasten papers together with it very well. Perhaps the roots will yet be found to contain medicinal properties. The leaves contain many tough flax threads. The flowers, of which every stalk bears a great many, contain so much fluid honey that it can be poured out. You can fill a teaspoon out of three or four flowers. If this honey fluid is collected and then slowly boiled, a syrup is obtained that tastes like honey. The flax blooms at Christmas here—in the middle of Summer.

So far, the attempt to separate the threads from the other component parts of the leaves in an easy way has not been successful enough to make the labour of doing so a profitable industry. All attempts so far to discover suitable machines for so doing have been attended with unsatisfactory results. The Maori women take a sharp mussel shell, hold it between the toes of their naked feet, and then draw a flax leaf underneath it through between the toes. In this manner the green stuff of the leaves is scraped off and a white flax produced that, with rubbing and beating, becomes very fine, and takes on a fine silky lustre. This labour is, however, too slow, and not adapted to commerce, on account of the high wages current in New Zealand. For this reason, this remarkable and useful plant is mostly burnt, and rots away, to make room for corn and meadow land. It certainly is there for a purpose, and until the proper time comes, all attempts to utilise it will be useless. But when the time comes—when the dear God (who orders everything in wisdom when least to be observed, in order that we children of men may exercise our powers with the intention of discovery) chooses to show men how they shall go to work—a new and important branch of industry will arise in New Zealand. It is not probable that this plant would thrive in lands that have not so moist a climate as New Zealand has.

The surrounding sea, although it rages and mightily roars in storms (and it looks quite different to what it does in the estuaries of the great rivers in North Germany), in calm weather, on a fine day, is something very lovely. It, too, has plants like the earth, only they are differently formed. Some of them are as high as the trees of the forest, and grow in groups like copses. If you look out of the boat into the clear, deep water, you seem gently to sway over the tops of high forest trees. The leaves are not green, but brown; the stems are not thick, but consist of long, thick tubes, which cling to the rocks with their thick roots at the bottom of the sea as mosses do to dry rocks on land. Some of the tubes are furnished with little balls full of air, which float them upwards. Others have large, round leaves just like snakes; others, again, have leaves that look like a large carpenter's apron: both sorts are internally filled with coarse air-vessels. If you cut one of the apron-like leaves through, you see a web of cells like the cells in a honeycomb. The outside brown skin of the leaves is tough, but the inside is brittle, and easily broken with the hand. If you work your hand backwards and forwards inside, and break all the cells, you have a great empty sack, which you can blow out and tie up in an airtight manner at the top. It then looks quite full, but contains nothing but wind. When it is dry, you can let out the wind and turn the sack to use, as is shown further on.

Sometimes you see an innumerable quantity of black birds like a huge swarm of bees, about the size of crows, partly swimming on the water, partly flying low down. The Maoris call them Titi; the Englishmen have named them mutton birds (I have forgotten the scientific name). These birds breed on uninhabited islands, of which there are a great many scattered about here and there in the neighbourhood of Stewart Island. In each nest there is one egg nearly as large as a goose egg, although the bird that lays it is not much larger than a common crow. The parent birds take a long time to hatch the one egg, and at last bring out a young one. The parents feed this so well that when it is grown it is twice as large as the old birds. The young one then consists of about two-thirds clear fat and one-third tender flesh and bones. The flesh, as long as it is fresh, is of excellent flavour, and the fat when melted looks like the fat of geese, and is of similar taste. But with time both flesh and fat take on an unpleasant train-oil taste. Perhaps with better management this might be avoided. The feathers, too, are good for pillows and mattresses. They are as soft as down, but they must first be allowed to hang in baskets in airy rooms to get rid of the fishy smell. Evidently these birds are made for human use. In April, the beginning of Autumn here, the young ones are fully grown. The natives then go to the islands and take them out of their nests, which are small holes in the ground, by thousands. The old ones appear already quite ready to leave the young ones, and these are too fat and heavy to fly, and, therefore, easily caught. As long as the Maoris were unacquainted with proper salt, naturally they did not know how to salt them, but they understood before the Europeans arrived how to preserve the flesh in air-tight vessels. They boiled the young birds and put them with the melted fat into the before-mentioned sacks made out of seaweed and fastened them up air tight. In savage times human flesh was similarly preserved. The heavy kelp bags are not strong enough to bear transport, they are, therefore, enclosed in bark and bound up with light sticks. Large ones intended as presents for high chiefs are ornamented with feather work and embroidery. Birds thus preserved, although they will keep good for years, have an unpleasant taste of fish and seaweed. Proper salting in barrels would doubtless be better, but the Maoris do not yet understand this.

How far the breeding grounds of these birds extend towards the south, the east, and west, I do not yet know, but Ruapuke lies on their northern border. At his request I have sent my scientific friend and countryman, Dr. Julius von Haast (ennobled by the Emperor of Austria on account of his scientific services at the Vienna Exhibition), some sealed preserved sacks of these and other southern birds. He is superintendent of the Museum at Christchurch on Banks Peninsula.

The sea is here, as it is all over New Zealand, rich in fish. It is only in calm, fine weather, which we do not often have in this windy district, that one can go out to fish with boat and lines. The ordinary fishes of different sorts that are caught here weigh two or three pounds. But if the sea is calm enough to allow one to go out into deep water to fish, some weighing fifty pounds and over are caught. They are shaped like carp, but I dare not say whether they belong to that species or not. They are of a pleasant flavour. All the fish which are caught here are better flavoured than those caught in more northern seas, and the oysters of Stewart Island are held in high estimation. The reason of this is that the water is cooler; on the other hand the fruits of the north are much more pleasant than those growing here because the air in Summer is there warmer.

Among shellfish I call attention, as being remarkable, to a large univalve called Paoa by the Maoris. (The vowels flow into one another so that each is heard, and sounds as if one said Paua slowly in German.) It is five and a-half inches long, four inches wide, and in the deepest place one and a half inches deep. The animal quite fills the shell. The shell covers the upper side, while the under side clings to the rocks in the sea, like a snail, and moves at will. This mussel is caught at low spring tides (the days directly after the new and full moon). The flesh is firm, and, boiled, has a flavour like that of a pig's head. As long as I had teeth I was very fond of it, but I can no longer bite it. The shell has inside a green, cloudy, shimmering colour, like mother-of-pearl, and is an article of commerce. It is shipped to England, and used in the manufacture of buttons, which are sent back here as well as to all other countries.

Another sea creature, called by the Maoris Ngaio, deserves to be mentioned here as a curiosity. I believe it belongs to the class of sea acorns, but it appears to be a very superior sort. It is undoubtedly a plant, and just as undoubtedly an animal. It grows with a stump on the bottom of the sea on rocks, as mosses or lichens grow on rocks on dry ground. A number of stems grow out of the root-foot, of the thickness of a lead line, perhaps two feet, or more, long. Every stem has, at the upper end, a thick knob, of the size of a duck's egg, with a mouth attached to it. So far it is a plant; but if you cut the knob, inside, growing along with the plant, the flesh of a living animal is found, that not only fills the knob but extends as marrow of the stem in animal substance right down to the root. In stormy weather, when the waves are high and deep, a few are torn loose from the rocky sea bed and cast on the shore. For a long time I could not overcome my dislike to eat these plant-animals, but when, in the course of time, I did so, and got used to the flavour, I ate them with pleasure. The animal flesh when boiled and separated from the rind of the plant, consists of skin and a delicate substance which consists, perhaps, of nerves. They taste like a boiled egg flavoured with oil, and have a very good flavour. The taste must, however, be acquired.

In heathenish times, the Maoris had a community of goods. Every clan (a subdivision of the tribes), generally under a minor chief, lived and worked together — the potatoes which were harvested, the carrots which were dug, the birds and fishes they caught, belonging to the community of the clan. Naturally, the chiefs, or those who were otherwise powerful amongst them, always got the best. For the same reason, for all requirements of any individual—as, for instance, at marriages—the entire appropriations of the clan were available. Gifts were made to the high chiefs by all the clans of his tribe: what the chiefs desired no one dare refuse them. Sometimes there were prisoners taken in war, who were kept as labourers and, when convenient, killed and eaten. If there were many slain, a part of the human flesh was boiled and preserved in air-tight bags, or sent as a present to friendly tribal or clan relations. The women, although generally more industrious than the men, were not oppressed, as is the case amongst many savages. All women, even those who had but few clothes, conducted themselves with noteworthy modesty, of which the men, however, are most neglectful. When the women were not occupied outside, they sat at their spinning. The flax threads, spun by hand, were entirely woven with the finger. It was very tedious work, and the web quite different to that made by a weaver.

Before the Maoris were acquainted with European cooking utensils, they cooked entirely with hot stones. A round hole was made in the earth, and firewood laid over it; on this stones were heaped up, and the fire then lit. Whilst the wood burnt, the stones fell into the hole; some were lifted out with sticks, other let lie. The provisions were then wrapped round with wet grass, and the hot stones laid on them. On this fresh grass was again laid, and the whole covered with earth. Such a steaming and rich-smelling heap was a lovely sight to children and hungry people. Warlike heroes were accustomed to comfort themselves with the thought that, when they fell, such a savoury bed was already prepared for them. Cannibalism had only been quite left off here a very few years ago, and now only provisions were cooked among the stones. In my journeys amongst the Maoris I have often eaten meals so cooked, and I consider that this method of cooking meals gives a very good flavour. I have often seen them rubbing fire out of two sticks, for at that time a fire produced in this manner was considered holier than an ordinary one which was lit with matches obtained from Europeans, and it was considered necessary to heat the cooking stones in this manner. A somewhat broad piece of wood, in which a groove was cut lengthwise, was laid on the ground. A man then rubbed a sharp-pointed stick backwards and forwards in the groove. Soon a smoky smell was noticeable, then the fine dust which was rubbed off began to smoke and then to glow. Now the burning sparks were wrapped in fine dry grass and waved to and fro by hand in the air till flames broke out. It was not permitted to blow with the mouth, because this would have made the fire unavailable for cooking.

The villages lay, in order to have dry ground underneath them, mostly on sandhills near the sea. In every village, mostly inhabited by a clan and their relatives, there was a common house, in which everyone could sit and sleep. Families lived mostly in little private houses. The common house was twice as long as broad, and, on the whole, a roomy building. At the fore-end, roof and side walls reached two or three yards further than the forward wall, and formed an open porch in front. The pillars and rafters of such houses were ornamented with artistic carving, the figures often as grotesque as those in London *Punch*. The door which leads from the porch into the house was about two feet high and broad. To the right of it, and a little higher, were the openings for light and air, of the same size. If you crawled into the opening

you came on a passage about three feet wide that extended the
whole length of the house. On both sides, and filling all the
remainder of the spaces in the house, were platforms about one
and a-half feet above the ground. These consisted of sticks as
thick as a finger closely laid together, which were fastened to a
joist, and formed a floor like basket-work, on which one could
either comfortably sit, lie, sleep, chatter, or loaf. If it was cold,
one or two small fires were lit inside; but no cooking was done
there. On the right side of the passage were two or three strong
posts, which bore at the top a long, strong beam, on which the
upper ends of the rafters were fastened, while the lower ends
rested on the side walls. Roof and walls were covered with reeds
inside, and, if they were of ancient date, were ornamented with
artistic patterns. Outside, the roof and walls were made of
grass, on which in most cases the winds had blown up white
sand.

The Maoris have well built figures and, as long they are not
ill, a strong constitution. Their legs are a little shorter than
those of Europeans, their bodies a little longer. For that reason,
they can sit down on the flat earth with the knees in front of the
breast as easily as on a chair, and with the same ease can rise up
from the ground—which a European had better not try. In the
south, the colour of their skin is nearly as light as that of the
southern Europeans. Old people had their faces, as well as the
most of their bodies, tattooed with artistic spiral lines, strongly
marked and blackish in colour. The younger ones, however, had
somewhat lost the art of tattooing, and to the still younger ones it
was distasteful. When I say I discover art in tattooing, I do not
mean that the natural beauty of the human countenance can
be heightened by it, but the contrary—as the beautiful, natural
shape of man is most dreadfully deformed even amongst highly
civilized people by artificial means. I mean merely that real art
is displayed in the tattooing of the old Maoris ; the loss of this art
shows a falling off in the Maori nature. It appears, moreover,
that they could not always have lived in so dirty a condition as
the one in which I found 'them and have already pointed
out, otherwise they could not have maintained such stability of

constitution. The consequences of this decadence could not long remain without disclosing themselves.

I found when I kept an exact register of births and deaths that there was only one birth to three or four deaths. It appeared that this decline in bodily strength arose from their having out-lived the spiritual ideas of an earlier and better time, and as they were not in position to renew their own youth, unavoidable extinction must have befallen them, unless help came from outside. Mothers suckled their children until they were three or four years old, and sometimes older, and for that reason there were fewer births. A few babies had already learned to suck smoke through their parents' black tobacco pipe, saturated as it was with tobacco juice.

The power of recuperation amongst the Maoris was so weak that if anyone became ill there was no hope of his getting better. A small hut was then built for the sick person in a lonely place, in which he lay all alone, receiving more or less attention, according to the number of his relations, being often much neglected, and was left alone until he died. Ordinary people who died were at once buried, or otherwise put out of the way; but chiefs were bent together immediately after death, the knees being placed under the chin, and then placed in a wooden box, specially made which was fastened on the top of a strong post. These posts were then placed upright in a good house and left for a few years, till all soft parts of the body had wasted away. The whole house was of course strictly tapu. Near relations, who on account of their rank were superior to tapu, were allowed to enter it when-ever inclined. After a few years the box was opened by a man who had power to take off the tapu, and the bones were burnt. The idea of packing the sacred body thus closely pressed together arose from the conception that it then was in the womb of the Goddess of Night or Death, who was the original mother of man-kind. Later on I shall have more to say about this goddess.

The Maoris believed in a life after death, but their concep-tions of it were so comfortless that they gave no consideration to it. According to the old religion there was a Kingdom of Death, which was called Po (night), in which the gods and the chiefs who were raised to gods dwelt. The Goddess of Death lived here—Hene Muotepo, the great Goddess of the Night (Hene means properly virgin, but stands here for goddess), who drew her children— mankind—after her. For the common Maoris of later generations this blessed place appeared to have become unattainable; they bethought themselves, therefore, of a nearer underworld, called Reinga, the entrance to which lay on the northern promontory of New Zealand. Of rewards in the next life for deeds done and opinions held in this life they knew nothing. In the entrance was a cleft, and in it stood two ghosts as watchmen, named Taupiko and Tawhaitiri, who leaned over from each side against one another, and between these two the souls of the dead had to glide. An active soul could slip through, but a helpless one was seized and annihilated. The empire of the dead lay in a deep valley underneath the earth; in the middle was a lake, and on its banks the souls lived again in bodily form. When a soul arrived it seated itself on the point of a mountain which was reflected in the lake, till it was seen by someone below. It then called out, asking " Do you belong to me ? " If this was not the case it shook its head, and waited till a relation spoke; it then threw its head back for a sign of Yes; then replied the relation, " Fly down," and as it did that it received its bodily form again. But here it was mortal, and then went to a still deeper place of death. High chieftains might in this manner reach the blessed Kingdom of Death—Po—where their ancestors lived as gods; but the common people arrived, after many wanderings, through the common Kingdom of Death, back to earth again, and appeared in the form of blue blowflies or butterflies. The latter were, therefore, commonly called wairua tangata (wairua, soul; tangata, man). This was their last existence. It seemed, also, that some souls of the lower people were not even good enough to go to the under- world, but were condemned to remain at the place of their previous existence. They dwelt in the ruins of fallen buildings, of which there were many that belonged to people already dead. These were, therefore, dangerous places, and no living soul dared to go near them. They were inhabited by man-eating ghosts, and if anyone went too near they led him in and slowly ate away his vitals, till at last he died of hunger. A different kind of spirit inhabited the priests called Tohunga (perhaps from Tohu—sign), by means of which they professed to heal sicknesses, give protection from witchcraft and wicked people, and to reveal secret events through oracular words uttered whilst in a state of convulsive enchantment. Belief in witchcraft was so universal that every sickness was attributed to the witchcraft of wicked people, to tapu, or having come too near a man-eating ghost, against which the priests or proper wizards could afford no relief. There was, however, another and a better kind of Tohunga, perhaps a remnant of the true priests, of which the wizards were only an off-shoot. The best Tohungas had nothing to do with witchcraft and soothsaying. It was their duty to preserve in their memories the old theology, heroic sayings, and the genealogy of the nobility, and to perpetuate these to successors who had a natural adaptability for retaining them. We may, therefore, call them the "wise people." Later I was myself admitted into their secrets without any ceremony.

One must not imagine there were any deep-meaning secrets. I had opportunity of learning from the mouths of the wise Maoris a language free from foreign intermixture. These "wise men" are now all dead, and I am the solitary successor alive in the south. There were further Tohungas for tattooing, architecture, carvers for ornamenting public buildings and canoes, but in the south these were already all dead. Idols the Maoris in New Zealand never had. Lately, however, I learnt that there is an idol in existence at Nelson, in New Zealand, which was brought with them by the immigrating Maoris from Savai (Samoa Islands), and that it is kept as a holy relic and shown to no vulgar eyes.

It is already mentioned that because there was no literature from which the language could be learnt I was obliged to prepare one from oral narratives. Narratives of daily occurrences taken down in writing became in time insufficient to enable me to penetrate far enough into the spirit of the language and the spiritual ideas of the people. I inquired after folk-lore. I heard that such existed, and a few old people were pointed out to me who were acquainted with it. These were, however, reticent, but I continued to make inquiry when circumstances permitted it, and sought explanations of fragments which I had already learnt until they at last recognised me as one who was initiated, and then opened to me the treasures of their wisdom. This happened a few years later, but it is better that I refer to it here in order that the reader may obtain a clear insight into the spiritual views of the people before we come to their conversion. Many a Winter evening I sat with two or three of these old " wise people," and we discussed their old religion and the old gods and heroes of heathendom. I wrote down their narratives in the Maori language and studied it in private.

If, in a dark corner of the earth, one is for the time being the only man with scientific culture, even though that be but small, one attains to a certain amount of distinction. This was the reason why I was drawn into correspondence with Sir George Grey when he was Governor of New Zealand for the first time (it was carried on through Mr Tuckett). Whilst I was collecting the mythological tales of the Maoris here in the south, Sir George Grey did the same in the north, and in the same manner—namely, by writing down the sayings of the old " wise people " as uttered by them in the Maori language.

Later, he had his collection printed in the Maori language and sent me a copy. It appears therefrom that the old mythology and history of the heroes, both in the north and south, agree with one another in all essentials : only in the later folk-lore, which appears only to refer to pleasant events, is there a marked difference.

Later on, I translated my collections into English, and they are now printed in the scientific transactions of the New Zealand Institute. There is no room for the tales; only a few items out of their mythology may find a place here. In these translations I have carefully abstained from all doubtful and foreign interventions, because that would have been disadvantageous to their being properly understood. Scientific men, who gather such reports from different peoples in order to compare one with another, require only the raw material. Here, however, I may make comparison with the Mosaic records ; but the comparisons need only be taken for what they are worth.

CHAPTER XI.

ON THE MYTHOLOGY OF THE MAORIS.

THE mythology of the Maoris embraces a larger area than New Zealand. All the peoples of the South Sea Islands call their principal god Tangaroa, with the exception of those of the New Hebrides and a few other groups. The meaning of this name is uncertain. It may come from Ngaro (concealed). In New Zealand he is god of the sea. He is said to appear when the rays of the sun play on the breaking waves and paint rainbows in them. He was married to the earth goddess, who had the name Papatuanuku (papa means flat; tua, above; nuku, wide landscape), but the meaning is uncertain. Once in Tangaroa's absence his nephew Rangi (heaven), the god of heaven, seduced his wife, the goddess of earth. When Tangaroa came back, Rangi was obliged to fight a duel for this injury done to him. Each was armed with a spear. The nephew Rangi threw his spear first, but the uncle eluded it and struck the nephew through both thighs and lamed him. Tangaroa was satisfied, and handed over his wife to his nephew, so that now the god of heaven (Rangi) and the goddess of earth were looked upon as being married.

It is quite apparent that there is a deep meaning in this myth, which, however, had long vanished from the Maori "wise people." It may mean the creation of the sea, and the springing up of the dry land, as in Genesis i., 9, 10, from which time the earth was watered from the heaven above. The resemblance truly does not seem very clear, but in the following more comes out that makes it clearer.

As Rangi, the heaven, was lamed, he could no longer stand upright, and was, therefore, obliged to lie flat on the ground. Now everything was dark and still; no light could shine, no air blow. "Darkness moved over the face of the waters." Still in this way heaven and earth produced many children. Most of them, however, were cripples and of monstrous shapes. Some had, however, healthy limbs, and were of a superior kind. Amongst these the

K

most noteworthy are Tane (interpreted man, later god of the woods); Paiao, god of the clouds; Tawhirimatea, god of the winds. In time the children got tired of the darkness and of the immovableness of things. They called a meeting, therefore, to consider what was to be done to get light and freedom. Some suggested they should kill their father (heaven), and content themselves with their mother (earth). Others advised that the father should be let live, but that he should be set upright and fastened up. This advice was taken. Only one of the children objected (the god of the winds); he was conservative and opposed to all change. He advised they should let the old one and other matters alone, but he was out-voted. After the resolution was come to, they went to work to lift the heaven and divide it from the earth, at which the old one bitterly complained that he was being badly treated by his children.

Tane and Paiao (cloud) were the most active in lifting their father up, and Tane fastened him so that he was obliged to keep the heavens standing. "And God made the firmament, and divided the waters which were under the firmament from the waters which were above the firmament, and it was so." (Gen. i., 7.)

It may appear strange that so changeable a god as that of the winds should have shown himself to be so conservative at the consultation. This is to be explained in this manner: Tawhirimatea in the beginning was a quiet youth, but when he was over-ridden by his brothers, and his parents were torn asunder against his will, he became restless. He swung himself up to heaven and spoke with his father about his children's injustice to him. He came back in a contentious mood and began at once to war against his brethren on all sides. He hunted Paiao's clouds about, stirred up Tangaroa's sea for him, and broke the branches of his trees in the woods.

When the heavens were fastened up, and the bearers of it had come down, Tane looked up to his father, but the old man looked black and sorrowful. Then Tane made bright ornaments, climbed up to heaven again, and covered it with a glancing colour. When he came down again and looked at what he had done he thought his

appearance was too uniform.   He then climbed up again supplied
with other ornaments.   He took the fish up to heaven (the milky
way), painted the two Patari (two bright stars in the southern
sky in the neighbourhood of the pole), put the stars in their places
so that they might serve to show the time of the year.   " And let
them be for signs, and for seasons, and for days, and years."
(Gen. i., 14.)   Then he came down and looked at what he had
done, and behold, kua pai (it was good).

Now, Tane looked at his mother, who had no ornaments so
far.   He lifted her crippled children, and planted them as plants
and trees.   The latter he set first of all with their legs (branches)
on the ground and the heads (the stumps, with roots as hair) in
the air.   Then he went to one side and looked at what he had
done, and it did not please him : the trees and plants had not an
agreeable appearance.   Accordingly, he took them up again and
turned them upside down, with their legs (the branches) in the
air and their heads in the ground.   Then he stepped on one side
again and looked at what he had done, and said, kua pai (it is
good).

Although Rangi (the God of Heaven) and Papatuanuku were
separated, their mutual love still continued.   He wept tears of love
on to her in the shape of dew drops, and sighs of love rose from
her bosom up to him in the mists of the woody mountains.

It is remarkable that the sun and moon have no representatives
among the gods.   The names Ra (sun) and Rangi (moon) may have
some connection with one another.   The moon is called simply Te
Marama (light).   In the old mythology the representations are
always spiritual and sublime; for that reason, there are no idols
and no prayers to creatures.   Why this is, whilst the other South
Sea Island peoples have so many gods (to which peoples the Maoris
belong), may be here explained.

It is true Tangaroa was considered the original father of
gods, but by reason of the prominent part Tane took in the
development of creation and in the institution and final destiny
of mankind, he was thought less of, and at last his dominion was
diminished to that of the sea alone.   Tane, amongst all the South
Sea peoples, and especially in New Zealand, is considered the

next in place to Tangaroa : his destiny to be god of the woods appears to have developed later. I have been astonished that Meinecke in his " South Sea People and Christianity" could not find him in the New Zealand mythology, although he sought for him there. The information which was available for him must, therefore, in this respect, have been very superficial. If you compare the history of Tane, as follows, with the first three chapters of Genesis, you will sometimes take him to be Elohim (God), and at others man (Adam). His name, Tane (man), is then seen to be of importance.

After Tane had ornamented his father and mother (heaven and earth), he wandered alone through the woods, and sought amongst the birds and the fountains a helpmeet for himself, but found none. " But for Adam there was not found a helpmeet for him."

Then he turned to his mother, the goddess of earth, and she advised him to make the form of a wife out of earth, and to breathe life into it, which he did. The woman thus formed he called Hinehaone (in the present language Hine is the name of a virgin ; ha, breath ; one, loose earth). This figure does not appear to have had much life in it. Yet Tane and she produced a daughter named Hincatauria (ata, morning ; uria, fiery glance : therefore, morning glow). The name Hine adhered to women who had many names in their childhood, and the name sometimes adhered afterwards. The mother, Hinchaone, then disappears out of the narrative. When the daughter, Hineatauria, grew up, Tane took her for his wife, but she did not know that he was her father. She had many children, whose names appear to mean frailty and mortality, and these are considered the first of the human race, as Tane and Hincatauria are considered the first parents of the race.

Once Tane made a journey to the upper heaven, inhabited as it was with different beings, and visited his older brother Rehua. Who this Rehua was, or what he represents, I have not been able to discover. The origin of the idea had long vanished from the Maori " wise people." Only this was known, that he lived up in the tenth heaven. He is not named amongst the children of heaven and earth, and can, therefore, not have been a brother, properly speaking. He was called Tane's tuakane. This word means an elder brother, or else a descendant of an older family line. If the Maoris have brought the original ideas of their old religion from Western Asia, which appears probable, the angels as a class must be here meant by tuakane, as older brothers of mankind. When Tane arrived at the first heaven, entrance was refused to him by the inhabitants, who did not know him, the meaning evidently being that Tane had set the bounds of this heaven, which the inhabitants of the lower regions were not allowed to pass. But, conscious of his strength, he swung himself aloft, and had to encounter the same interdict at the second heaven. Thus it went on until the tenth heaven, when he met Rehua. The brothers recognised one another with tears of welcome in verses of great poetic beauty. The actions and conversation which followed appear to mean that Tane, although he did not undervalue his own worth, recognised the superior holiness of his brother. As it goes on the folk-lore becomes confused, perhaps because we have only fragments, and can no longer get at the original ideas. What was going on in the earth in the meantime is of considerable importance. During Tane's absence Hineatauria asked her mother-in-law, " Why is my husband absent so long ? " " What," replied she, "your husband ? He is your father." And then she told her the story of her birth. She took this so much to heart that, overcome by shame and penitence, she took a solemn departure from her mother-in-law with a prayer that she should tell Tane to undertake the education of her children, and then went into the under world, Po, or night. Thus death came into the world by the shame and penitence of the mother of mankind. When Tane came back to earth he asked his mother, " Where is my wife ? "   " You no longer have a wife," said his mother ; " she is gone into the world of night, and has commended the education of her children to your care." Then Tane went into the underworld himself, if possible, to bring his wife back. For a long while he wandered around alone in the land of the shades till at last he found a house. He spoke up towards the front pillars of the house. No answer. When leaving the house, sad and downcast, he heard a voice saying in the inside, "Where are you going to, Tane?" " I follow our sister," replied he.   A peculiar expression, the word "our" includes the person addressed.   Then said the voice :

> "Go back, Tane, to the world of light
>   To educate our fruit ;
> Leave me here in the world of night
>   To sorrow for our guilt."

Since then, the mother of mankind is also goddess of death, and has now the name of Hinenuiotepo (hine, virgin — here goddess—nui, adjective great ; o, genetive ; te, article ; po, night or kingdom of death), the great goddess of death ; she now lives in the kingdom of death, and draws her children, mankind, after her.

In this mythology of the Maoris, I have only mentioned a resemblance to, not an exact coincidence, with the Mosaic record. This resemblance may be accidental, but it may arise from Western Asiatic sources, where something similar is still to be found in old inscriptions.   You find there also, as well as in the folk-lore of many other people, reports of and allusions to the flood.   To this I have not been able amongst the Maoris to find any satisfactory allusion.   Perhaps a great darkness is confused with a great flood, a substitution which may well have occurred amongst a bold seafaring people in the course of time, as a great darkness would be much more terrible to them than a great flood. There is such a report, which is considered to belong to a very ancient time, and has no connection with any other folk-lore. Without any indication it begins and ends as suddenly, and all its deep meaning has been forgotten, so that I took it for an incomprehensible fragment of some old poem.   The names that occur in it have various meanings, so that I can derive no indication from them.   I, therefore, for the most part omit them.

Tutakahinahina was a man who could walk on water.   Before he died, he ordered a supply of firewood and provisions for his house.   Then he died, and was buried in the house by the wall, with his face turned down and his back up.   The grave was surrounded with a fence.   The sun was now held back (here the names of many beings are given who held the sun back), and the world was shut up in darkness. The darkness was so great that nothing could be seen except by the light of the fire. Tutaka-hinahina's family could live because it was supplied with the necessary firewood and provisions. The rest of mankind used what they had and could get at, and then had to perish in the darkness. When in Tutakahinahina's house the firewood was used up, they were obliged to use the fence of the graveyard. Then his son Teroiroiwhenua heard his father speaking in the grave. "This is where I am buried—look where there is a mound." While he listened, he heard the gnawing of the maggots in the grave. Then he saw two maggots creep out of the grave, a male and a female. He seized the male one—(he let the female one go)—and roasted it in an oven, heated with holy fire, especially kindled, by rubbing, for the purpose. Then came Tametea (since Tawhirimatea, god of the winds) and moved the oven. A shimmer of the returning light came at once. First the birds began to sing, then the men to rejoice.

The old mythology of the Maori, although it is a heathen one, is sublime, and points to a higher degree of culture than that in which the Maoris in New Zealand then were, and as long as they lived and moved in the midst of these sublime conceptions, in a measure, they could thrive as heathen. It is in no way maintained, even from a worldly point of view—Christianity has a far higher aim,—that a heathenish religion, even one of the best, is sufficient for certain people. A heathenish religion has never, and never can, elevate a people so that it can compare with enlightened Christian nations in progress of useful and higher knowledge and science.

Inflexible heathen opinions, like cherubim with blazing swords, always barred the way to Paradise, and obstructed the path to the Tree of Life. Where such hindrances arise in Christendom, it is not from the teaching of Jesus Christ, the Son of God, and His Apostles, but from a misunderstood Christianity that must become converted and illuminated by the Holy Spirit. The mythology of the heathen has arisen from poetic inspiration. It is, therefore, sublime ; and as long as a people thoroughly live in it, it may well impart a spiritual impulse. The external life, however, always lingers far behind the poetic aspiration. If we regard the old mythology of a people from our own standpoint, and admire the sublimity of the gods and heroes, we may easily overlook the inward corruption that is mixed up with it, and consider too little the cruelty, the vices, as well as the outward and inward unclean-ness of the mass of the people. A heathen religion, even when it teaches the loftiest virtue, always lacks strength to turn people to what is good in practical life. There is no purity of heart, no intelligent probity, no heartfelt pity, for one's fellow creatures, and, above all, no peace in life, no comfort in death in the natural man. If such moral failings are also to be found in Christendom— but far from such depravity as is found among the heathen,—it arises from the fact that by so many Christianity is only adopted externally, just as a heathen religion is adopted by the heathen ; and it would always become worse : many of the adopted noble sentiments and manners would disappear, vice would become bolder, manners would become cruel and heathenish, if God did not take care to keep a salt of the earth alive amongst the so-called mystics and pietists. By them the inward and outward essentials of Christianity, the consciousness of dependence on God, our Saviour Jesus Christ, the father of peace and goodwill towards all men, is maintained in the mass of Christendom.

Reasonable men, who dislike pietists because they (reasonable men) have allowed themselves to be led astray by small-minded and ignorant slanderers, will find that this is true, if they will examine the matter without a foregone conclusion and in an intelligent way. By that salt of the earth inside Christendom, the Gospel of Jesus Christ is sent to the far-off heathen. " That they may turn from darkness to light, and from the power of Satan unto God ; that they may receive forgiveness of sins and inheritance among them which are sanctified." By its means raw savages are made into respectable men, so that they are prepared for useful and beautiful progress and friendly relations with the enlightened peoples of older Christendom. Thus, in accordance with the counsels of God, a new-born manhood is developed from a lost one. Far-away heathens, through it, become " fellow-citizens with the saints and of the household of God, and are built upon the foundation of the Apostles and Prophets, Jesus Christ Himself being the chief corner stone, in whom all the building, fitly framed together, groweth into a holy temple of the Lord."

" The Kingdom of God cometh not with observation." One shall not say see here or see there, in this or that Church community, for " Behold the Kingdom of God is within you." It is in the superficial Christian and in the better heathen. It is the inward yearning after a higher life, the respect for goodness, uprightness and truth. But it is overgrown with worldliness, disputes, folly, and sin, and a want of acquaintance with the inner Christian life and its working in practical life. A garden overgrown with weeds may bloom in a luxurious green, amongst which here and there a few leaves of good plants may be prominent, but it is not a sight which pleases the eye of a practical man. If the weeds are rooted up and taken away, the good plants at first stand up, but in a weak manner. He who has once experienced a thorough cleansing of the heart through Jesus Christ will understand how miserable his own goodness was. In a few days the light of the sun gives them a healthy green and a proper growth. Christianity must be inwardly accepted, and the heart will, unhindered, enter into a junction with Jesus Christ, and will daily enjoy his mercy as a plant does the light of the sun. It cleanses us from all wickedness, and renews in us the image of God. It then works from inward outward into practical life, first in the hearts of pious people, and from them, the salt of the earth, into the mass of the people. The Kingdom of God is then inwardly in the hearts of pious people, and, through them, in the nation— as Christ, as the Kingdom of God, was amongst the Pharisees and Jews. Let us, therefore, " put on, as the elect of God, holy and well-beloved, bowels of mercies, kindness, humbleness of mind, meekness, long-suffering, forbearing one another, and forgiving one another."

CHAPTER XII.

ON THE ORIGIN AND HISTORY OF THE MAORIS.

NOW we must discover how the Maoris came to this far-away island, New Zealand, in the wide ocean. The natives of New Zealand, when first seen by the discoverers and their followers, were still in the stone age. Their stone axes, cut with much labour and trouble, were fastened on to wooden sticks with strips of New Zealand flax, and with such rough tools they had to build their vessels, and that without nails, as they had no iron or other metal. To build a vessel, they had to cut down a tree, then, with immense labour, to cut it off at the upper end, then to hollow out the stem like a trough, and hew the lower side into a proper shape like a ship's bottom. In such vessels (called by the Maoris waka, by the Europeans canoe), how could they get across to New Zealand, over a wide sea, with rolling waves? But we must remember that in earlier times, as has been already pointed out, they possessed more lofty ideas and a higher cultivation than they had in later times. Now, they have retained a lofty, bold spirit, although they have long since lost their former culture. The sea forced them to be bold seafarers. Their high courage and united manhood did not shun the labour to hew down the loftiest trees in the woods with stone axes—and there are very high and thick trees here—to hollow them out, and make them into canoes. Thin and pliant tree stems were then split, and planks hewn out of them. These were then fastened with strings, drawn through holes made for the purpose, to the sides of the canoes, in order to raise them. In this way they made vessels of respectable size, with which they could trust themselves with confidence in rough seas. Sometimes two such canoes were lashed together with cross-beams, which made a sort of double ship, on which a kind of deck could be erected.

The Maoris of New Zealand are, however, only a branch of a people who have spread out over thousands of islands which lie scattered in the great so-called Pacific Ocean. All had the same religion, language, and customs, although each of them has

perpetuated itself in a somewhat different manner in each of the
island groups. According to their traditions, it is reported that
in former times an intercourse existed between the different island
groups. Certain arts were known, and new ones were sought for,
which might be met with on certain far-off islands. It is true
such sea voyages, in such unhandy vessels, and on a great wide
sea, were not without danger; but God has placed a heroic
courage in the human breast in order that in battle with untamed
nature he may make the kingdom of earth subject to him. Such
battles, as long as man is not degenerated by luxury and vice, or
made slavish and cowardly by oppression, awaken pleasing feelings
in the manly breast, and dangers are more inspiring than terrifying. As long as the Polynesians (this is the name of this people
of many islands) exercised their heroic courage in bold but
peaceful sea voyages and made new discoveries, their families
could live in peace, be fruitful and multiply. But the heart of
man is altogether corrupt, and qualities that are good in themselves easily change to bad ones. The heroic courage which
should make untamed nature subservient to the use of man and
do service to God was turned against their fellow creatures, who
are made after the image of God, and who should live together
peaceably as brothers. Men kill men like wild beasts, who kill
for pleasure and have no knowledge. With time the natives of
New Zealand had turned into such cruel savages.

I cannot here enter upon scientific investigations, but this
may be remarked, that some who have carefully compared the
mythology and traditions of the South Sea Islanders with the
ancient history of Western Asia are of opinion that the inhabitants
of these many islands, to which the New Zealanders likewise
belong, were originally a people of the Aryan race, and lived in
the neighbourhood of the Persian Gulf. That thence they either
emigrated or were driven to India, and that there an intermixture with the inhabitants of that country took place. That
from thence, at the beginning of the Christian era, they spread
out into the Indian Archipelago, where they underwent a further
mixture with peoples who had come from the rivers of Central
Asia, and thence they spread into the islands of the Pacific.

Foreign mixtures appeared very acceptable to the people. When English whale fishers came to New Zealand a number of half-caste children were soon born.   When the whale fishery ceased, and no more Europeans came to New Zealand, and the natives were left to themselves, the half-bred children grew up with Maori ideas, and learnt only their mothers' language; but by their means the appearance of the people, especially here in the south, where there is the largest mixture of half-blood amongst the population, was considerably altered.   This actually happened here, and a stronger spirit is to be observed in the renewed mixed race.

It is remarkable that the language of the inhabitants of two large islands so very far removed from one another as New Zealand, in the far south sea, and Madagascar, on the south-east coast of Africa, appears to have had a common origin.   Look only at the numbers

	1	2	3	4	5	6	7	8	9	10
MADAGASCAR	Eser	Rua	Taru	Efad	Rinó	Oné	Keitu	Varlo	Seve	Fura
NEW ZEALAND	Tahi	Rua	Toru	Ewha	Rima	Ono	Witu	Wharu	Iwa	Ngahuru or Tekau

(From J. T. Thomson's Transactions of the New Zealand Institute.)

Formerly the Maoris first counted up to eleven, which they call tahi tekau ; twelve was then tahi tekau ma tahi (an eleven and a one); and so on up to twenty-two (rua tekau); their hundred, or rau, therefore, contained $11 \times 11 = 121$.   Now they have taken the European method of counting and thrown out the ngahuru, and call their ten their first tekau.

According to the numbers which occur in the old stories, they appear not to have taken their first aggregate up to eleven, but to ten.   I am, therefore, inclined to think, especially as they have so easily appropriated the division by ten, that, originally, they called the simple ten ngahuru, and in the second aggregate of their system of reckoning tekau as tahi tekau, ten ; rua tekau, twenty ; and so on.   The tekau has a remarkable resemblance to the Greek deka, as the rua has with the Latin duo.

Judging by this relation of language the Malagaski in Madagascar, the Maori in New Zealand, as well as the whole population of the South Seas, must have had a common origin, and have emigrated from the same country, probably from the East Indian peninsula, the Deccan, especially as it is known that the inhabitants of this coast in the most ancient times were skilful sailors, but the inhabitants of the eastern peninsula were not. One branch of this people took its way south-westerly to Madagascar; the other went in an easterly direction over the East Indian peninsula, in the direction of the Moluccas, into the Pacific Ocean. According to their traditions they fixed upon The Navigator Islands, in the Samoan Group, as a permanent place of settlement, which was afterwards regarded as a centre of operations. Thence they spread out (eastward from the Fiji Islands, which contain a mixed race of Maoris and Australian Blacks) over the whole of the Pacific to the Sandwich Islands in the east and New Zealand in the south. This could easily be done, as they were expert navigators, as in all directions, even all the way from India, the sea is strewed with islands.

All the natives of New Zealand maintain, throughout the whole length and breadth of the land, that their forefathers came from Hawaiki (Savai of the Navigator or Samoa Islands) about thirty generations back (they can trace the ancestors of their high chiefs by name as far back as that) to New Zealand, which they named Aotearoa (long uprising world). The names of the canoes, according to their traditions, are still held in remembrance. If you only reckon a generation from a father till the birth of the following son as twenty-five years, you have a space of time of 750 years. Some reckon more, some less. It appears, however, that New Zealand was inhabited before this emigration. It is not yet decided whether the earlier inhabitants belonged to the Australian negroes or the South Sea peoples. At all events, New Zealand was known to the latter before the emigration.

It is remarkable that the related peoples, the inhabitants of Madagascar and those of New Zealand and of the South Sea Islands, now so far removed from each other, have all at the same time as peoples renounced heathendom and accepted Christianity. It seems more than an accidental coincidence. Does everything develope itself, including the history of peoples, by accident and without any plan, preconceived and of a higher kind, or does everything occur in accordance with God's providence and direction, and in accordance with a plan. Which is the most reasonable to believe? "God has made of one blood all nations of men for to dwell on the face of the earth, and hath determined the times before appointed, and the bounds of their habitation." (Acts xvii., 26.)

I have already stated that the Maoris, as long as they lived in the sublime ideas of their old religion, could in a measure, thrive under heathendom. But later generations had long since allowed the lore of the old gods to sink into forgetfulness, and it was only known to the " wise people," but by them without any spiritual meaning. Their morals, therefore, became very depraved. Instead of living in the faith of sublime ideas, they lived in painful fear of lower evil spirits of a man-devouring kind—who dwelt in ruined buildings of tapu, because a breach of this entailed death as a consequence, of witchcraft of evil-minded men, and in constant fear of being killed and eaten—for they ate one another. Their sentiments had become so inhuman that they could eat dead bodies, stinking and putrefying, with pleasure, and without any feeling of disgust.

Schiller's verses were here verified :—

> Woe to the stranger whom the waves
> . Cast on that unhappy shore.

To roast and eat a number of strange men—that is, those belonging to another tribe—was as great a pleasure to them as it is to lovers of the chase in civilized lands to have a grand dinner party when they have had good sport.

It must have been about 1820–1830—I knew a few who were present—when the Maoris in the south first came into touch with the Europeans. The captain of a whaling vessel placed a few of his people in an uninhabited bay in Stewart Island to catch fur seals, whilst he went whale fishing with the rest of his crew. The natives, however, did not approve of this. Soon a number of men and women went across from Ruapuke to Stewart Island, fell upon the sealers and killed and cooked them. They then looked for their provisions. At that time they were quite unacquainted with European things. They took the flour for white ash, and amused themselves with throwing it at one another and watching the white dust fly. Then they found something that looked like provisions, and they chewed it till foam came out of their mouths (it was soap), but it was not to their taste. Still worse did the tobacco taste, which they, therefore, called heaven's gall (aurangi). A vessel held some black seed (gunpowder), which they scattered about as a useless thing. Then when they had satisfied themselves with the flesh of the dead men and in the evening sat around a bright fire—oh, what a fright!—lightning and flames of fire suddenly broke out amongst them. The fire had lit the powder they had thrown away. Some time afterwards some canoes with all their crews were lost, and no one knew for a long time what had become of them, until later some whale fishers came from Australia who became friendly with the natives, and these brought the news that an American whaling captain known to them, when he found that the men he had left on Stewart Island had been killed and eaten, whilst sailing about, meeting some canoes, had sailed them down.

Not long before my arrival, and before Christianity had obtained so much power amongst the blood-thirsty natives that they gave up cruelty, and lived peaceably with one another, the inhabitants of the southern island, who themselves had almost eaten an entire tribe in the south, were hard pressed by a tribe from the north under the leadership of the celebrated chief Te Rauparaha. Part of the hard-pressed tribe fled to the south to Ruapuke and neighbourhood. But they were not allowed to remain there in peace by their more powerful foes. A band of them came overland and made floats of the stalks of New Zealand flax, and embarked at the mouth of the Mataura, which empties itself opposite the island of Ruapuke, and in the neighbourhood of the mouth of the river fell upon a village of the local tribe. Most were killed at once and immediately cooked and eaten by the hungry warriors. The remainder were kept as prisoners in the meantime. Amongst the latter was a woman who, later on, lived as a good Christian at Ruapuke. She has often told us of the horror of the attack. Her children were torn from her breast and thrown on the glowing coals, and the poor mother was compelled to look quietly on, for she knew well that if she disturbed the rough warriors her own head would be split. The warriors thought they would be able to refresh themselves here after their toilsome journey overland, but they were deceived. Some of those attacked had escaped, and quickly carried the news to the surrounding villages. A band quickly assembled at the island of Ruapuke, where the high chiefs lived. These went to the Mataura and fell upon the enemy, yet wallowing in human flesh. Many were at once killed and eaten; a few were kept alive as slaves. I knew a few of these and baptized them. They then received their freedom and went back to their northern home. Such cruelties were formerly quite ordinary occurrences. Just as cruel was their child murder. Affairs of love, as they are carried on by young people of civilized races in honour and modesty, were quite unknown to the heathenish Maoris. The old people, not only the parents, but those of the whole district, arranged the marriages without asking what the young people's inclinations were. This did not hinder young people, when so inclined, from indulging their fleshly lusts. Children which were born of such unhallowed unions, at the command of the old people were put out of the way as kittens are put out of the way. Even married women sometimes put their new-born children out of the way, either because they did not like them or because attending to them was troublesome. They did not kill them outright, but placed them in a lonely place and let them cry themselves to death. And now, in the space of a life time, these cruel New Zealand savages, by the simple preaching of Christ crucified— although the Word of the Cross in old Christendom was called by certain Jew-like Christians (in name) in the time of St. Paul a "stumbling block," and by some narrow-minded worldly-wise people "foolishness"—are so changed that the magnificent prophecy of Isaiah xi. applies to them. A weak missionary, who could command no earthly power, can lead the changed, erstwhile cruel savages, and can live in friendship and love with the formerly treacherous and unclean heathen, now, however, clothed and in their right mind, and sitting at the feet of Jesus. The little children of the missionary are now attended to by people who were previously cannibals and murderesses, and that with more motherly kindness than they could feel in their heathenish state towards their own children.

"The wolf also shall dwell with the lamb, and the leopard shall lie down with the kid ; and the calf and the young lion and the fatling together ; and a little child shall lead them. And the cow and the bear shall feed ; their young ones shall lie down together : and the lion shall eat straw like the ox. And the sucking child shall play on the hole of the asp, and the weaned child shall put his hand on the cockatrice' den."

May the time soon come when the following verses from Isaiah xi. may apply, not only to the new communities, but to old Christendom :—

"They shall not hurt or destroy in all my holy mountain : for the earth shall be full of the knowledge of the Lord, as the waters cover the sea. And in that day there shall be a root of Jesse, which shall stand for an ensign of the people : to it shall the Gentiles seek : and his rest shall be glorious.

CHAPTER XIII.

THE SPIRITUAL ADVANCE OF THE MAORI.

ALTHOUGH sunk in cruel savagery the faint recollections of the sublime conceptions of an earlier and better time were still locked in the Maori breast. As in the north of New Zealand occasional conversions took place through the missionaries, and as the Maoris noticed and were astonished at the inward joy and the noble life of those who were converted, this was felt to be in accord with the sentiments of these conceptions. It was, therefore, possible that the whole Maori population from one end of New Zealand to the other should be seized by an unexampled spiritual desire for Christianity, by means of which wars, murders, cannibalism, and, above all, gross cruelty and vice, should be abandoned. It has occasionally happened that a great elevation of mind has permeated a people, when there is occasion, for instance, to make great sacrifices; as when the Fatherland is threatened by overwhelming enemies, but the power of God alone, through the gospel of Jesus Christ, can effect such an elevation as will permanently turn a people to better aims. It is then awakened to an inward desire for a higher life and spiritual being. Although this in-dwelling strength of God has only extended the gospel of Christ by means of spiritual weapons wielded by weak men, and thus gained victories over the powers of darkness amongst the peoples of Europe, yet as they inwardly live in the gospel, they have produced civilization, with the astounding discoveries and advances of our age flowing from it as a result. In this strength of God, which gives the longing heart eternal life, the world for all time will be overcome and conquered.

And now, to relate how the savage Maoris here in the south of New Zealand became civilized Christians, we must go back to the time when I found them here and lived amongst them. Raw savagery they had already renounced before my arrival through the means of the already-mentioned spiritual movement, and had adopted an outward form of Christianity, but they did not understand the spiritual part of it. Their sacred services were works without thought, those of the teachers equally as well as those of the learners. In their then condition, more could not be expected from them. In time, I succeeded in arousing more attention, so that they began to think over what was heard and read. They began to get more earnest. They resembled the eunuch from Ethiopia, who sat reading by the lonely way in his chariot, when Philip met him, and said, " Understandest thou what thou readest?" He said, " How can I, except some man should guide me." Thus the Maoris here. When they began to understand, they came with the timid question, " Cannot I be baptized?" Such questions at first did not come from those of high position, who were looked up to, but from old, simple, otherwise quiet women.

The first who was baptized by me was an old sick woman on her deathbed, whose eyes were lighted up with the peace of God in Jesus Christ, through which she had received the seal of eternal life. The second, if I remember rightly—for I have no data, as my papers were all burnt,—was the wife of the Irishman whom I have previously named. She was a pious and enlightened woman, and had been married to her husband by the Bishop of New Zealand when still a heathen. I was then unacquainted with the communal customs of the Maoris, according to which all transactions were undertaken with the consent of the whole community. Under these circumstances, as Christianity had not been long introduced here, it (baptism) was an affair of the native teachers. The reason that no objections were raised to these two first baptisms was because the first was looked upon as a baptism of necessity, and that, as the wife of a European, they had no authority over the second.

Not long afterwards a few elderly women sought me out, who had attentively listened to my discourses, and whose hearts God had opened, as that of Lydia, at the place of prayer at the water in Phillipi (Acts xvi.). These wished to be baptized. I gave them every day an hour's instruction. After a few days they stayed away, and when I asked the reason, it was whispered to me that it was forbidden. At the same time, a boat sailed for Waikouaiti, the Wesleyan mission station, the object of the journey being withheld from me. I soon learnt that, at all events in the eyes of the teachers, I had raised a strong feeling of enmity. The applicants for baptism belonged to the Wesleyan party, but they were unimportant old women, whom the teachers would not have recommended for baptism. So far, only a few notable and some easily-taught young persons like the teachers had been admitted to baptism by the Anglican bishop and the Wesleyan missionaries. I kept silence, and continued the instruction leading to baptism. When, in time, the boat came back, nothing of the result was allowed to escape, and I refrained from making inquiry, as I knew that missionary Creed, who was now at Waikouaiti, and with whom I had been in danger of being lost in the wild mountains, would not take sides against me. Matters thus remained for a while.

The teachers then came and commended to me the old women for baptism, as well as their old husbands, also the Christian consecration of their long-existing marriages. After a few weeks baptism was solemnly administered. The teachers themselves declared that the ceremony had a sanctifying influence. Soon others, mostly whole families, were recommended for baptism, who also received it after a suitable time spent in instruction.

The teachers were originally instructed to make use of their position to place obstacles in the way of my administering baptism, and to represent to their missionary what my intentions were. They administered their office without advantage to themselves, except that by means of it they were held in greater respect, which was worth something. They did a great deal of good, in so far as they spread the spiritual movement all over New Zealand and kept it alive.

According to our conceptions they were naturally very ignorant, for they had received no instruction worthy of the name. Even their reading was not fluent. If they had to read a chapter with which they were unacquainted before the congregation they had to prepare themselves beforehand—with such labour the sense and meaning of what they read often escaped them. It often happened that they broke a word in two in the middle and made two out of it, or that they joined one syllable of a word on to another, which gave it quite a different meaning. Once a teacher came to me and asked how the sun could be turned round. I could not at first understand what he meant. Then he showed me Matthew v., 39—" Whosoever shall smite thee on thy right cheek, turn to him the other also." Now in Maori tera (compounded of te cra) means this or the other (all words are neuter), and te ra means the sun. He had, therefore, divided tera and made sun out of it. According to heathen ideas, for a Maori of rank to allow such an insult as a blow on the cheek to go unrevenged was as impossible as to turn the sun back. This question was an honest one, whereas most of the questions which the presumptuous teachers put to me were to try me. You see what weak tools God uses in his well-ordered economy, "that nothing may be lost," to advance His Kingdom amongst the Maoris. He knew how to draw most of the missionaries out of a class where the talents given them would otherwise be lost. As workers in God's service appointed by the missionaries I honoured the teachers, although their presumption was often annoying. Especially presumptuous were travelling teachers, because they considered themselves wise and wished to show themselves wise, and submitted catching questions to me to try me. A few of them once came from Waikouaiti. After they had been a short time seated, one of them asked, "What is the name of the place where the Jews held race-meetings?" I answered the Jews had none. After a few questions to ascertain if that was my real meaning, they thought to catch me in my ignorance, and one after another called out, "Olympia!" "Olympia!" I said they were wrong, that Olympia was the place where the Greeks held their games, and that they were quite a different people to the Jews. Instead of understanding what they read in the New Testament, they only learnt names and places, in order to be able to ask as teachers in the congregation, "What was the name of the sick servant of the centurion at Capernaum?" "What was the name of the man who provided the boards for Christ's coffin?" and such-like stupid questions. When travelling teachers came who brought freshly-learnt names with them (often quite wrong ones), they came to try me with them to see if I knew them, too.

The teachers, and with them many others who considered themselves clever, were presumptuous and ignorant, and catching with useless questions; but one must not, therefore, think that underneath there did not lie an earnest striving after the kingdom of God and His righteousness. They could pray. It was only sometimes difficult to recognise under the rough coating the deep longing for holiness that by means of their spiritual stirring up had more or less taken hold of their hearts. We, of the old Christendom, from childhood up, are so walled in by Christian customs and habits that we know how to conceal the sins of our heart—such as self-sufficiency, spiritual pride, and such presumptions as may be repulsive to others under a polite exterior. But the Maoris, grown up as raw savages and unpolished children of nature, knew of no such concealment. Their presumptions were not repulsive, but easy to their minds, and they came out freely with them. The deeper spiritual impressions, on the other hand, were new and uneasy; these, therefore, came less to the surface.

In time I gathered the teachers, both Anglican and Wesleyan, for regular hours of instruction. I read the Gospel of Luke along with them, explaining and examining in order, by better knowledge, to lead their minds away from useless speculations, In time they came to value this instruction. They were pleased to understand what they read. They often thus found material for their discourses, which had often consisted of matters that had no connection with one another and were quite meaningless.

No further hindrances were placed in the way of my baptisms. The teachers, however, so managed matters that the applicants had to go to them in order to be recommended to me. In the first instance I had to put up with this, but I allowed no directions to be given to me. For a time the newly baptized people retained the old appellations of Anglicans and Wesleyans, but they were now under my particular charge, like new-born children in need of the proper sustenance of the reasonable pure milk of the gospel.

The desire for baptism, which more and more found expression, really arose from an inward need of the heart. It had its origin in the general spiritual movement of the entire people, by means of which a yearning for an imagined, but not yet known, higher life was awakened in them, and that yearning the new movement caused to burst forth. They knew well that on baptism they must forsake sin, and that before God and man they must live a conscientious, pure, and Christian life; that their words and acts, even their inward thoughts, would be closely watched by those who were not yet baptized; and that their errors would be cast up to them. To many such thoughts were full of terror; with others the inward stress was strong enough to overcome the fear. It was the love of Jesus Christ that moved their hearts; not so much that they loved Jesus, but much more, that Jesus loved them (sinful men), and had by His life and death saved them.

A drawing of the Spirit, as if by two silken cords of love, proceeds from Jesus Christ in the drawing by love of the hearts of sinful men. One proceeds from His cross, where suffering and dying He was lifted up; the other one from His lofty throne on the right hand of the Father, from whence He prepares a place for us; and both are united in His loving heart. The old death goddess drew the Maori into the world of night; Christ draws us into heavenly light. Where the souls of men, full of yearning, turn with anxious longing to a higher life, and then, with no mixture of self-sufficiency, to Christ, they feel and follow this draught, and find in the holy communion of Jesus Christ a heavenly existence—life and blessedness. And this blessed communion is so mysterious, and yet so comprehensible, so sublime, and yet so simple, that every one may have it, from the king on the throne to his meanest subject in a poor hut; from the cultivated man in his superior culture to the uncultivated one in his plainness; from the learned man with his full treasures of knowledge to the unlearned one with his simple Bible; from the scientific discoverer to the wild heathen. All may find purity of heart, inward peace and joy, comfort in sorrow, and consolation in death.

Instruction for baptism consisted mainly of that of the apostolic belief and the Ten Commandments. Many words of the language had not previously the meaning which they have acquired since the language has become a Christian one. Thus, then the word atua—then meaning the other, standing now for the highest being, meaning God—previously meant everything that was different to ordinary experiences as a ghost; an appearance in the air, an European steam engine, and so on. Sin (hara, nothingness) was then differently understood to what it is now. Cruelty, ignorance, and especially all vices, were then only sin when they disturbed the internal life of the community, but practised against strangers they were deeds worthy of praise. It was no sin to rob and oppress widows and orphans, especially amongst the lower classes. But to burn an old fencing post for firewood on which the clothes of a dead child of noble blood had hung, and cook meals with it, especially when persons of lower caste had eaten of them, this was a deadly sin. Yet in spite of all such errors man is made after the image of God, and however deeply it may be overlaid with a hardened crust, marks of the original image are still to be seen in the deepest thoughts of the heart. Accordingly I found in the depths of my scholars' hearts a leaning towards the everlasting nature of God a desire for a share on our part in His eternal love, for moral duties, purity of heart, justice and truthfulness, heartfelt pity, and kindness.

In the second of Romans (verse, 14, &c.) it says: "For when the Gentiles, which have not the law, do by nature the things contained in the law, these, having not the law, are a law unto themselves: which show the work of the law written in their hearts, their conscience also bearing witness, and their thoughts the meanwhile accusing or else excusing one another." When this original law is moved by the knowledge of Jesus Christ, the old man is put off and the new one put on, fashioned after the manner of God in righteousness and holiness.

The baptized people were under my particular charge. Every week I met them in separate gatherings, besides the ordinary ones, in little divisions. This soon had this result, that each would speak out freely about the state of his soul. In this manner the already begun, but yet very weak, young life was nourished and strengthened. There are, or there used to be, in Germany people who said that, instead of so much spiritual instruction, the missionaries should lay more stress on enlightenment and civilization. This is a piece of wisdom that appears excellent when sitting in a comfortable room, but is not suitable for practical life. Everything has its proper time, also the civilization of the converted heathen. A civilized life requires many labours which cannot be neglected, such as raw heathens are quite unaccustomed to, and are such as they cannot so suddenly understand. Money must first be earned to buy clothes with (their own weaving is not sufficient for it), then follow daily washing and combing, then washing and mending of clothes, building of better buildings, keeping them clean, and a thousand other daily-occurring troublesome matters, all of which are quite strange to the natural man, and, therefore, impossible. If the missionaries were to begin with this, they would find their labours end in nothing. First, the heathen must be converted by a change of heart—"Turn from darkness to light, from the power of Satan to God, and obtain forgiveness of sins." Then, when their thoughts for a time have moved in higher and purer conceptions, the fruit of the conversion causes the desire for a decent life to arise in them, and with this desire come courage and industry and a willingness to work. Now is the time for the missionary to. counsel and lead them. These are matters of experience.

Let him who thinks he can entirely, or for the greater part, make the heathen civilized by moral teachings, try it himself on the degraded and sunken poor of Germany, and he will find that all such labours are in vain. The so-called mystics and pietists manage things better. These come to the sunken poor with the love of Jesus Christ in their hearts, which, in common with Him, they bear to the poor sinners. Their hearty sympathy opens the hearts of those who have gone astray, their brothers and sisters, and they let a ray of the light of Jesus Christ on to them. This light falls on the better, scattered feelings of the heart, and awakes a desire for salvation in Jesus Christ. New hope arises in them. After they have been fed for a time with the sincere milk of the Gospel of Jesus Christ, and thus strengthened, a newness of life arises in themselves, and new courage to improve their condition. Now, for the first time, they can be helped with moral counsel. It is the same with the converted heathen.

The community was still a divided one. The newly baptized people, it is true, felt themselves under my care, but in the same spirit as before, and they were still called Anglicans and Wesleyans, and were addressed as such by their respective teachers. There was no community of spirit, not even that of mere companionship. The inhabitants of each little village would each have a separate divine service for themselves. They had, so far, not the least inclination to go on a Sunday to a village, which was close by, and build up a larger congregation. The best method of producing union of spirit would have been, if I could have done so, to induce them all to assist and build a sacred building—a church in common, but that was impossible. In order to awake unity of spirit, we must have a common church. I resolved, therefore, in the name of God, and relying upon His help, to build a church myself. First I went on to a hill, beneath which our settlement lay, and knelt down there, and under a great bush dedicated the place in prayer to our Father in heaven, who sees in secret, as a house of God. Then I went, as soon as I had time, into the nearest wood to look for building timber. In distant woods I found slender young trees which would answer very well for the building, but these were too far away for me to be able to carry them. In the nearest woods there were only short, and mostly crooked, stems, and I had to be content to hew these straight and carry them where desired. It was heavy labour, especially as in the wood and on the road to it all was pathless and overgrown with thick undergrowth. The natives wondered at my labours, of which, although they were intended for them, they could not see the use. None was willing to help me without wages, and I had no more money. I needed some timber which required to be longer and straighter than any that I could obtain here, also a few boards. I then asked a European, of Stewart Island, who was engaged in the timber trade, how much a certain quantity of sawn wood and boards would cost. He told me the price, and I told him that when I received money I would perhaps give him the order to deliver the timber. There the matter rested, as I intended. But after a few weeks the man came in his boat and brought me the timber. I pointed out to him that I had expressly said, when I received money, and so on. He said that I should give him a certificate that I owed him the money (I have forgotten how much it was, but think it was £7). Now, I wanted the wood so badly, and the payment seemed so easy, that I accepted his offer, although in time, when no money came, it caused me much inward trouble. Especially I did not wish that my acknowledgment should circulate in trade amongst the scattered Europeans here.

I now went cheerfully to work to carry the timber to the place, and to cut stalks and rushes for roof and walls. As such labours had to be carried on between my journeyings over the island to the different villages, and only a short time was left to prepare my most needful food in the roughest fashion, I often fell asleep after supper from sheer weariness, and in spite of all exertions, could not undress and go to bed in an orderly fashion. After I had hewn the timber— of course, only in a rough way— into the right shape, I stood the building up. At the same time God so brought it about that I received from a land surveyor in

Otago (Mr. Tuckett was long absent) a present of tobacco. Now, a few old Maoris were willing to help me at building for tobacco. They thatched the roof and walls inside with flax stalks, and outside with reeds. The building had a really church-like appearance—of course, in a rough way—with a tower at the western and a cross at the eastern end, and a place for a choir in a symmetrical lean-to. Inside there was a chancel and an altar. There were no benches, because the Maoris were accustomed to sit on the ground. Such church-like peculiarities were necessary to distinguish the House of the Lord from other buildings, and give it a superior appearance, in order to awaken a desire for a holy communion and fellowship of saints.

The church was at last finished, and could be dedicated. The year, as far as I can remember, was 1846. I invited all the inhabitants of the island to come in, and many did so. The solemn service, so different from their thoughtless ones in the stuffy community houses of the villages, seemed to impress them; for on the following Sundays the church attendance increased. The teachers wished to retain the assemblies in their own villages intact, but most of the former hearers went away to church; they made short work with those who were left behind, and then came themselves. Of course, in the week days, I visited the different villages as before, and only held the congregational services in the church on Sundays.

Originally it was my custom when I referred to Bible passages in my sermons to name the place where they were to be found. This made a rustling in the New Testament to find them. So far, I had allowed this to happen, although I was obliged to stop for a little; but all at once three or four old women who could not find the place, rushed up to me with outstretched arms, with their Testaments, for me to turn up the places for them. This was too much for me, and I ceased to give out the places.

It was evident that a community of mind was awakened, and in time there was less talk of sectarian differences, although now and then disputes broke out.

The reader may well press the question on me, as it often pressed itself on me, how I could answer it to my conscience to build where others had laid the foundation. Now, if five, or even two, talents had been given me (Matt. xxv., 15) I might well have besought the North German Missionary Society to send me to some other country, and to some other heathen people; although that would have been no easy matter, for sometimes years passed by before I could receive an answer to my letters to Germany. But 1 had only one talent. I do not say this from modesty or mere empty talk, but from conscientious conviction. I have a certain faculty for gathering rough material together; the circumstances were very favourable for it here; but when the congregation is once made I find little ability in myself to build it up internally. I was now sent to New Zealand. The mission field was already possessed by others, who did not belong to our missionary society, but were just as good disciples of Christ as we were. I did now what Christ wished the servant with one talent had done—1 put it in the bank, that when He comes He may take His own with interest. I mean by this that the field here was white to harvest; the labourers here had not the knowledge how to reap, just as one who had hitherto had no scythe in his hand would be unable to mow. I was now here, and I could do it. Therefore, I put my talent in the bank, that in the name of Christ I might go contentedly to work, and bring souls to Him, without founding a church of any particular denomination—neither Lutheran, Reformed, Anglican, or Wesleyan—not even a permanent missionary station of the North German Missionary Society. The further development I left to the Head of the Church alone.

CHAPTER XIV.

MISSIONARY JOURNEYS.

OF the general spiritual development of Christianity in the Maori peoples I have already spoken several times. A further movement in a small way began here in the extreme south, whither so far only a small amount of inward result had been experienced. This spread out from Ruapuke and extended over the scattered villages in the islands and on the coasts of

Foveaux Strait. The news of the numerous baptisms in Ruapuke and the quiet pious demeanour and the blessed inward peace of those who were baptized flew from place to place and created a movement amongst receptive spirits. Soon Maoris desirous of salvation came from the scattered villages in their boats to Ruapuke to see the new life and to request baptism for themselves. In every case they were kept here one or two weeks to receive instruction and to prove their earnestness, and then when found to be upright in their intentions they were solemnly baptized. They then went joyfully on their road back to their dwellings, and became a salt of the earth and a light to their neighbours. In time most of the scattered districts received in this way little knots of baptized Christians. It was natural that I should soon feel a desire to visit the scattered children in baptism—it made no difference that many were older than I, they all called themselves my children—to see how they progressed in their new life, and to nourish and strengthen them in their Christian walk and belief. I made many journeys for that purpose to the surrounding districts in the Maori boats. Before we enter upon these journeys, it will be necessary to explain the place whence the Maoris had their boats, for the canoes hollowed out of tree stems had already gone out of use.

In earlier times, till just before my arrival, there were many whales and seals, and ships came from many countries to catch them. People came here also from the British colonies in Australia and carried on the whale fishery with boats from the coast at places where the whales came at certain times of the year to cast their young in still water in quiet bays, or, as one says here, to calve. At other times they killed the seals, whose skins are valuable, when basking on the rocks. When the whales and seals were mostly destroyed, so that the catch was no longer profitable, many of the sailors and sealers remained here and made themselves at home amongst the Maoris. The chiefs allotted them wives, and they accommodated themselves to Maori methods of life, but they awakened a disposition towards industry. Some carried on a small trade. Others built boats, or made sails, which they sold to the Maoris for pigs and potatoes. These were also, when a whaling ship put into port, exchanged for clothes and European goods. Sometimes brandy was received in exchange, but it was soon drunk, and sobriety again became the order of the day. There were, therefore, foreigners (pakehas) among the Maoris in their different villages. What many of them had been in the notorious Australian colonies I never asked. They lived peaceably and respectably amongst the Maoris as decent fathers of families.

The scattered villages lay (I must state it, as it was in the past, as European immigration has changed it all, even most of the names) partly on the northern coast of Stewart Island, partly on the southern coast of the large. Middle Island. Journeys from place to place were always made by boat.

Such journeys were not without danger, for mighty waves roll through the wide strait, and make strong tide rips on the uneven rocky ground, especially where ebb and flood tide meet. A boat appears a very small thing amidst the high foaming waves; but the Maoris are expert sailors, and the journeys are only made when, as far as can be guessed, the weather is likely to be fine.

Let us first go to Stewart Island, the mountains of which can be seen from Ruapuke standing high up across a distance of twenty miles of sea. On coming near to them you pass through a group of small wooded islands of no great height. You then see rocky bluffs and inlets strewn with islands. We now pass into a great inlet called Paterson Inlet. The entrance is at the side, because a large peninsula called the Neck (because it is only joined to the land by a neck) lies right across the mouth. Inside of this island you find yourself in a tangle of woody bluffs and small islands all of moderate height. Beneath them are larger and smaller basins of water, in which the woody landscape is reflected. From a boat the prospect is not sufficiently extensive. Let us climb a height on the Neck of the above-named peninsula, and at the place where for thirty years past the school has stood, which serves likewise for church, where my daughter now lives, married to the preacher and schoolmaster. From this height there is a view of which one never wearies, gazing over the bays and their many islands and rocky bluffs, between which glides here and there a white sail, or a fisherman's boat. At the sides climb the mountains, one behind another, rising higher and higher, all thickly wooded almost up to the highest point. The highest mountain is about 4000 feet, being higher than the height of the Brocken in the Hartz mountains. The appearance of the Hartz mountains is softer, but not so sublime as the bold upward spring of these mountains, in their fair wooded garb, with the sea at their feet. The high tops stand out bare from the wooded hills (like bald heads over a growing beard, I might say, but such a comparison is an injustice to their beauty). The great inlet reaches from east to west, halfway through the island, and is continued as a depression in the land to the West coast, thus dividing Stewart Island into two great mountain groups of granite formation.

The Maori name for Stewart Island is Rangiura (from Rangi, heaven, and ura, to redden, as the blushing of cheeks), and doubtless the soft red of evening often pours a graceful flood of light over the landscape of Rangiura.

Although there is much building going on, and cities are rising up as if they grew out of the earth, Stewart Island can supply the south with timber for a long time to come. It appears particularly well adapted for it. On the other hand, its wet, cold summers are but little adapted to agriculture. Perhaps the thick woods are the cause of this, for when the woods are thinned, the soil is still covered with a sort of half-preserved green kind of vegetable growth to a depth of three to five feet, in which no field or garden plants will thrive, because their roots cannot reach firm soil underneath it. There are now a few saw-mills in the woody bays, and small vessels carry the timber to European settlements. Then, however, when I used to visit my children in baptism, the Maoris lived in a hopeless state of poverty, because their old heathenish religion and later religious customs had lost all power over their conduct. To this the sailors, who had become incorporated amongst them, contributed in no small measure. The hearty acceptance of Christianity dispelled this hopelessness when it was brought to them. The Maoris then lived in little villages of twenty to thirty inhabitants. The huts were not nearly as good as those of Ruapuke, where the families of the chiefs lived, and their habits of life were poverty-stricken and dirty. In most of the villages I found a few of my baptized people. I remained for a week or longer in each of the villages, nourished and strengthened the believers, lifted the fallen up, and prepared others for baptism, who were then baptized with all the solemnity that the poverty-stricken huts allowed. I then proceeded further.

When I look back upon my early missionary journeys, although imperfect and defective influences always had a disturbing effect on me and prevented me from being unduly uplifted, I always find that they had a strengthening effect on my spirit. I will not compare them with St. Paul's missionary journeys in Greece and Asia Minor, not even in the smallest measure. This much, however, the Maoris and the Greek-speaking people had in common. They had outlived their heathenish religion, and were, therefore, prepared for Christianity, which offered and gave to their seeking hearts full satisfaction. In other respects there was an enormous difference. Paul and his companions had to do with an enlightened, wealthy, and vigorous people. The Maoris, on the other hand, were sunk in ignorance, poverty, and hopelessness, and for that reason were nearly dying out. In their case it was proved that the Gospel of Jesus Christ is a power of God to the salvation of all who believe, and able to lift them *in this life* out of their sunken condition.

Sometimes, on my arrival in a village, a pig was killed, and as long as it lasted it was well appreciated. Still, it was not often that the Maoris had a pig to kill, as most of them went to the before-mentioned Europeans in payment for boats, sails, and tackle; at other times there were fish and sea-birds. It happened sometimes in the poorer villages, when the weather was stormy, that no boat could go out to fish, and that for a week we had nothing to eat but dry potatoes, and nothing to drink but water from the brook. Sometimes I was the only visitor. At other times I was accompanied by others from place to place, and the huts were sometimes so over-crowded that at night we slept, thickly packed, on the earthen floor. The smell that arose from such a bed was no sweet one. Fortunately, the walls were not too tight to prevent the admission of fresh air. Still, a missionary, yet in his full strength, enjoying good health, who had gone out with the expectation of encountering hardships, did not trouble himself much about it. Then it was always refreshing, after a week of dry potatoes and cold water, to come to a place where one of the Europeans lived. A clean seat was here available, not, it is true, on a chair—tables and chairs were very scarce in the district,—but on a sailor's chest, which was drawn up to the fire, and there I was entertained with salt pork and unleavened bread baked in ashes.

Cleanliness and better fare were not the only pleasures I enjoyed in the huts where a father of European birth kept house. The Maoris had few children, and these had a dirty, flaccid look. With the families of mixed blood it was different. Here I met a Maori housewife, sparely but cleanly dressed, surrounded by numerous half-bred children just as clean and with rosy faces. A person fond of flowers, who has long wandered through dry places, and then finds a blooming rose bush with buds and blowing roses, could have no greater joy than I experienced at the sight of these lovely children. A pleasure fills the feeling human heart, and one hopes that these children may thrive, by the blessing of the grace and friendship of our God, through Jesus Christ. The cause of these children thus blooming was that the families were cared for and ruled by parents who had been born and had grown up under the influence of Christianity. Negligent Christianity is always better than sunken heathendom. The cleanliness and neatness in such huts may not always have been so well preserved, but, to a certain extent, specially prepared for my arrival; still, it was a great advance in manners, for the pure Maoris could not for a long time, even on the occasion of the visit of a missionary, adopt the good custom of washing themselves. The feeling that they were dying out (more of this hereafter) had destroyed their hope. Such Maori women who had the good fortune to obtain European husbands felt lifted up out of their state of listlessness into a better method of life, and became joyful mothers of children. They were seized, too, by the spiritual movement of the new

M

teaching—namely, of Christianity—and it was their most earnest desire to be baptized with their husbands and children, and to be honourably married.   Whatever the husband had previously been, the children were so amiable that " The hearts of the fathers were turned to the children, and the unbelievers to the wisdom of the just." I met everywhere with a hearty reception, and was attentively listened to.   The Bishop of New Zealand (Dr. Selwyn) had already been before me in some of the villages, and had already baptized a few half-bred children and married the parents properly; still, there was plenty for me to do.   When a mixed family was thus baptized, and the parents properly married, they all felt so blessed that they formed a Christian family.

On the other side of the Foveaux Strait, the south end of the Middle Island, the formation of the land is different to what it is at Stewart Island.   The south-east end is a wide plain.   In front of this there is a row of small mountains standing quite solitary.   These run from the high mountains of the Western Alps in a south-easterly direction along the sea coast, and are separated by the mouths of wide rivers.   These have the plains on one side and the sea on the other.   The island of Ruapuke is the last link of this chain of mountains.

As far as the coast was inhabited the conditions were the same as at Stewart Island.   The Maoris lived in small villages remote from one another, in a state of listlessness, from which they were awakened by Christianity.   What has already been said about the inhabitants of Stewart Island may equally be said of them.   I will only relate one recollection I have of them. Once when I went for the first time to a village on the coast, I found the people very favourable to church services.   The population was a little more numerous than in other villages, and they had no Europeans living amongst them.   As on my arrival at Ruapuke, they were divided into two parties, Wesleyans and Anglicans; each party had built a little church to itself—naturally only miserable places thatched with grass, and as a proof that the opinions of each were acceptable to the other they had built them close together, so that a person in one could hear what was spoken and sung in the other, and these two churches together bore the name of Babel. When I asked what induced them to use this name the reply was made that Dr. Selwyn, the bishop who had been here before, had himself suggested the name to them. The simple people had not noticed the irony, and in all good faith had called their church Babel, and I did not interfere with their simplicity. I was requested, so that all party feeling might be at rest, to hold meetings in one church one day and in the other the next. 1 willingly consented, with the one condition that all should assemble at the place where I held the meeting, and should seat themselves in such a manner that there should be no distinction of parties. This was agreed to, and we had a beautiful union, elevating gatherings, refreshing hours of instruction, and at last the sacrament of baptism was administered.

There were Pakeha Maoris—that is, foreigners or Europeans who had become domiciled amongst the Maoris in other places on the coast. Some of them had little vessels with which they carried on a whale-fishery.

For a long time the reader will have remarked that the Maori ways of living were very dirty ones, and will think that with conversion some cleanliness and decent customs should have been introduced. He is right, but everything has its proper time, also the improvement of the Maori manners. It does not come all at once. The conversion, when an adaptability for its reception is present, or is awakened by the Spirit of God, works inwardly in the heart. Manners, as a fruit of the Spirit, must be learnt by sustained effort. Without a previous conversion and a renewal of the heart in truth this would be impossible. The wild savage is used to dirt and untidiness, and feels at home in it. At times he can wallow in gluttony, and at other times suffer hunger without it giving him much trouble. He need only work when he feels inclined, and can idle for as long and as often as he chooses. If useful and beautiful things from the civilized world come within his reach, and he can obtain them either by begging, robbing, or stealing, he does it, but to work for a civilized life, and for its attendant advantages, and that without ceasing, that he can and will not do. From his point of view he would be a fool to exchange his careless, wild life for a civilized one. The latter

requires a hundred labours and troubles with which he will have
nothing to do. Change of heart alters this. God-fearing men,
who in old Christendom have been born again by the Grace of
God to a lively hope in the resurrection from the dead in Jesus
Christ, know well what new strength for self-improvement the
conversion effects; how one transacts his business with love and
pleasure in the sight of Jesus Christ, and what a desire for purity
of heart and person, and a consistent life is thereby obtained. It
is just the same with the conversion of the Maori. They now felt
the desire to enter the ranks of civilized men and people, and were
willing to undertake the labour and trouble that a civilized life
requires. *Now came the time to lead and help them in it.*

Let us look for once at the heart of the Maori at the time of
their conversion. What was it that moved them so mightily?
Was it fear of hell, or a warm longing for heavenly blessedness?
It was neither. To the heathen Maori life after death was quite
an indifferent matter, and a desire for piety required first to be
awakened in them by Christianity. I believe, in most conversions in
old Christendom likewise, neither the fear of hell nor a desire for
blessedness is the moving cause. It is true that many a bold
sinner, when on his death-bed, experiences a cowardly fear of hell,
even although he may not have believed in any before, and he is
ready to promise everything that conversion requires. But such
a conversion is not to be trusted, for when the danger is past the
old ways of life are generally continued. The thief on the cross
was not converted by fear, but by his heart being drawn, being
near to the Saviour who died for sinners. The moving cause of
conversion lies deeper than a mere desire for reward or fear of
punishment—heaven or hell. It lies in the nature of man made
after the image of God. Whether they are moral or immoral men
of old Christendom, be they fine people or raw heathens of the far
lands and islands of the earth, deep in the human breast lies a
fearful unrest, which may, it is true, slumber, but which from
time to time will make itself felt in shuddering and uneasiness,
and also in love and a deep yearning for a higher life and being.
If, now, the gospel of Christ is brought near to this anxious
seeking of the creature, such as is centred in man; and if the

hearts can lift themselves above the previously conceived vain opinions, and be open to the influence of the Spirit of God; then the divine relation is accepted and taken hold of.

> Those natures which on meeting quickly take hold of one another we call related to one another.—*Goethe.*

The Maoris, as well as the peoples of the South Sea Islands, had outlived their heathen religions, and they groaned under a medley of religious forms. In this condition, and before they had completely died out under their hopeless views of life, God so brought it about in his wise providence that the gospel of Christ should be brought to them. On my arrival in New Zealand their diminution from dying out was quite noticeable. Here in the south I found there was one birth to three deaths. This had quite discouraged the people; and, even for savages, they were in a state of helpless poverty. They did not even possess the necessary food and clothing to be able to stand the frequent severe weather. As Christianity, especially when conversion takes place, gives the mind a cheerful and hopeful upward swing, the general elevation which the Maori people experienced is explainable, and is the reason why so many conversions followed on my weak labours. It was the anxious seeking of the creature that finds its desire in Christianity.

In civilized Christianity if anyone is converted or born again of the Spirit a great change takes place in his heart, and his general conduct shows the fruit of the spirit—"Love, joy, peace, long-suffering, gentleness, goodness, faith, temperance." Such a change for the better takes place in the converted Maori. The former has, however, enormous advantages. He has drawn in Christian manners and customs with his mother's milk, and has grown up surrounded with them. The Maori, as a heathen, has inherited nothing. He has grown up in uncleanness, roughness, cruelty, deceit, and treachery. His Christian knowledge is faulty, and what he has is newly learnt, and not yet interwoven in his life. His Christian experiences are to a great extent formal, and his virtues do not yet arise from a free spirit, but are mostly the result of forced resolution. In order to express his feelings, he freely uses parables. The figure of "That spiritual Rock that followed them, and that Rock was Christ" (1 Cor. x., 45) was a lovely thought to the Maori.   He compared himself to a shell that adheres to the rocks and cannot be torn away by the waves of the sea, or to a seabird that floats over the unstable waves, thrown about hither and thither, swimming or diving, which then flies and seats itself on a rock, and there stands with firm foothold.   A man converted in old Christendom is a deeper Christian and a better man than the converted Maori, but the change for the better is just as great in the Maori as in the other, if you consider what he has been.   As a heathen, he was " so grim that no one could walk in the same street with him," now he is a meek disciple of Christ.

" Come unto Me all ye that labour and are heavy laden and I will give you rest.   Take My yoke upon you and learn of Me, for I am meek and lowly in heart, and ye shall find rest unto your souls.   For My yoke is easy and My burthen light." (Matthew xi., 28-30.)

CHAPTER XV.

HOW I WAS RESCUED FROM MY LONELINESS.

WE are still in the years 1844 and 1848, during which years I worked alone amongst the Maoris.   At this time this neighbourhood was lonely and remote.   The nearest settlement was at Wellington, Cook Strait, then only a poor small place, 500 miles away from here.   The intended settlement in Otago, over 100 miles away from here, was put off because the New Zealand Company in London was short of money to carry it into effect.   My friend, Mr. Tuckett, to whom the foundation of the settlement was committed, had resigned and returned to England.   Whales and seals had been recklessly killed, so the catch was no longer remunerative.   Ships, therefore, came here but seldom, and at last I began to feel myself very lonely in this dark corner of the earth.   I never doubted that some time I should receive means for my support from our North German Missionary Society, but it was impossible to tell when

there would be an opportunity to forward it.   I just had to trust
in God and make the best of it.   I was under the necessity of
producing my own food from the soil and of cooking it myself,
and sometimes it was very scarce.   Potatoes, it is true, could
easily be raised, but not farinaceous food.   Boiled peas sometimes
took the place of bread, but I had not many, as in my desire to
improve the condition of the Maoris I always gave away the
greater part of my crop for seed.   After so doing I was displeased
to find that when they had gathered their harvest the first year,
instead of planting their seed they cooked and ate it.   In following
years I was obliged to go into their gardens and plant it for them
myself.   I began to keep goats, pigs, fowls, ducks, and geese.
These made my settlement quite lively, and raised my hopes of
an improved way of living.

> Hope and a little good,
> And a good conscience, too,
> Are a great good, it's very true.

I found, however, in time, that attending to such a household
took more time and labour than I could well afford, and I had to
watch to prevent my domestic animals going astray.   Besides
household duties and attending to my vegetable garden I was
obliged to cook and wash, and in such a manner that I could hardly
retain the cleanliness of my own person, one of the principal virtues
of civilized life.   In time the many labours became too much for
me, especially as the food was so poor.   Of a variety of food, such
as in Germany even in poor households is considered as very
meagre, there could here be no thought.   I had to give up the
mid-day meal because there was no time to cook it, and content
myself with two meals a day—morning and evening.   Flour was
not easily to be had; it cost money, and I had none.   My health
began to give way and my strength to fail.   Once, I remember it
yet, because at that time it made a deep impression on me, I baked
some bread which was to last a week.   But in the evening when I
began to eat I could not restrain myself, my will was powerless,
and I devoured all the bread at one meal.   Of course on the other
days of the week I had to go without bread.   Sometimes I tried
potatoes in Maori fashion, placing them in water till they rotted

into starch. You can then wash the rotten part away from the starch and make a kind of biscuit of the remainder. Still, it has a foul smell and taste, and is not conducive to health.

My mental powers had developed themselves late in life, not from school years up, and their steadiness in many small matters which make up character was still unsettled. Here I had to forego entirely all intercourse with cultivated men. It happened therefore, that the many labours, with insufficient nourishment, weakened my body, and this affected my mental powers. My thoughts began to turn to a confused melancholy. This may have found expression in my writings. At all events the Wesleyan missionary Creed at Waikouaiti, with whom I had been lost on Banks Peninsula, and with whom I exchanged letters, remarked it. He wrote to me that I had need of the recreation of a journey, and I should come to him for a time. I felt myself a most earnest desire, after I had been three and a-half years here all alone, once more to meet cultivated Christian people. Accordingly, at the end of the year 1847 I made the journey in an open Maori boat. At that time, as there were no large vessels, the Maoris were not afraid to make long sea voyages in their open boats. Sometimes the waves were high, and it took great care and skill to steer the boat over them. Every evening we landed at a place where Maoris lived, and after staying a few days went further on until at last we reached Waikouaiti. In such a manner in those days journeys used to be undertaken the whole length of the coast from place to place. At that time, with such a sparse population, we considered everyone within a distance of 200 miles as neighbours. Since the European immigration our acquaintance is limited to the immediate neighbourhood.

I was well taken care of by the amiable family of missionary Creed, and I thought at first that my health, both of mind and body, would be restored. I was, however, deceived. The melancholy thought that I must leave this beautiful family life and again enter upon my life's work at Ruapuke, where I must take care of myself, and assist the Maori families in their awakened desire for Christian life, prevented my health establishing itself. A helpmeet as wife, who like Martha, in Luke x., would be cumbered with much serving of Jesus and his poor brethren, would be the right person in the right place.   If I seemed externally to be better the inward pain was far from healed, when, after a stay of two months with the missionary family, I returned to my settlement at Ruapuke.

When I was now alone in my hut, and all looked so desolate, melancholy again nearly overcame me.   I prayed till I recovered courage.   It was then clear to me that if I was to carry on the necessary missionary work, it was impossible that at the same time I should produce my own food, cook, wash, and preserve cleanliness, so that my health might be maintained.   I was satisfied that our missionary society would send me the means for my existence with pleasure, when God showed them the way. Under these circumstances I made the important resolution to go into debt.   I had previously borrowed a little money from a man on Stewart Island.   I ought previously to have remarked that letters of credit had been forwarded to me, from Hamburg, in case German ships should come here.   But no more ships came to this desolate region of the earth — the whales were destroyed — and no one here would accept the letters of credit.   I went, therefore, to the Irishman whom I have already named, and made a contract with him to board me, promising to pay him when I received money from Germany.   I obtained a hut close to his from the Maoris, which we soon made habitable.   My meals were now brought to me regularly three times a day.   It was rough country fare, not nearly as good as common people get in Germany.   Still, I gained strength, because I had no longer to do cooking, washing, and such like labours.   I could now attend to my proper missionary work, as well here at Ruapuke as on the neighbouring islands and the coast.   Besides the missionary labours, I occupied myself with study of the Maori language in connection with the old mythology and heroic tales. You cannot learn a foreign language in two or three years so thoroughly that you always place the right word in the right place, which is very necessary for a correct understanding of it. Such studies were pleasantly refreshing in the midst of my labours as a missionary, and my natural cheerfulness returned.

Letters from Inspector Brauer of the Missionary Society, in Hamburg, informed me that I was not forgotten, which letters, after long wanderings along the coast from Wellington, reached me at Ruapuke. I was informed that assistants would shortly be sent to me, and that the first, Brother Honoré, would shortly be sent out. From this I concluded, as a matter of course, that he would bring some money with him, and that I should be able to pay my debts, which began to trouble me more and more.

After a delay of four years, 1848 (so noteworthy in the history of Europe), the New Zealand Company in England, in connection with the Branch Society of the Free Church of Scotland, took up the settlement of Otago again, and ships with the first emigrants arrived. Although 100 miles away the effects were felt by us. Our Maoris often went there in boats, partly to see what was going on, partly to get work and earn something, in order to buy European clothes and household utensils, for the desire for Christian manners—the result of their conversion—made itself felt more and more. Connection with the civilized world was thus restored to a certain extent. My old friend, Mr. Tuckett, who now lived in London, sent me a supply of valuable books ; also some tools, nails, and other things useful for building, because he knew, although I was no mechanic, that I knew how to use them, and he thought such things would be useful to raise the Maoris in the social scale. He was right, but as long as I was alone I had no time to make use of them. With conversion, which was making a progress that filled me with joy, and which resulted in many baptisms, a new spirit awoke in the Maori, which made them willing to work for a civilized life. This was especially noticeable amongst the women, amongst whom there were indications of an ardent desire for a decent house and family life. They observe this in the superior, but still very deficient, family circles where a European parent ruled. I had little or no skill to help the women. Moreover, an unmarried missionary cannot entertain too close relations with the family circle of the women.

At the end of 1848 Brother Honoré arrived, without any money. When I asked him how the missionary society could possibly send him to New Zealand without any money, he replied it was said in Hamburg that the New Zealand mission did not cost any money, and for that reason the East Indian mission took all they had. That was too much for me. So far, I had laid little stress on the hardships I had suffered, because it is expected that a missionary shall bear them. But that they should think, because from the commencement I had been so careful in New Zealand, and had suffered hardships for years, that, for that reason, it should cost no money, whilst New Zealand is a very expensive country to live in, that, certainly, made me feel very bad. My displeasure may well have made itself felt in the letters I wrote at the time and later on.

I know that missionaries are sent out, and do acceptable work, too, with the understanding that they shall earn their own living amongst the heathen. They must, however, go to a country where this can be done; but here in the raw uncivilized south of New Zealand this could not be done, if one did not wish to become as uncivilized as the natives. Here nothing could be earned and nothing obtained in any other way. But other Europeans were living here amongst the Maoris without receiving an income from home? Yes, but in an uncivilized way; and could earn something by trade, for which a sea boat was necessary, and the skill to handle it; or at boatbuilding or sailmaking. I was a farmer, and farming operations are not yet carried on here. I could have taken up with such a life as the Pakeha Maoris lived (Europeans who had become Maoris), and have pictured it to myself as follows:— Like other Europeans I should have to take a Maori wife to cook and wash for me, and to work in the garden; but as I was too poor to give her suitable clothing, she would despair of attaining a Christian condition of living, and would remain in a state of savage filth. I should then have to see her going about with one of my shirts on, and nothing over it, from under which her dirty legs would present themselves; her hair would be uncombed, and she would either have a short pipe stuck in her mouth, black with tobacco juice, or else have it stuck through her ear like an ear-ring. Now, such a family life the friends of the mission would hardly wish for me, even those who think that missionaries should live very cheaply and in a state of poverty. My missionary work would be a very lame one, and no stability could be the result of it. I could then have done nothing for the *civilization of the converted people, which must necessarily go hand in hand with the progress of Christianity.* Furthermore, I was in no way disposed to lower myself to such a state of existence. If no other way of life should present itself I would rather go to the north and hire myself out for a time as a farm labourer.   But it need not come to that yet, for my faith that our missionary society would send us help stood firm. My difficulty must be known to them, especially as there was now a post office in Otago, and letters were not so long on the way. I knew nothing, however, of the difficulties under which the North German Missionary Society then laboured

As a preliminary, Brother Honoré and I had to take our meals from the Irishman, and every week got deeper and deeper into debt. This could not go on for ever. We had now tools sent from London by Mr. Tuckett, and went into the wood, felled trees, sawed beams and boards, and built a new house. For this district, where there were nothing but low huts, it was a stately building. There were, however, many things wanting in it, which in our ignorance of architecture we did not then understand. Later on I came to see that a house is not sufficiently well built if merely it does not topple over, but the danger of fire and the conditions necessary to health must be carefully attended to. Our house was wanting in both respects. We had to make our chimney out of clay. Now, in low huts and in wide chimneys clay is good enough ; but our house was high, and the chimneys were, therefore, high and narrow, and when these cracked in drying it could not always be noticed. Our floors were too close to the earth, and that had the disadvantage that, with the heavy and frequent rains of the district and the prevailing moisture, it was detrimental to the health of the inhabitants. I can only look back with inward grief on the time and labour lost in erecting this building.

We lived in the new house, and as time went along the debt became more and more pressing. Besides the cost of board, I had borrowed some money from a man in Stewart Island. I had been here five years already, and had received no proper support from the Missionary Society. Brother Honoré had brought me a little underlinen and some simple clothing. Brother Heine, at Nelson, had once sent me a £5 note. A Bremen ship had cashed my acknowledgment for £7 which I had negotiated here. A letter now arrived from the North German Missionary Society. It contained an official direction from the Mecklenburg Church congregation to ordain Brother Heine at Nelson. The German congregation there located had chosen him as their pastor. That so long a journey—over 500 miles from here—cost money the people in Germany appeared quite to have overlooked. Nevertheless, I undertook the journey, relying upon God, without any money; for, besides Heine's ordination, something had to be done on my part to obtain support from the Missionary Society, and I intended to try whether the German merchants in Nelson, where we Germans were somewhat known, had sufficient faith to cash a draft for me. The official direction to ordain Heine may be, thought I, a fingerpost erected by God to show me the way. "The counsel of the Lord is wonderful, and excellent in working."

I went with a Maori boat to Otago, and lived there without expense with the natives, which I could always do. From thence, as opportunity offered, I went in a boat to Port Chalmers, the port of Dunedin. In the post office at Port Chalmers I found two letters for me. One was a Government letter, with the intimation that the Government had made me registrar of births, deaths, and marriages for the south. This was not of much importance, for only Europeans came under the Act, and European settlers proper there were not yet in our district. So far, the office was without salary. Still, I took it for two reasons. One was because I loved the Governor and recognised that his intention was kindly (he knew how to value a missionary in a homeless region), and, secondly, because the office gave me a position amongst foreigners as an official—Paul knew how to make use of his position as a Roman citizen. The other letter was from my old friend in London, Mr. Tuckett, and contained the news that he had sent me a flour mill, which could be driven by oxen. His intention was very kind, but the mill came too soon, for so far we had neither corn nor oxen. Besides, the mill could not be sent in an open boat to Ruapuke. Still the consignment, in the difficulties under which I then laboured, was very welcome, for I saw that I could turn it into money in the city of Dunedin, to which place the mill had already been forwarded.

At Port Chalmers there were no natives, I had, therefore, to live in a hotel till an opportunity offered of going to Dunedin by boat. As I had no money, and did not wish to let my poverty be known (for fear I should be taken for a swindler), I asked the landlord to take care of my little baggage till I returned from Dunedin. Payment for my board could thus remain outstanding. At Dunedin (at that time an unimportant place with a few small wooden houses, now it is a large city) I soon found a buyer for my mill, who gave me £40 for it (less than it cost) and a free passage to Wellington in his vessel. Now, the first difficulty of want of money was overcome.

> When the need is sorest,
> God's goodness at its best
> Is then most clearly seen.
> At last, it must appear,
> God's hand His own doth lead
> In wondrous way and blesses all their need.

Of course I wrote at once to Mr. Tuckett explaining the circumstances under which I had been obliged to sell the mill.

CHAPTER XVI.

MY HELPMEET.

IN Dunedin I lived as the guest of the chief surveyor, Mr. Kettle, whose acquaintance I had previously made on my journey to Waikouaiti. I found that my name was otherwise well known here. I received invitations from Captain Cargill, the superintendent of the settlement (after whom our provincial city, Invercargill, in the south, is named), and from the pastor, Dr. Burns (nephew of the Scottish poet, Robert Burns, of world-wide fame). The pastor showed me copies in his book of baptismal and marriage certificates given by me to half-caste families who then belonged to my wide district, but now to his.

From Dunedin I soon went back to Port Chalmers, paid the landlord, put my baggage on board ship, and then went overland to visit missionary Creed at Waikouaiti, as the vessel was to call there on her journey to Wellington. Mrs. Creed gave me a sealed letter to her friends at Wellington. I thought, possibly, it might be such a letter as David sent concerning Uriah, which might possibly not put my life in danger, but might jeopardize my previous hermit-like life. Arrived in Wellington I met Brother Wölkner, who had been sent out by our Missionary Society as assistant to Brother Riemenschnieder, and was now on the road to meet him. (After a time he joined the Anglican Church, and later suffered the death of a martyr at the hands of the natives.)

From him I learnt that our North German Missionary Society had undergone a great change, and that the management had been shifted from Hamburg to Bremen. I could not remain long in Wellington this time, because it was of great importance to me to learn whether I could obtain money in Nelson against bills of exchange from merchants who were known to me, for on that depended the future existence of our mission at Ruapuke.

The town of Nelson during my five years' absence had not altered much, it still looked like a village; but the progress in the adjacent farming country was much greater. The Mouterie district, where we had attempted to establish ourselves, was at first given up as being too remote. The nearer Waimea Plain, which was a wilderness before, was now changed into cornfields and homesteads. The brothers Kelling, from the Mecklenburgh district, had a fine farm in full swing. A few of the German labourers possessed their own allotments—others were on the way to acquire them. Most of the German mechanics lived in the city, and in worldly circumstances were in a similar position to those of mechanics in small towns in Germany.

All, both the citizens in the towns as well as the labourers in the country, had ample supplies of provisions in their houses, so that their emigration had certainly very much improved their circumstances.

Some of our German residents here had come out with us, and were, therefore, old friends; the others had arrived in another ship during my absence. They were all from Mecklenburgh, and for that reason the Mecklenburgh congregation had sent me the power to ordain a pastor for them. The ordination took place in the city of Nelson, and all the Germans attended the service. My friend, Mr. Tuckett, already often mentioned, who had formerly lived here, had relinquished his roomy dwelling house to the German congregation. There was a large hall in it, where tables for drawing field charts on had previously stood. This hall was well adapted for use as a church, and the surrounding rooms for dwelling-rooms for the pastor. The Germans were about to build a public building in the country, to serve both for school and church.

The bond of union amongst the Germans was the church; in other relations they were on the road towards blending with their neighbours the other inhabitants of the British Islands.

Nelson, which lies in a deep gap between high mountains, has always remained a sleepy place. Even later, when it became the capital of a province, it manifested so little political life that it received the nickname of sleepy hollow all over New Zealand. Is it possible that the German admixture may have been conducive to the political quiet of the place?

At home I have occasionally heard people who have never been actual foreigners express displeasure that Germans in foreign countries so soon neglect both their German language and manners, and assume both the language and customs of the foreigners. That is true in New Zealand, but not only Germans do it, but others do the same, and I have been acquainted with many foreigners who have come from different countries and peoples. Yet I am certain they are right. Why should they always be considered and treated by their neighbours as strangers, which must be the case as long as they shut themselves up in exclusiveness? If, on the other hand, they adopt the language and customs of the country—including the more solemn keeping of the

Sabbath—they are all considered and treated as comrades and citizens of the country. The inward German feelings of the heart are not extinguished in the first generation. They may remain true to their home Church convictions if they are numerous enough to form a congregation. This gives no offence in New Zealand, because no denomination has any preference—all have equal rights. They must not, however, take upon themselves to look down upon those of other opinions or condemn them. As long as the first generation lives it may be well, too, to hold public divine service in the German language, but following generations will better understand and prefer the language of the country.

I remember in my childhood to have learnt in my Hanoverian catechism, under the head of Patriotism, "How ought we to regard it if we earn our subsistence in another country?" Answer : "Then we ought to look upon it as our second Fatherland, and we owe the same love to it as if it were our own Fatherland." "Seek the peace of the city whither I have caused you to be carried away captives, and pray unto the Lord for it : for in the peace thereof shall ye have peace." (Jer. xxix., 7.)

After the business in Nelson was done, included in which was the marrying of Pastor Heine to a German maiden, and I had drawn money against bills of exchange (I believe about £75), I commenced my return journey to Wellington. In Wellington I had the pleasure of meeting Brother Riemenschneider, who, as he had heard of me through Brother Wölkner, had gone there to meet me. He had waited for me for a few days, and had, therefore, soon to start on his return journey. I lived with Mr. Watkin, superintendent of several Wesleyan communities here. He had but little room in his house because he had a numerous family, but as he had previously been a missionary himself (in the Fiji Islands), he knew that a missionary did not think much of sleeping on the floor without bed or bedstead, indeed, he much prefers it to sleeping in a public house.

How wonderfully the influences which the children of men exercise on one another come round again ! One evening, when the superintendent and I were sitting in his study before the fire (it was Winter), and were comfortably smoking our pipes, the conversation turned on the subject of how God had led me to be a missionary. I told how, before I knew anything about missions, leaflets on the subject had come into my hands through the intervention of God. The first article which 1 had read made such an impression on me that I could still repeat the contents after many years. It was translated from the English, and the subject was the heathen in Fiji. I did this because he asked after it with so much attention. And now it appeared that he had written the article himself.

Another incident which took place here, and was of importance to our mission station at Ruapuke and the district, must not be passed by. Christianity can condescend to the sunken heathen, but, and it may well be noted, not to allow them to remain in their filthy condition, but in order to elevate them into civilized human beings. The desire of becoming such was noticeable amongst the converts at Ruapuke, especially amongst the women who desired better circumstances for their families. I had often supplied help and advice, but I had not the skill to do so ; Honoré just the same. For what can unmarried men do amongst the affairs of women and those of a family ? A skilful and suitable wife for a missionary was, therefore, a necessity for our mission station. 1 was already thirty-eight years of age, and no longer of a disposition to make love in a tender fashion. A marriage such as that of Isaac in Syria with Rebecca, and with the same sacred intentions, was more in accordance with the circumstances.

In the 10th chapter of Luke there is a beautiful story of two sisters. One, Mary, loves quiet contemplation, sits at the feet of Jesus, and listens to His speech. The other, Martha, was cumbered with much serving of Him, probably with a little impatience, which may well be forgiven to such natures. Such impatience, even if sometimes untimely as it was then, is occasionally wholesome in the way of equalizing different dispositions. Now, such a woman with a character like that of Martha, which would find its proper occupation here, I had already longed for as a wife. There are always such women to be found in Christendom, who always find plenty to do because it is their heartfelt desire to serve

Christ in the person of His meanest brethren. With such a one I became acquainted in Wellington. She was a young cultivated widow (an Englishwoman), without children, and without relations in New Zealand, and she had already had experience in dealing with the Maoris, and knew their language. Her name was Elise Palmer. I could give her a sphere of operations, and that was my dowry.

On visiting the house in which she lived, 1 was reminded of the above-named marriage of Isaac with Rebecca. A small maid of the house showed me a picture—I know not whether it was childish innocence or a roguish trick, which it might later, perhaps, have been considered to be—and asked me if it was not pretty? The picture represented Rebecca when she was being asked (it was written underneath), " Will you go with this man ?" She replies, "1 will go with him."

Elise Palmer was a friend of the wife of missionary Creed at Waikouaiti, and it was by her the proposal of marriage was introduced. When I made the proposal, she replied that we knew so little of one another, that the suggestion had not sprung from our own inclinations, but had been made by others. " Then," said I, " it is said good marriages are arranged by the angels in heaven, and Mrs. Creed is as good as an angel." That had the desired effect.

In order to get married I had to have a certificate from the registrar. The registrar-general, to whom the sub-registrars have to send quarterly returns, was in Wellington. As I was appointed registrar for the south, and came to him for my certificate of marriage, it gave him a suitable opportunity to show me how to prepare the official papers and keep the register of my district. It is true that in my district there were so far no registrations, because immigration had not yet extended that far (which, however, might soon happen), still, as I was an official, the expenses of my certificate were remitted to me, and every saving was an important matter.

After a few days our betrothal was concluded by marriage by Superintendent Watkin. We then went on board the ship, where our luggage had previously been taken, which lay ready to sail, and at once started for Otago. The vessel was going on the business of the New Zealand Company, and Mr. Fox, the chief agent of the company, gave us a free passage in her, which again was a saving.

In two days we landed in Otago, and as for a time there was no opportunity to go to Ruapuke, we sailed in a Maori boat to Waikouaiti to visit the Creed family of Wesleyan missionaries. Mrs. Creed did not take it ill of me that I had called her a good angel.

On 1st December we landed at Ruapuke. It was already the custom in all missionary stations in New Zealand to address the wives of the missionaries with the English name—mother. My wife was accordingly addressed by the title of "mother"—the mother of the community.

At first the housewife had enough to do to arrange our house, and introduce a respectable method of life, and I had much to do in the community at Ruapuke, from which I had long been absent. The tone of the community had become a Christian one, although the baptized people were still in a minority. These had sought and received baptism from a fervent desire of the heart, and formed the better class. It could not but happen that others, who had no real hearty desire for the "Kingdom of God and His righteousness," still preferred to belong to the better class, and were willing to forsake their heathenish ways and confess the Christian faith. Later on, when it came to be dishonourable to be a heathen, it could not be prevented that unworthy people were sometimes baptized. Still, no open sins were permitted either by the teachers or the community; in fact, the community was much more severe in the matter of Church discipline than we were, because we would rather bear with the weak ones with love and kindness, which the community did not understand. They were still young converts, and had not put on, " as the elect of God holy and beloved, bowels of mercy, kindness, humbleness of mind, meekness, long suffering." Both the severity of the community and the gentleness of the teachers had its advantages, which I did not then see, for I sometimes rebuked the community because they scared away and drove into the wilderness those erring sheep whom Jesus would willingly seek and bring back, and they were thus liable to be devoured by wolves. The punishment was a temporary exclusion from all religious services (resolved upon by the community), and it was in the unanimous feeling of the community a disgraceful punishment, which was very much feared. When I look back upon the time when the feelings were still hard and rough, I can well see that the severe earnestness of the community was a wholesome discipline, and had the effect of making the weak ones careful. At the same time the fallen ones knew that they had an advocate in me, who could command the respect of the community, and thus they learnt what love was, and with touched hearts could turn to the Heavenly Advocate, Jesus Christ.

Three months after my return I made a round journey in my missionary cutter, and visited all the scattered places on the coast of Stewart Island and the mainland. There was plenty to do in all places, to lift up the fallen, to strengthen the weak ones, to admonish the faithful, and instruct the applicants for baptism, and I then concluded with the sacrament of baptism. After a month's absence I came back to Ruapuke. It was the day before Easter, 1850, and on the evening of Easter day our house caught fire, the one which Honoré and I had built with so much trouble the year before. The chimney, which was built of clay, had cracked in drying, and with a dry wind and a strong draught the sparks had set fire to the woodwork of the house. Whilst we endeavoured to extinguish the fire, which was impossible, we lost the time to save our things. Everything was lost, including all my books and papers. For a time we had to suffer great privations, but these troubled me less than the pain in my conscience. I was to blame for the misfortune. I had built the chimney. I should have thought of the danger of fire when I was building. All our labour and trouble and all our belongings were lost. My wife and Honoré had to suffer for my blunder in building. That no reflections were cast on me made my pain so much the deeper. Even yet I cannot look back upon the time without shuddering. No description of our sufferings may, therefore, be expected. The dear God made our trial so light that it was bearable. Brother Honoré and I built another house, but not so high as the first one. We made the chimney so wide that any cracks in the clay could be seen whilst it was drying. In time plentiful help came from Bremen, where the management of the mission station was now situated. Trade between Europe and New Zealand increased, and it was easier to help us.

CHAPTER XVII.

A BATTLE FOR CULTURE.

IT has already been remarked that the converted Maoris were far from being able to attain the holiness of Christianity and the life of Christian morality to the same extent as those who are converted under the old Christendom. Still there was just as great a change for the better from their savage and sunken condition as was the case with converted Christians who had been brought up in Christian ways. The results of conversion amongst the Maoris showed itself in a desire that was awakened in them to resemble Christians in their manners of life. It is true this was impossible to the older ones, but the younger generation were capable of cultivation. A beginning had to be made in the family life, and there there was room for improvement. Now my wife took the matter in hand.

Let us take a look at the conditions of family life. Of cleanliness in household matters there was not the faintest trace. If the husband was absent it was considered good manners for the wife not to wash herself. She then became so abominably dirty that it would be an insult to a pig if one had said she looks like a pig. It was considered a virtue that she should not wash herself to meet anyone else but her husband. All smoked tobacco. The whalers had introduced the custom. Men and women, boys and girls, all smoked short clay pipes as long as they could get tobacco, on which they were very intent. Even sucklings began to draw smoke through their mothers' pipes. It must also be remarked that children were often not weaned until they were four to six years old, and then no longer lay in their mothers' arms, but stood upright on their sides. In the degradation into which the Maoris had fallen the mothers had lost even the courage to wean their children. For that reason, and on account of the incessant tobacco-smoking and other impurities and deficient nourishment, they had very few children. They dared not punish the children, no matter how disobedient and naughty they were, because the parents in their then heathenish, brutal condition, were liable to such fits of rage, especially when other people interfered, that it often ended in their striking them dead.

If a child was sick the parents would not let it sleep, because they thought it could be kept alive by constant waking. In such a way many a sick child was shaken to death, and then complaint was made that the mother, from want of watchfulness, had allowed the devil to steal the child. At first, before I understood their meaning, I understood the complaint according to our Christian ideas—that the mother had not been watchful in prayer. I then endeavoured to excuse and comfort her by saying that it was not the devil had stolen her children, but the dear God had taken them to Himself in heaven, and that, when they went to heaven after death, they would find the child still living there. This was a consolation to the mother; but I found it was not want of watchfulness in prayer, but negligence in not shaking the child enough they complained of.

One morning, after my wife had undertaken the superintendence of the manners and customs of the female part of this little world, a man came to us and said his little child was dying. My wife and I at once went. In the house we found a circle of old women who were helping the mother to shake the child that it might not fall asleep. In this way they thought the breath of life might be retained. My wife at once took the sick child to herself, and sat down with it, and commanded silence in the house. No loud word was spoken, no sound made. The sick child soon fell into a gentle slumber. Now, everybody thought it would die; still none dared to dispute the command of my wife. She remained there the whole day nursing the child. In the evening it was better, and she could give it back to the mother, with strict injunctions not to interfere with its natural sleep. This sick child later on grew into a strong man.

There were more of similar delusions, arising, perhaps, from their previous degradation and the process of entering upon a new life. My wife, therefore, found plenty to do in introducing enlightened Christian ways into the family habits and household customs. There was plenty to do to make a beginning, to introduce something like comfort into the huts, and to bring the clothing of the women and children into order. This was not only necessary for the sake of appearance, but for the sake of health; for in the transition from heathendom to Christianity, and the passage from savagery to civilization, the children were at one time covered with too warm rags, and at another left exposed to the weather without any.

Of course the bad inherited customs could not be got rid of at once. It took much labour and patience, but "Cast not away, therefore, your confidence, which hath great recompense of reward; for ye have need of patience, that, after ye have done the will of God, ye might receive the promise (Heb. x., 35, 36).

The community houses, in which everyone could sit and sleep, and where there was a very disorderly method of lying about, fell into disuse, because each family built a small hut, in which a commencement towards cleanliness and order could be made. These new houses were very easily built, and only lasted a few years; but this was of no consequence, as from time to time better buildings were made.

We now began to grow corn. Rye was not adapted for our climate and soil. The straw grew as tall as a man, and the ears were a foot long, but they contained only a few shrivelled grains. Wheat, on the other hand, throve very well. At first we cultivated only with spade and hoe; later on we had first-class implements. My valued old friend in London, Mr. Tuckett, with whom I always continued to correspond, took an active interest in the Christian civilization of the Maoris, and sent us a valuable two-wheeled cart, ploughs, harrows, two hand-mills, and the necessary power for driving them either with oxen or water. We had previously broken in some oxen, and accustomed the young ones to the draught from youth upwards.

The Maoris were, it is true, willing to work for advance in civilization, but when they saw the heavy agricultural implements and heard the whirr of the machinery driven by oxen, they thought it was going a little too far. Men who could sail their boats on the high seas work with oxen! This was too much for their high pride. We had a great deal of prejudice to overcome and a great many matters to explain. The chiefs, too, were secretly afraid that the inferior men would become their equals. Indeed, if the chiefs had not become Christians themselves and experienced the strength of Jesus Christ in their hearts, the battle for civilization would have been lost.

When, later, horses were introduced, they all took great pleasure in riding. The men considered it as manly as sailing boats, and the women became good riders.

Only a few of the men could overcome their distaste to working with oxen, but they were all willing to work with spade and hoe. After a few years we had extensive wheat fields in Ruapuke, and it was a pleasure to see men, women, and children all employed in the fields, sometimes at the harvest, sometimes at the threshing. The corn was ground in the mills already mentioned. The girls had long ago learnt to milk cows, so there was now bread, milk, and butter in the houses, food which had previously been unattainable. The standard of health began to improve, the births to increase, the deaths to diminish. Soon more produce was raised on the island than could be used, and an important export of potatoes and carrots took place. There was good sale for these on the opposite coast, to which the first settlers from Otago had already come. The money received was of great use to our Maoris to enable them to buy clothes and necessary household utensils. Ruapuke was the central point from which these advances in industry and manners radiated, but they extended to the scattered villages elsewhere, as visitors often came from thence to look at the new mode of life, and took back with them a desire to copy it. Still, Ruapuke was so much in advance of the other places that it was likened to Egypt, inasmuch as there was always corn there.

The children were not allowed to smoke tobacco any more, or be naughty in other ways. If chastisement was necessary the infliction of it was committed to me. This was done so conscientiously that children over whose heads a punishment was hanging submitted themselves to it willingly, because they preferred rather to bear the short smart on the back than the trouble in their consciences any longer. Such chastisements were always accompanied by loving admonitions, and the result of them was a love that still continues in their breasts, although they have long since become men and women.

If my wife went out to visit a village, as soon as she was noticed a cry arose, " Mother comes," and every housewife at once seized her broom and began to sweep her house and place her few things in order, so as to be able to stand inspection. This was a considerable advance on what I have previously noticed—namely, that for a long time the Maoris could not understand the good custom of washing themselves and cleaning their houses on the occasion of the visit of a missionary, as was done in those families where there was an European head.

All growing girls, one after another, learnt household duties in our house, which all of them ardently desired to do. Once a little girl asked to be taken in, and when the request was refused, because the house was full, she crept under the table, held on to the leg of it, and said she would not go, and we were obliged to let her stay. The children became so much attached to us and our ways, that some Maori mothers used to say that their children no longer belonged to them, but others used to say " What would become of our children if the missionaries were not here." We generally had ten or twelve of them in the house. Every day, with other children, they had two hours' instruction, the rest of the time they helped, partly in the house, partly in the garden and the field. A girl drove and lead the oxen, while I held the plough. For so large a household we had to work to bring food out of the earth. We could not manage so well with the boys, because their inclinations were for the sea, and as soon as they were old enough they became sailors. The girls, however, did not consider it beneath them to occupy themselves with the oxen as the men did. They made good drivers, and the Maoris found it astonishingly convenient to have the things they used to bear on their backs carried for them.

Once we went to the wood to get firewood. Close by was an old Maori occupied in his potato patch. It was old Titus, on the subject of whose baptism Brother Honoré had formerly written to the committee (and his report was published). It was not enough for him that he should renounce the stated heathenish manners and superstition with a simple " Yes," but he declared out loud—" I utterly renounce all these things." And when he was asked, in accordance with the confession of faith, if he would be baptized in this faith, a simple "Yes" was again not enough for him, but he said—" I will be baptized into this faith." Now old Titus was busy in his garden, and as we drove close by and began to load up firewood he sat down to look at us. He had never seen a cart before, and being an old man he recollected the old heathenish time before there were any European novelties introduced. The load got higher and wider, almost larger than a Maori house. Old Titus looked on wondering. At last, when we started to drive away with it carefully, up he jumped and laughed and danced till the woods rang.

The church services were attended by all who could go with the heartiest goodwill, and those who could not go consoled themselves with the sound of the bell, which summoned the devout ones to church. Children were confirmed, and many of the grown people were communicants. Naturally, unpleasant-nesses sometimes arose, for we had to do, not with holy angels, but with sinful men, yet inexperienced in Christian life and conversation. But the progress made was refreshing.

So I think now in the evening of my life, when I look back upon that time of youth, and overlooking the weaknesses, see only the bright side. At that time I did not find it so enjoyable. I lived and moved in the work, and knew it thoroughly, and in all things I saw imperfection, failings, and sin. With sinful men it always looks so. It also happened that the many labours absorbed all my strength, and with the exhaustion of body and mind I was more disposed to look on the dark than the light side of things. Brother Honoré found his field of labour on Stewart Island. I had to perform divine service, teach the school at Ruapuke, and attend to the spiritual welfare of the people, and besides that daily undertake hard manual labour. You cannot get a mechanic here as at home, and if anything is broken you have to repair it yourself. Let nobody at home think that if anyone of the artisan class wishes to become a missionary he does it in order to lead a comfortable life. The opposite is the case. In his isolation such a missionary thinks but little of outward hardships and internal denials. He feels that he is fulfilling his calling and has full contentment in Jesus Christ, as now all the talents which God has given are in full use, which in his former cramped state, hemmed in on all sides by laws written and unwritten, could not be the case.

I did not then know that the willingness of the Maori was to be attributed to the fresh zeal of a recent conversion, and that when the fire of new spiritual light, ignited by conversion to Christianity, in time burnt more dimly, worldliness would mingle with progress in civilization. Communities in old Christendom, amongst which revivals have taken place, have to go through similar experiences.

Our North German Missionary Society was willing to help our Maoris in their advance towards civilization. At my suggestion they sent us artisans, whose passage money they paid, but who had to maintain themselves on arrival. First came a young shoemaker. He found plenty of work, and payment for it. Besides his shoemaker's shop he built a little tannery. Cattle were being slaughtered here, so there was no lack of hides; and the bark of an indigenous tree of the beech kind made very good tan bark. The good result induced me to send for more artisans. A married carpenter was sent who could do mason work as well. I thought the Maoris would be able to get better buildings, because the houses they built for themselves were leaky and crazy. Here I made a great mistake. The Maoris could now and then pay for a new pair of shoes, and have the old ones mended, but when it came to building a new house in a workmanlike way, it cost so much more than a pair of shoes that they were far from rich enough to be able to afford it. In order to support his wife the carpenter was placed under the necessity of doing other kinds of labour. This grieved me, and I, therefore, willingly gave my consent to his going across to the mainland, where there were already European settlements, and carpenters were in request.

An agricultural labourer, who was sent out to relieve me of the exhausting manual labour, and also to instruct the Maoris in agriculture, wrote to me from Otago, where he had landed, that he was offered three or four times as much wages as he had received in Bremen, and requested me to release him from his engagement, if he would return the passage money. Of course I released him, as, under the circumstances, his service at Ruapuke would have been an unwilling one. Our shoemaker no longer felt himself comfortable on the lonely island amongst the natives, when good work was available for mechanics on the mainland; and, besides that, our Maoris, who often made journeys across in their boats, could easily get foot-wear there. All these people, as well as their relatives who came after them, have made a good living in the south of New Zealand.

The Maoris take little interest in matters from which they do not see that they derive much advantage, but they are so much the closer observers of everything that may be of use to them. A few had learnt to mend old shoes; others could saw boards and build simple little houses; we could, therefore, do without our artisans. Their presence and labours were not without advantages as an incitement to copy them, and our Maoris made progress from year to year.

The gospel of Christ was introduced at the time of Christ taking the form of a man by miracle—by miracles which were adapted for the persons with whom he was then associated. Such miracles are no longer adapted for our time, but there is yet a divine miracle-working power in Christianity. Is it not a miracle, when before our eyes wild stinking heathen and cannibals, by means of conversion to Christianity, and just because through it they have experienced the power of God in the Gospel of Jesus Christ in their hearts, become from inwards outwards civilized men, and can now step into the ranks of the civilized people ?

"Give thanks unto the Father, which hath made us meet to be partakers of the inheritance of the saints in light: Who hath delivered us from the power of darkness, and hath translated us into the kingdom of His dear Son: in Whom we have redemption through His blood, even the forgiveness of sins." (Col. i., 12, 13, 14.)

CHAPTER XVIII.

ADVANCES AND CHANGES.

THE previous chapter embraces a space of about ten years— from 1850 to 1860. At the beginning of this time the people came to church unwashed and uncombed. The dresses were various, but not elegant. It was a time of transition from Maori to European customs. It attracted no attention if a man went to church with merely a shirt and waistcoat and nothing else. At the end of this time this would not be allowed to happen. All came washed and combed, in clean and respectable European attire. If some clothes were patched, it was done neatly, and it did not look at all bad if the patches were of a variety of colours. The dwellings were so constructed that cleanliness and respectability could be maintained in them. The cooking, too, was done in a civilized manner. The standard of health had been so far raised that the birth rate was higher than the death rate.

The following space of time, in which our previously wild Maoris emerged from the low scale of society in which they had so shortly before lived and became fit to rank with Europeans, will soon bring my recollections to a close.

Religious and social advances continued to go on in a quiet way, but neither old nor young could forget that in their uncivilized life they had far less to do, whilst now they had to be constantly at work. The old ones were, and naturally remained, narrow in their spiritual conceptions; for that reason they paid more attention to the form of religion than to a free spirit of inward piety. A younger generation, better instructed and with wider views, now grew up, but in them more worldliness appeared than real piety. A taste for cleanliness and neatness soon expanded into a love of fine clothes and new fashions. New pleasures were introduced—namely, a love of music and riding. The women, too, were very good riders. This might well be considered innocent pleasure; still, the thoughts became worldly, necessary labour was often neglected, and hardly-earned money could have been better spent than on gaudy ornaments. But still the worldliness of the young people, with Christian life and conduct, was far preferable to the early uncleanness and ignorance of the old people.

As I have just mentioned dancing, I am reminded that so far I have said nothing of the old heathen Maori dance. It appears all nations dance. It must, therefore, be implanted in human nature, just as music, poetry, and other human gifts are. The principal dance among the heathen Maori was the war dance. If an open battle was to be fought (a different thing from a treacherous ambush), when the armies were opposed to one another they endeavoured to raise their spirits by a song and rythmic movements. The song became louder and the movements more vigorous, but always keeping true time, till their courage rose to madness. Then the armies rushed on one another in mad rage, and a furious slaughter was the result. Such battles were mostly of short duration. Here in the south, on my arrival, only the friendly dance for pleasure was in use. Still, this was akin to the war dance. Women could take part in it; arms and breast were bare. It began with a movement of the arms and head, to the accompaniment of a low song. So far, there was a certain grace in it. Soon the song became loud and harsh; the movements were more vigorous, and extended over the whole body, whilst the features were dreadfully distorted. Sounds were produced by slapping and striking the naked arms and breast with the hands, similar to those which would be made in throwing deadly weapons at an enemy. They made a gurgling and rattling in the throat, such as fallen enemies might make. The whole ended in loud laughter. In Christian times such dances were no longer used. The European settlers were accustomed to dance, and the Maoris, when they had an opportunity, looked on, and were pressed to join in the dance, which they did, and thus learnt. Young men who had served as sailors and seen foreign cities brought back simple musical instruments with them, on which they could play a little. In this way the European dance was introduced into the Maori villages, and performed by both sexes with appropriate modesty.

I have already said there was an export of wheat and potatoes from our little island. Later on that of cattle and riding horses was added to it, which were taken away by coasting schooners to the European settlers. Still, this could not go on for ever, for as new farming operations were entered upon on the opposite coast our Maoris could not compete with the experienced Europeans, and their products found, therefore, less sale. Still the export, as long as it lasted, had to a certain extent set our Maoris on their legs. We had, therefore, to look around for other branches of industry. For a time wheat was still grown for our own use, but in the course of time even this was given up. Inhabitants of small islands always by nature prefer the sea to the land, and those of Ruapuke made no exception. In consequence of this it happened that every Autumn a great many young fat mutton birds were caught on the many uninhabited islands of this district. These were preserved and were in great request amongst the Maoris living in the north, as there are none there. In the early times our southern Maoris could only send a few in their open boats, and that not without danger. But now all along the coast there were European settlements, and little vessels went from place to place, and goods could be safely sent by the merchants. The Maoris, therefore, found it much more convenient to salt down a large quantity of these mutton birds and send them north, receiving for them in exchange either money or money's worth in flour, sugar, and such like, than with great labour to raise wheat and grind it in their mill. Industry and co-operation found thus its equivalent.

The island of Ruapuke, on account of its many rocks and boulders which lie in all directions, is but poorly adapted for the plough. On the other hand, the soil (granite formation), when the heights and flats are cleared of the wild growth and sown with good grasses and clover, is well adapted for grazing. For rearing cattle the Maoris showed little inclination. This industry could, therefore, not be carried on to advantage. Rearing sheep might answer better, for these sensible creatures want here but little supervision, as they cannot run away from the island, and there are here no savage animals, and there is no proper Winter. When I came back from a journey, during which I had some dealings with European settlers, I brought as a present for my daughter, then a little child, a few lambs as playthings for her. These soon grew to sheep and did so well that their number doubled every year. In a few years there was, therefore, a flock in view. Still, it was not wise and good that I, as pastor, should keep a flock of sheep here, as not a foot of land belonged to me. I advised the Maoris to buy sheep from the Europeans and bring them across. I should have preferred the whole island commonage to be devoted to it, everyone holding according to his ability. But the common people had little taste for it, as they could not yet see the use of it, and wished to spend their little money some other way. The nobility, however—the high chiefs and their family branches— went into it, and a couple of hundred sheep were bought for them and brought across to the island. I added my few sheep to this flock, and a calculation was made what the respective share of each in the flock was. When, in the course of years, the flock increased, the common people, too, derived benefit from it in earning something for washing, driving, shearing, and handling them; besides, after they had become practised in shearing here, they could go on to the large sheep runs in shearing time and earn good wages. When now the wool of our sheep is sold every year, and the labour and other expenses paid, the money remaining is divided amongst its owners, everyone according to his proportion. (I have only a small portion.) This makes it possible for me, with my scanty income, to live here, and, further, it is right that I should derive a portion of my subsistence from the Maoris, even though done indirectly.

Amongst the old Maoris the desire to become Christians arose from an upright heart, even though with little knowledge, because it filled the void of heart from which they suffered. With the younger ones, the now growing generation, who were the most numerous, as the older ones were dying off, it was less a matter of heart. It was enough for them that they belonged to a Christian community, as it were, by inheritance. Their conduct was always that of Christians. It could not be expected that the first zeal of new converts should always continue. In the north of New Zealand, where the Maoris were more numerous than here, the reaction became the more noticeable, and prophets arose who considered themselves inspired and specially called. These endeavoured to give Christianity a form amongst the Maoris according to their own ideas. None attempted to cast it off again. Later, when a few people rebelled against the English Government, there were not wanting Maori prophets who preached rebellion and promised victory, and so disfigured Christianity that it suited their wild notions. As it was to their interest to get all the Maori tribes to adopt their views and join their party, some of such prophets came to the south. They adopted the European title of doctor, because they claimed to be able to heal the sick. But our Maoris were such faithful subjects of the English Government, and such simple Christians, that if they wished to find listeners amongst them they had to preach biblical Christianity. By it, too, they knew how to test their alleged power of working miracles in the way of healing the sick. This naturally aroused curiosity. The standard of health, in consequence of the improved manner of life, was a good one. Only a few old people, who perhaps suffered from bad digestion, were easily persuaded that they were ill, and after a few days, during which they had to content themselves with very little, and that light food, were represented as being cured. At the same time they knew how to re-suscitate the fear of the previous, but now renounced superstitions. Empty old dwellings and ruins of houses, whose previous owners had died, and which had, therefore, a weird aspect, were pointed out with dreadful forebodings as the haunts of unclean spirits. Nightly meetings were held to banish the spirits, and solemnities practised by candlelight which had some sort of resemblance to the holy communion. As some of our communicants had taken part in these rites they were excluded from the Lord's table. Since then I have been very careful in the admission of applicants to the communion. I had long seen that the enjoyment of it strengthens the faith of living members, but does not awaken faith in dead ones. Since then we have had only a very small number of communicants.

Such a reaction as we experienced is the rule in human nature. The early spiritual elevation of conversion creates in deeper souls a quiet, truthful spirit, but they are always in danger of falling into temptation, still more so those converted from heathendom.

With superficial persons, however, who are only externally drawn into conversion, it results in a formal and powerless frame of mind. It is true the old superstition, in which the Maoris had been brought up from childhood, was renounced, and that with uprightness of heart, but its deep root had not been torn out of the mind. When these roots were encouraged with great cunning by these false prophets of the north, they shot up into poisonous growth. In those years the standard of health had been a matter for congratulation, but now sickness and death began to work again, and the painful fear of their superstition could be seen to be the cause of it. The sensible Maoris saw this in time, and the false prophets no longer got a hearing and were obliged to absent themselves. Still, it cannot be said that the old superstition is quite rooted out of the heart. In my youth, even in Germany, there was still a great deal of superstition on the subject of witchcraft, wizards, and ghosts, how then could it be expected that Maoris recently converted from a heathendom swarming with witchcraft and ghost stories should be altogether free from superstition?

There are no heathens proper now in my whole missionary district in the south of New Zealand. The whole native population, as well at Ruapuke as in the scattered villages, may be looked upon as a Christian community. The same may be said of Brother Riemenschneider's charge in Otago and the surrounding district, which is adjacent to that of the southern community, although two and a half days' journey removed. For that reason many visits cannot be made, especially as no money for journeying came our way. Previously Riemenschneider worked in the North Island, but came to Otago later on, as he had to give up his charge on account of the disquiet resulting from the war. Of our spiritual charges, it may be said " The spirit is willing, but the flesh is weak." We missionaries strove with God for our yet weak spiritual children, that Christ might win a footing in them, and that in good hope that as He had begun the good work in them He would perfect it till the day of Jesus Christ.

CHAPTER XIX.

HOW IT LOOKS TO-DAY.

IT has already been mentioned that some European men— sailors who had left the whaling ships—lived amongst the natives with Maori wives, and that in these mixed families there were some lovely children of the half-blood. In time the parents of such children died, and the poor orphans— especially those on Stewart Island—were brought to Ruapuke by the relations of the mother. For this reason we had a considerable number of children on our island. With the many and necessary manual labours which I had to perform, it was not possible to give them such instruction at school as was to be desired. Fortunately, our New Zealand Government came to the conclusion that it was their duty to supply the Maori youth with instruction in the English language. For as long as the Maori remained ignorant of the English language, and, therefore, had no access to English literature and the local newspapers, they would be obliged to remain a restless people, disassociated from the settlers. With difficulty a part of the small sum that was voted by our Parliament for Maori schools was obtained for this far south, where we had a small school fund of our own. A few years before the Government had bought the whole of Stewart Island from the local natives for the sum of £6,000, under the following conditions:—Two thousand pounds was at once divided amongst the local natives.

Two thousand pounds was retained by the Government, that the money might not be squandered, and the interest annually paid to five high chiefs of the local nobility; the rest was retained to provide schools for the southern Maoris. The accumulated interest of the last sum now amounted to sufficient to build a school at Ruapuke, where most of the children were. The southerners had, therefore, an important claim under the new Education Act. The school was opened in 1868. Owing to the increase of orphans on Stewart Island, the number of scholars amounted, at the beginning, to 50. These left the school after one or two years, married, and established households. For that reason the number of scholars became considerably less, and with it the income of the teacher diminished, as the Government paid according to the average attendance. The first teacher left us after about two years, and I saw clearly that with our small income no good teacher would come to our island. Accordingly I offered to take the school myself, which was agreed to by the Government. It was no longer necessary, in order to encourage the Maoris to industry, that I myself should lead the way in manual labour. It was necessary, however, that I should work almost every day to earn my own living. As my income was now increased by the salary of my office, I would at last be free of toilsome manual labour. Still, I found later on that when the head is weary with the labour of the school, there is no better recreation for me than working in the fresh air; but this may not be the case with people who are not so much used to manual labour.

It is no easy matter to instruct the Maori youth in the English language. The sounds in the Maori language are simple in the highest degree, those of the English are most difficult. If in a simple village school in Germany, where the word grammar had never been heard, one were to begin instruction in Greek at once, it would present no greater difficulty than teaching the Maoris English does. And yet the difficulty may be overcome; but there is need of patience, and the labour is tiring to the teacher's head. When the first generation learns to speak the foreign language, but imperfectly, they can come to a very good understanding with the English settlers, and in the succeeding generation things go along better, and the difference of race is not so noticeable.

Our Maoris could now step into the ranks of civilized people. What a difference between formerly and now—between heathendom and Christianity. In heathen times the sick people were placed in isolation, that they might not interfere with the comfort of the living. A little roof was built over them, something to eat and water to drink was placed at their side, and they were then left to their comfortless end. Now, since the community has become Christian, and has acquired Christian customs, they can die in the blessed faith of our Saviour, Jesus Christ, and that, under the care and in the presence of their dear ones in their own dwellings. Verily Christianity makes men into men, fashioned after the likeness of God. Those resident in old Christendom should think of this when they say missions to the heathen are useless, and yet are not themselves devoid of noble human feelings.

The old Maoris died off one after another. They left but few children, and although these, under the improved conditions of life, grew to advantage, they had but ltttle strength of constitution. Many died of consumption—some in childhood, others in early years of manhood. It was the effect of the sad, sunken state, into which the Maoris had fallen before they could be vivified anew by Christianity. The number of Maoris proper became smaller every year. With those of the mixed blood matters went the other way. It is true some of them fell victims to consumption inherited from their mother; still, on the whole, they possessed greater strength of constitution. They had inherited a spirit of enterprise from their fathers, which was wanting in the Maori proper, and were, therefore, better able to throw off despondency. When they grew up they married; sometimes among their own people, sometimes Maoris, sometimes Europeans. They were far more fruitful than the Maoris proper, but no so prolific as the Europeans who had settled here.

In our community the half-castes were by far the most numerous. For the old Maoris the island of Ruapuke was an important place, for the younger generation, and especially for the half-castes, it had lost its importance. The young men grown up with the sound of the roaring sea singing in their ears, had little taste for agriculture and cattle raising, but they were so much the bolder sailors. After they had learnt English at school, they took service as sailors, saw something of the wide world and gained extended experience. Then they came back, married the young girls, and built little vessels. But now they came to the conclusion that the little island of Ruapuke, dear as it was to them, was not adapted for them, because it had no harbour and their vessels were, therefore, in constant danger of being wrecked. On the other hand, the island of Stewart Island, twenty miles distant, offered them the desired harbour. The young families, therefore, one after another left Ruapuke and settled in the beautiful harbours of Stewart Island. Many of them were born there. The Government, which had previously bought the whole island from the local natives, gave each of them a piece of land for their own. In this way there arose a beautiful settlement of half-castes. The blending of the European blood with the Maori (the latter is nearly white in the South) has produced a beautiful race with fine European features. They now have a good Government school, and my only daughter is married to the teacher, who is also preacher, and attends to the spiritual wants of the community, so that the old connection with the mission is thus continued. The men go with their decked vessels into the fishing business, the dredging of oysters, and the catching of seals, and occasionally, too, take cargo along the coast. They are thoroughly acquainted with the local seas, know all the tides, the whirlpools, and the havens of refuge into which they can run in case of a storm arising suddenly.

Through the emigration of the young healthy families to Stewart Island, our small island Ruapuke has become much depopulated. Those left behind are almost all old people, who have no enterprise and little spiritual life. The families of the high chiefs belong to it, who live in a state of proud poverty, and whose income and expenditure would have got into confusion if I had not exercised a kind of supervision over them. If they only had some enterprise, or if I were not too old to do it myself, they would clear the fruitful meadows of the island, the heights and flats, and places between the jutting rocks, of the wild growth, and sow them with clover and grass seed, leaving, however, the woods undisturbed, as they are useful. Then, instead of two thousand sheep, of which the flock at present consists, they could easily have six thousand or more. But they cannot be roused to such undertakings.

As I have again mentioned sheep, I am reminded that many readers would like to hear something about the interesting New Zealand sheep runs. When the enterprising immigrants from Europe became acquainted with the country of these southern parts, they found that in addition to the forests there were many open grassy places, which would answer admirably for sheep runs. The wild-growing cattle grasses were, it is true, too coarse for sheep to thrive on, but they could be burnt away, and the soil sown with good European grasses and clover. The soil also contained good indigenous grasses, different from the European ones, but related to them, that could not previously get through to the light. The Government, who had bought all the land from the natives, was now ready, as there was no peasant class, to lease such areas of land at very low prices. Thousands of acres were taken up under such leases. Lessees with money and brains were soon found, for both these qualities were necessary for such undertakings. They went to Australia, and brought large ships full of sheep back. At that time it took a great deal of money and labour to take the sheep to their destination after they were landed, but these difficulties were overcome. At first the flocks were only small, but they soon increased—(in Ruapuke they doubled every two years through the annual lambing)—so that the sheep were reckoned by thousands. The still empty wastes now served for the use of man, as a large quantity of wool was exported every year. The holders of such sheep runs, if they were clever, became rich. So far, all was well; but an evil arose, because the rich sheep owners became too conservative, and took it very ill when newly-arrived settlers came and purchased pieces of the land they had leased from the Government, with a view to settling on them. Many of the lessees who had money, or who could borrow it, purchased their previously leased lands in large areas. Now a wholesale land fever swallowed up the country. Other rich people came and bought large areas of land, so that it became difficult for a small peasant to acquire a suitable piece of land. The large landowners over all New Zealand obtained a powerful conservative influence in politics in opposition to the liberals, who wished a small peasantry to be the rule—-everyone with his own farm—thus creating the same evil that exists in England, where soil and land belong to the rich, the farmers only being lessees, and the peasantry living in great poverty. Such evils the liberals in New Zealand wished to avoid.

After the sheep runs, especially here in the south, had made successful progress for years, quite an unexpected misfortune befel them. You read in ancient histories that rabbits have destroyed countries (the weak little creatures), and that may well be true. As there was so little game in New Zealand, only birds, a few lovers of the chase decided on importing rabbits. These were let loose in a lonely place, and the people were prayed and threatened not to disturb them till they had become numerous. And they increased beyond all expectation. No river, no mountain could keep them back. Fortunately they could not cross the sea, and our island Ruapuke was spared the plague. On many once green sheep runs is now not a blade of grass to be seen. All is eaten by the rabbits, and the sheep must starve. They try to exterminate them with poison, with dogs, with every imaginable weapon. You read that here 10,000, there 20,000 were killed without making any appreciable difference. Still this land plague affects only the great sheep runs where there are but few people. In the neighbourhood of towns and villages they are easily kept under. These towns, villages, and sheep runs are only of recent date. In the earlier years of my residence here these districts were pathless wildernesses. The European settlers of the south of New Zealand are mostly Scotchmen belonging to the Presbyterian Church. They have brought with them their historic God-fearing and pious way of life, and as our Maoris were converted to Christianity long before their arrival, and had already made considerable advance in civilization, they lived in a beautiful unity with the settlers both in social intercourse and religion. It did my heart good to see it. Here in Ruapuke we are separated from the new towns and villages by twelve miles of sea, but many of the scattered members of my community, especially those on the mainland, have them in their immediate neighbourhood. In addition to the good that the settlers have brought with them there are the public houses which the Europeans will always have—a temptation, but still no greater temptation than the public houses in Germany are. Now a young community just risen from heathendom should be taken as great care of as a virgin whom one would wish to protect from the temptations of the world.

As soon as the settlers in any place are at all numerous, a church is built out of their own means. There are no church tithes here, and the community must support their own pastor. The blessing of God rests on this active and heartfelt piety, for "They work in quiet peace, and their outward condition endures." "Righteousness exalteth a people, but sin is their undoing. Godliness is profitable for all things, having the promise of the life that now is and that which is to come."

The Government has charge of the schools. They are unsectarian, and now, to please the Catholics and the Freethinkers, are without the Bible. This want is supplied by the Sunday schools, to which all children, rich and poor, are attracted. They are held in different schools, and pious teachers read the Bible in classes with their scholars, and present its contents with a warmth of heart such as could not be done in the day schools, where so much has to be learnt. The teachers meet once a week for conversation, edification, and preparation for the next Sunday. I write this from my own observation, and because, as a visitor, I have often had an opportunity to be present at it all. Once every Summer the Sunday schools have an outing, as it is called here. They gather in the church, and then march under the leading of the teachers out of the town into some beautiful, roomy, open place. Here they are regaled with cakes and tea, and they amuse themselves with innocent games. Their parents and grown-up brothers and sisters attend (the labours of the day being over), and they form a large party of men, women, and children. It is a beautiful treat, and without intoxicating liquor of any kind. What an army of children you see here! The number of the children in villages in Europe in proportion to the grown-up people bears no relation to that which is the rule in New Zealand. God's blessing, " Be fruitful and multiply," applies very fully to the European immigrants.

Our North German Missionary Society, in the beginning of their labours among the heathen, acted in their New Zealand mission in accordance with the words of Christ, under the guidance of God, it is true, and without their knowing it—" Let. not thy right hand know what thy left hand doeth." That means doing good without looking for thanks in a selfish way. A missionary society may well rejoice at the development of their community from heathendom, and may then consider it as theirs, even though it no longer needs their guidance.

But how goes it now with our New Zealand community, gathered by Riemenschneider in Otago, and by me in the south, and the adjoining province? With the help of God, the raw, stinking heathen have become changed into civilized Christians, who in no respect are inferior to ordinary Christians in old Christendom, and they considerably surpass the converted natives of the North Island.

Now, however, they are surrounded by numerous European settlers, who, in their social affairs, have formed themselves into Christian communities. It would be an error if barriers of sectarian differences were erected here. Our Maoris are, therefore, incorporated into these Protestant communities, which we submit to with great pleasure. Under these circumstances the mission of our North German Missionary Society can have no future. They decline, therefore, with pleasure the task of building permanent communities. They have brought souls to Christ without requiring self-seeking thanks. They will have their reward in heaven. Hundreds of souls have become believers who would otherwise have died in comfortless, hopeless heathendom, and have departed with the consolation of eternal life. They will thank their mission friends in heaven —all of them who helped in the mission by prayer,

gifts, labours, and counsel.   What is written in a German hymn
will be fulfilled-—

> There him will I grateful thank
> Who pointed out the heavenly way,
> And a million times still thank
> Him that he showed it me.

For myself I ask no recognition, because so much has to be
deducted for many failures and sins in my labours, that I should
occupy but a poor position.   It is enough for me that I have been
an unprofitable servant, who desired to do what he ought to have
done, but did not do it.   In Jesus' words, relative to unprofitable
servants, there is the meaning that from servants—and in
comparison with our heavenly Lord we are miserable servants—
only labourers' work can be expected, and that their labours would
have no result if God did not always put them right and repair
their errors.   In my own case this saying is a true one.

"For by grace ye are saved through faith, and that not of
yourselves.   It is the gift of God, not of works, lest any man
should boast."

As I have lived so long amongst the natives of New Zealand
(36 years), and have carefully studied their way of life from the
time of their savage heathendom, and through their development
into civilized Christianity, I must say something about their
dying out.   It cannot be denied that they are dying out (my
experiences extend only to the south of New Zealand), whilst
their kindred of the mixed blood—the result of the union of
European whaling sailors and New Zealand mothers—live on
and increase in number.

What is the cause of this dying out of the Maori, whilst
the Europeans who have emigrated to New Zealand are remarkably
vigorous and fruitful, and the above-mentioned half-castes live
and increase?   I cannot agree with the saying that a weaker race
of men must die when it comes into contact with a stronger one.
It is contrary to my experience, and I doubt, therefore, whether
it is the case in other parts of the world where the natives die
out.   When I arrived amongst the Maoris in 1844 I found the
death rate so high that there was only one birth to three or four
deaths.   At that time, in comparison with the Maori population,

there were only a few sailors who had been left behind by European and American whalers. These had only been here a few years, and lived scattered amongst the Maoris; they could, therefore, have no effect on their health.

The Maori physique was that of a strong, well-grown, bodily stature, and yet it died out. The race resembled a young person dying of consumption. As such a person, even in Europe, no matter how well grown he may be, goes to an early grave, without any other reason, just so was the Maori race dying out here. The whole race, of which the individuals died in the bloom of their early years, was dying of consumption. This cannot always have been the case. There must have been a time, even if centuries ago, when they lived in New Zealand, and when their bodily powers strongly developed themselves in the fresh air, and when they were healthy and fruitful, and increased in number. I am inclined to put their extinction down to two causes. In the first place their forefathers came from tropical countries, where the Summer is always warm. In New Zealand they had, with very healthy air, to withstand a great deal of rough weather. They might have been able to bear this if they had not been, secondly morally in a sunken state. When the old heathen religion, with its sublime ideas, fell more and more out of sight, and could no longer influence them to lead a virtuous life; when the chiefs, in spite of all their vices, both when alive and after death, took the place of the gods; when the vicious tapu (by means of which men and things on which it was laid became sacred, so that if a common person touched them it was punished with death) was more and more used to extend the power of the chiefs, cowardly fear took the place of noble human feeling. Their morals then sank, their methods of life became brutish and most unclean, and that was the case with the common people as well as the chiefs. The abominable cannibalism became more and more common. Without the smallest feeling of disgust they could eat a stinking corpse. Such a method of life is inhuman and unnatural, and must lead to ruin.

The air of New Zealand is of that kind that it strengthens the healthy who lead a reasonable life, but the occasional rough weather weakens those who are weakly and impure. The Maoris, being sunk in impurity and inertia, caught frequent colds which ended in consumption. Still, it is to be noted that the time of their dying out joins in with the arrival of the superior foreigners. I maintain that God, "who has decided beforehand how far and wide a people shall dwell," arranges matters thus in accordance with His wise and orderly government of the world. In our time it is the fashion, especially amongst the followers of worldly-wise people, not to admit that the dear God governs the world; still at the back of all the subtleties of the highest wisdom there is an unexplained power, as the deeper thinkers in philosophy confess. Yes, an eternal God governs, who takes part in divine goodness in the course of events, not only in large matters, but also in small ones. When a people is about to die out, He permits a stronger one to take its place, and that in order that those who henceforth shall possess their land may sweeten their last days, and well is it with the successors if they recognise and do this.

" Blessed are the merciful, for they shall obtain mercy."

ADDENDUM.

THE translator is loath to obtrude his paltry personality on so sacred a scene as the life of such a man, but to afford a very slight glimpse of it, by one who is unworthy to unloose the latchet of his shoe, he appends a short account of a visit he made to Ruapuke when little more than a boy (in 1873), and published at the time. Once more (in 1894), he visited the scene of his labours. His tomb marks his place of rest.

"Nay, in all these things we are *more than conquerors* through Him that loved us" (Romans viii., 37).

"He that *overcometh*, the same shall be clothed in white raiment; and I will not blot his name out of the book of life, but I will confess his name before my Father, and before His angels" (Revelation iii., 5).

"To him that *overcometh* will I grant to sit with Me in My throne, *even as I also overcame*, and am set down with My Father in His throne" (Revelation iii., 21).

"And he that *overcometh*, and *keepeth my works unto the end*, to him will I give *power over the nations:* And he shall *rule them with a rod of iron;* as the vessels of a potter shall they be broken to shivers: *even as I received of My Father*" (Revelation ii., 26, 27).

"And I will give him the MORNING STAR!" (Revelation ii., 28).

The Saints of God! their conflict past,
And life's long battle won at last:
No more they need the shield or sword;
They cast them down before their Lord.
Oh, happy Saints! for ever blest;
At Jesus' feet how safe your rest!

The Saints of God! their wanderings done,
No more their weary course they run;
No more they faint, no more they fall,
No foes oppress, no fears appal.
Oh, happy Saints! for ever blest;
In that dear home how sweet your rest.

The Saints of God! life's voyage o'er,
Safe landed on that blissful shore:
No stormy tempests now they dread;
No roaring billows lift their head.
Oh, happy Saints! for ever blest,
In that calm haven of your rest.

The Saints of God THEIR VIGILS KEEP,
While yet their mortal bodies sleep,
Till from the dust they, too, shall rise,
And soar triumphant to the skies:
Oh, happy Saints, rejoice and sing;
He quickly comes, your Lord and King.

THE TRANSLATOR'S VISIT TO RUAPUKE.

(Extract from Otago Daily Times, 11th January, 1873.)

Outlandish places not often visited by man, " Antres vast and deserts idle," have a certain charm for me. It is a characteristic, I suppose, common to the race, and the only difference between a Sir John Franklin, a Livingstone, or a Captain Cook, and an ordinary mortal, is that the one has the feeling developed to an irresistible force, and the other can quietly button it up and smother it witout any difficulty.

The recent trip of the " Storm Bird " from the Bluff to Ruapuke presented an opportunity of seeing a place that but few of our dwellers in towns have seen, and was not to be despised accordingly. Ruapuke is a small island about 4½ miles long, by 3 miles broad, about 13 miles distant from the Bluff, inhabited, as I understood, by about 70 or 80 Maoris, and one white man and his family—the Rev. Mr. Wohlers. This gentleman is a German missionary, and has been on the island since 1844. The communication with the outside world is very irregular, the only means of transport being by boat.

It was a lovely day, with a fresh wholesome sea breeze blowing when we got away from the Bluff wharf at noon, with about 80 excursionists from Invercargill, and steamed across the Strait against the breeze, the fore-trysail just drawing enough to steady the vessel. Among the passengers were a number of the natives of the island, who, happening to be at the Bluff, were glad of the chance to run across and back so easily. The Rev. Mr. Wohlers and the chief of Ruapuke, Topi by name, were also on board. Both of the latter I found very communicative, Mr. Wohlers answering my many questions as to the strange life he was leading, and the peculiarities of the place, with the greatest cheerfulness. Topi is an intelligent specimen of the Maori. He it was who was selected to pilot the Acheron in these waters when the coast was surveyed, under Captain Stokes. Other names are given in the Government charts as having " assisted " Captain Stokes, but poor old Topi's is not mentioned. I don't suppose he was much of a hand at the sextant and logarithms, but you may wager he knew every rock and sheltered cove, tide rip, or shoal, between the Solander and Otago Heads, and, after all, assisted to some purpose. Too often he had made the journey by boat without compass or chart, when safety depended upon a keen look-out and knowledge where a sandy beach lay or a headland jutted out, that a boat might run for on a dirty night, and be hauled up on the beach or lie in smooth water until a change of weather gave her dusky crew a chance to continue their journey. This is the school Topi learnt in—not so snug a one as the " Dido's " quarter-deck, but for practical seamanship and the

development of self-reliance, not to be despised, though trigo-
nometry was an extra.

For ten miles further we hold our course, Ruapuke
developing slowly from a undefined, misty sort of a land, into a
more shapely looking country. The outlines of the lower hills,
and the lay of the gullies, the trees and the rocks becoming more
and more visible until we pass between Bird Island and some
rocks that might make the passage by night unpleasant, round a
promontory into a little bay by name Henrietta.

The strong sea breeze blows right out of the bay ; while a
quarter of a mile away, on the other side of the neck of land that
here juts out, we should have to lie with steam up in case the
anchor should drag, and we should be plunging bows into the sea.
Here she lies as snug as if alongside the wharf. The bay is
sheltered from all winds but the south-west, and even in that
direction Stewart Island must form a partial shelter, although
the "fetch" is quite long enough to raise a very respectable sea.
Still, the fact that Topi keeps his cutter moored here all the year
round, would lead one to the conclusion that it never can be very
bad. Hardly is our anchor down, when the irrepressible boy,
who is not wanting on this occasion, lets his anchor go, and
hopefully waits until blue cod and trumpeter, the daintiest fish in
New Zealand waters to my taste, reward his labours.

The bay was named Henrietta before Mr. Wohlers'
arrival; and as he has been there twenty-eight years, it has borne
it no short time. In the age of tradition, it appears a vessel
called the "Henrietta" was wrecked there, and, *mirabile dictu*,
after the wreck, and haunting the remains of it, there appeared a
queer little animal that the—Liliputians I had almost written
instead of the Ruapukians, so grotesque it seems—had never seen
before, and for want of a better name, Henrietta they called
it. Mouse is the name it goes by with us, but Henrietta it is to
this day at Ruapuke. The community is so small, and the
intercourse with the outside world so infrequent, that the title
the animal was dubbed sticks to him. Had it not been for the
isolated condition of the place, it must long ago have given place
to the English name.

The missionary's house is a comfortable little cottage,
nicely furnished, and carpeted with native mats. Besides his 70
or 80 black children, he has a pretty fair-haired daughter, a
native of the island ; but, oh, enchanted Ruapuke, speaking
English with a German accent. Here again the absence of the
"social mill that rubs our angles down" has favoured the history
of the place being told in its language. It was holiday time, and
the school closed, or I might perhaps have heard the little Maoris
saying their multiplication table ; and, a sovereign to a cockle-
shell, the young rascals would have said it with a German accent !

The remains of a mill, with a pair of French burr stones,
were pointed out to me. They are no longer used, as the Maoris

P

found it was less trouble to pull across to Bird or Green Island, load a boat with the greasy mutton birds, and send the tit-bits to their friends in the north in exchange for flour, than to grow wheat in so windy and stony a place.

You might doubtless see in a small, isolated community like this many social problems worked out that demagogues and statesmen have quarelled over for ages. In a society of men so small social science is, as it were, reduced to its ultimate fibre, and the *reductio ad absurdum* of many a plausible high-sounding policy, is here ready worked out to hand. The Ruapukian protectionist would have placed a high duty on flour to stimulate the production of it, and native industry would have had to grow it, though it gathered its crop but every third year, and dug instead of ploughed its fields. All the stump orators that ever inflamed the passions of an excited mob would waste their eloquence at Ruapuke. The Maori knows it is cheaper—that it costs him a less expenditure of protoplasm—to exchange the greasy mutton birds for the flour of wheat than to grow it in his rich but too scant soil, with Boreas to mow it as it grows.

It would take a volume to tell all that might be seen in a couple of hours in a new place, if a man only has the eyes to see. The fresh water lagoon, more valuable to Ruapuke than our water works to us ; the fantastical monumental shape of isolated boulders, like the pictures of Druidical stones, deserved attention ; but the whistle blew, and reluctantly I bent my steps towards the beach, where I arrived just in time to see two wide-awake villains, who had pulled off their boots, carry the last of the girls into the boat. We hove up the anchor, and started off like a racehorse, before the wind, which had increased to a magnificent breeze. With all square canvas set, we tore along against the strong tide, and made the passage to the Bluff in an hour and three-quarters, having psssed a most enjoyable day.

THE MAORI IN HIS NATURAL STATE.

To show the qualities of the Maori (the natural man) in the state he was before being brought under the influence of Christianity (or but very slightly), there is appended an extract from the diary of the Rev. J. A. Wilson, a missionary to the North Island natives, who lived amongst them from 1832 to 1862. The first two instances display some of the highest qualities which man possesses—a noble scorn of treachery, with bitter sarcasm for a traitor, and the most intrepid coolness under heavy fire ; the second, the lowest degradation and the most disgusting ferocity of which man can be guilty. Of such contrasts, wide asunder as the poles, is man in his natural state composed. The one inspiring in the mind of the narrator, who witnessed the incidents, as it must in ours, the most unbounded admiration ; the other, the utmost shudder of disgust. The office of Christianity is to bring every impulse of the natural man (which we all are) under control, and make it subservient to the will of God, and this we cannot do of ourselves.

"For by grace ye are saved through faith, and not of your-selves. It is the gift of God, not of works, lest any man should boast."

Extracts from the Diary of the Rev. J. A. Wilson.

July 18, 1836.—Our messenger, Keno, is a neutral, and has often carried letters between Tauranga and Rotorua. Although well rewarded and kindly treated by us, he went yesterday to Tupaea, the principal chief, and said: "Chapman has sent men (bearers) to Nelson for goods. They return to-morrow. Send early to the forest, and you can plunder them."

To this Tupaea replied : " *You* have received the hospitality of the pakeha, and partaken of his kindness. *You* are their friend. I have never received their gifts or favours. *You* are the man. It is for *you* to do this."

I mention this to record the noble reply of a heathen, and the bitter satire in his rebuke. Tupaea's father had done a still greater act.

(An Incident in the Waikato War.)

December 27, 1860.—When I rose to leave, a chief from Kawhia said to me : "Last night we buried some of our dead in the rifle pits. Ask the chief of the soldiers to respect them. Let them remain undisturbed." I promised to do so, and added : "The general will allow you to remove the dead if you desire it." To this they objected, saying: "No; let them remain where they fell. The burial service was read over them in the night *during the fight*. The ground is tapu (holy) now. We wish them to lie where we have laid them."

Thus under no ordinary fire (for the troops expended in all 170,000 rounds of ammunition during the two days of their attack), at a distance varying from 150 to 250 yards, these people, without perturbation or fear, interred their dead, concluding with the noble burial service of the Church of England—a fact which probably has no parallel in the annals of war. The farewell honours to these bold spirits were literally paid by the guns of our artillery and the unbroken volleys of two British regiments. The burial of Moore (the theme of song) pales in the contrast.

April 2, 1836.—This morning the Taua (war party) arrived. They came without tumult or noise, with a quietness not expected ; but it was a lamentable sight. The Ngatimaniapoto tribe struck me as being the wildest and most forbidding. These wretches were carrying on their backs, in baskets made of flax, the flesh and bones of the men they had killed, that it might be eaten at Kawhia and Mokau, on the western coast. When speaking to some of them, a boy, with a man's head in his hand, came and

stood a yard in front of me, and held it up for me to look at.
This he did so often that I was obliged to drive him away. The
heads of the chiefs whom they had killed were displayed in
triumph, and I observed a little girl playing with one of them on
her knee, as our children amuse themselves with a doll. When
they had reached the water-side the chiefs sat down by our boat-
house to refresh themselves, and then the heads of the Maketu
chiefs were placed on low staffs about three feet high—I suppose
in order that the people at Te Papu might see them. But the
saddest sights of all were the degraded widows of the men who
had been eaten, now led away wretched and dishonoured captives.
Many of these poor creatures were following behind the cannibals,
who still carried on their backs the flesh, heads, or limbs of the
slain. Some of these miserables wept when they saw us amongst
them. I recognized the widow of Wharetutu; yet help in such
an hour was utterly beyond our power. The Taua cut down my
young Kahikatoa trees on a spot I had reserved for my garden,
and made their ovens, and cooked the flesh of their enemies.
This, with also burning some of the fencing, was the only outrage
they committed on us; their leaving the settlement uninjured
was owing to the influence of Te Waharoa. This chief came to
Te Papu in the early morning, and was with me before his main
body arrived. When alone I reproved him again for cannibalism
and cruelty. He replied: "I am going to breakfast; come and
take some of this flesh with me."

July 24, 1836.—As we walked from the site of the settlement
to Waharoa's encampment, we saw at a distance memorials newly
raised, marking the fall of a chief, or some other rangatira; but
when we came to the place itself, the horrors that met us are too
revolting and atrocious to dwell upon. It could only be compared
to a place where wild beasts were wont to shelter and devour
their prey. The bones of men lay promiscuously strewed in every
direction. Here a bare skull, and there a rib or ribs, with part of
the spine; and around the ovens might be recognised any or
every bone of the human frame. When I say that, according to
native testimony on the spot, sixty bodies of full-grown men in
their prime of life were taken to this den of cannibals—some of
these partly eaten being only partly cooked, and the remains still
lying about on the warm damp ground—it may easily be
imagined that the sight and stench arising from all this was
intolerable beyond expression. It was literally "a valley of
bones"—bones of men still green with flesh, hideous to look
upon! Among these spectacles I was arrested by the ghastly
appearance of a once human head. In mere derision it had been
boiled, stripped of the skin and hair, and put on a post with a raw
Kumara placed in the mouth. The wound that had caused death
was a long gash from a war hatchet on the temple.

Well might the Rev. Wilson write as he does on July 3,
1836.—The efforts of a missionary among a savage people in the

midst of war often appear vain. But it is not so. The ploughman ploughs in winter and toils in the scorching heat of Summer, leaving the result to God.

JUDGE MANNING (Pakeha-Maori) ON THE MAORI CHARACTER.

(Earl Pembroke's Edition, 1887, page 195.)

"The Maori rangatira whom I am describing had passed his whole life with but little intermission in a scene of battle, murder, and blood-thirsty atrocities of the most terrific description, mixed with actions of the most heroic courage, self-sacrifice, and chivalric daring such as leave one perfectly astounded to find them the deeds of one and the same people ; one day doing acts which, had they been performed in ancient Greece, would have immortalized the actors, and the next committing barbarities too horrible for relation, and almost incredible."

OBITUARY NOTICE.

(From Southland Times, 13th May, 1885.)

It is not always the men whose names are oftenest in the public mouth that make the deepest mark on the times in which they live. Politicians appear and pass away, leaving behind them little besides the memory of party strife—for the most part sufficiently inglorious—and unthought of in connection with the permanent good of their country. We record to-day the death of one, known certainly and revered by those acquainted with the early history of the southern portion of this island, but the extent of whose influence on the native race is probably little suspected by the community of the present day.

The Rev. J. F. H. Wohlers, as our obituary notifies, died at the Neck, Stewart Island, on Thursday, 7th inst., at the age of 73 years. Mr. Wohlers arrived in the island of Ruapuke, in the year 1844, a missionary from a German Society, to promote the conversion and civilization of the Maoris on each side of Foveaux Straits. Fortunately, in a paper read before the Southland Institute, and published in the Transactions of the New Zealand Institute of 1881, Mr. Wohlers has left a quaint and most interesting record of his labours. Ruapuke, when he came to the south, was an influential centre of Maoridom. The famous chief Tuhawaiki, or "Bloody Jack," had there his head quarters, and the population numbered about 200 souls. Mr. Wohlers arrived at an opportune time. The natives, having lost even the poetry of their old religion, had, under the superstition of "Tapu," sunk to the lowest depth of degradation. But the results of missionary labour in the North were being felt even in the remote islands of Foveaux Strait. The "vibration," as Mr. Wohlers put it, of the new spiritual movement created by Christian teaching was being

felt throughout the whole Maori population.   The arts of reading
and writing had in the north excited the Maori mind, well known
to be acute and active, to wonder and desire to be acquainted
with them.   Writing came upon them like a miracle, and, coming
along with Christianity, was accepted as a sort of confirmation of
its truth.   Yet it was the spirituality of the Christian religion
that had so far enlightened the minds of the northern natives,
and had abolished, wherever it had been received, murder and
cannibalism and other crimes.   It was the first faint note of this
new revelation, reaching the south by native agencies, that prepared the way for Mr. Wohlers' work, and made it safe for him
to dwell among the savages of Ruapuke.   We have not space to
record the traits and habits of the people at that comparatively
recent time, or the expedients adopted for their reformation by the
solitary white man who had so nobly thrown himself among them.
All this can be gathered from the interesting narrative that we
have cited.   Let it be said only that a magical change came over
the condition of the people.   Christian baptism followed.   The
real family life became established.   Cleanliness took the place
of filth, and industry that of idleness.   Pakeha sailors married
Maori women, and the husbands brought into the households at
least the reflection of the religion in which they had been brought
up.   Mr. Wohlers has spoken enthusiastically of the numbers and
beauty of the half-caste children that were the issue of these
marriages, and those acquainted with the present generation will
be able to confirm his statement.   Fortunately for Mr. Wohlers
and the cause he had taken up, he met in Wellington, in 1849, a
lady who became his wife, and who ruled somewhat like a queen
in the little community of Ruapuke.   Mrs. Wohlers was the means
of creating a social and economical revolution in the island, such
as only a woman filled with energy and strength of will could
accomplish.   Eventually a church was built, mainly, if not solely,
we have heard, by the missionary's own hands ; a school was
commenced, in which English was taught, and so the work of
amelioration went on.   The history of Mr. Wohlers' life is the
history of a great turning from darkness to light, and from
savagery to civilization of a considerable portion of the Maori
race.   It is a singular fact that Ruapuke, once the centre of rule
and of population in the Strait, should have become almost
deserted.   All, except a few families of the Maoris and half-
castes, have emigrated to Stewart Island, in the neighbourhood,
and principally cluster about the Neck.   At the Neck resides Mr.
Wohlers' only daughter, the wife of Mr. Arthur Traill, missionary
of the Presbyterian Church of Otago and Southland, and teacher
of the Native school.   The old patriarch whose life we have been
sketching died in the house of his son-in-law, having passed
peacefully away.   " The heart-felt sorrow of the Maoris," writes
a correspondent from the spot, " is very touching.   Both before
and since his death even the men might be seen kneeling by his

bedside and weeping unrestrainedly." He had been regarded by them as a father, and he spoke of them as his spiritual children. We term his a notable life, although it made little noise in the world. Simple, childlike, and devout, and with the weapons only of a good understanding and indomitable industry, he was yet called to a great work which he did nobly ; and we have no doubt his name will descend as a household word through many generations of the race he loved so well.

It remains only to be mentioned that Mr. Wohlers is survived by his devoted wife, and, as we have said, by his daughter, who is the mother of several children.

Extract from the Minutes of Presbytery, First Church, Invercargill, June 3, 1885, the day which the Presbytery met and was constituted.

INTER ALIA,—

It was unanimously resolved that the Rev. Messrs. Stobo, Alexander, and Stevens be appointed to draw up a minute relative to the death of the Rev. Mr. Wohlers, expressive of the Presbytery's sympathy with the bereaved members of his family, and forward the same to his widow, of which the following is a copy :—

" The Presbytery having heard of the death of the Rev. Mr. Wohlers, missionary to the Maoris at Ruapuke, desires to put on record its sense of his long and faithful labours in that mission. Although conducted among a decaying remnant, the great day, they believe, will make manifest the good that has been done, and the surviving natives who so warmly cherish his memory will ever continue, we trust, to walk under the influence of the truth which he inculcated. The Presbytery would express its sympathy with the bereaved widow and daughter, to whom they desire that a copy of this minute be sent."

ALEX. BETHUNE, *Presb. Clerk.*

EDUCATION DEPARTMENT,

WELLINGTON, April.30, 1885.

The Reverend J. F. H. Wohlers, Ruapuke.

Reverend Sir,—I have the honour, by direction of the Hon. Mr. Stout, Minister of Education, to acknowledge the receipt of the letter written by Mr. Arthur W. Traill at your request, forwarding your resignation of the appointment of native school teacher at Ruapuke owing to very serious illness.

I am to intimate to you that the Minister accepts your resignation with regret, and to say that your engagement will not be regarded as terminated until October 30, 1885, that your salary will be paid as usual till that date, and that you may consider that you have six months' leave of absence.

I am, further, on behalf of the Minister, to express to you the hearty appreciation by himself and the Government of the devoted labours of yourself and Mrs. Wohlers, throughout so many years, amongst the natives in the southern parts of New Zealand, and of the evident success that has attended your arduous efforts to teach and civilize them.

I have the honour to be, with much respect,

Your obedient servant,

JOHN HISLOP.

This letter from the Government of New Zealand to the Rev. Mr. Wohlers was written only seven days before his death. It is evidently in answer to one tendering his resignation as teacher of the native school, from which office, as his book informs us, he derived in later years sufficient income to relieve him from the need of maintaining himself by exhausting manual labour. To how few it would have occurred to resign at an age and under circumstances when he may well have thought his final resignation of all earthly offices was very near, let the reader judge for himself. To the honour of the Government, it is to be noted that they granted him six months' leave of absence on full pay. His action in this matter is only consistent with that minute conscientiousness that " payment of tithe of mint and anise and cummin," neglecting not " the weightier matters of the law, judgment, mercy, and faith," which marks his whole career. It comes from his deathbed as a faint perfume, almost of heavenly odour, fragrant as " incense from Sheba " and as the " precious ointment that flowed down Aaron's beard even to the skirts of his clothing."

" Precious in the sight of the Lord is the death of His saints " (Psalm xcvi., 15).

The translator concludes with a few words by Clement of Alexandra, one of the earliest of the Christian fathers, and himself a missionary to the heathen :—

" Orpheus, Amphion, Arion, and the Greek musicians, employed their skill in confirming the perverseness of man, and leading him to idols and stocks and stones. Not so the Christian musician; he comes *to destroy the bitter tyranny of demons,* to substitute in its place the mild and gentle yoke of piety ; to raise to heaven those who had been cast down upon the earth. He alone has *tamed man, the most savage of beasts,* and has indeed made men out of stones by raising up a Holy Seed from among the Gentiles, who believed in stones. Such is the *power of the New Song*—it has converted stones and beasts into men. They who were dead without any portion of the real life have revived at the mere sound."

www.ingramcontent.com/pod-product-compliance
Lightning Source LLC
Chambersburg PA
CBHW030124030726
47498CB00007B/2544